Praise for Krista Davis's *New Y...*
Domestic Diva

T0249355

"This satisfying entry in the series will appear to readers ...
enjoy cozies with a cooking frame, like Diane Mott Davidson's
Goldy Schulz mysteries." —*Booklist*

"Reader alert: Tasty descriptions may spark intense cupcake
cravings." —*The Washington Post*

"Davis . . . again combines food and felonies in this tasty whodunit." —*Richmond Times-Dispatch*

"Loaded with atmosphere and charm." —*Library Journal*

"A mouthwatering mix of murder, mirth, and mayhem." —Mary
Jane Maffini, author of *The Busy Woman's Guide to Murder*

"Raucous humor, affectionate characters, and delectable recipes
highlight this unpredictable mystery that entertains during any
season." —*Kings River Life* magazine

**Praise for Krista Davis's *Color Me Murder*, the first in her Pen
& Ink Mystery series**

"The mystery is pleasantly twisty . . . [an] appealing cast of
characters whose backstories lend themselves nicely to future
plots for this carefully crafted cozy series." —*Publishers Weekly*

"The theme was unique and new, the characters were relatable
and entertaining, the mystery was unpredictable, and the writing was excellent." —*Night Owl Reviews*

"I love a book that immediately grabs my attention and this
new debut series does that. This was a well-written and fast-
paced whodunit that was delightfully entertaining. The author
did a good job in presenting a murder mystery that had me im-
mersed in all that was happening." —Dru's Book Musings

Krista Davis is the author of:

The Domestic Diva Mysteries:

The Diva Cooks Up a Storm
The Diva Sweetens the Pie

The Pen & Ink Mysteries:

Color Me Murder
The Coloring Crook

The Diva
Sweetens
the Pie

Krista Davis

KENSINGTON BOOKS
www.kensingtonbooks.com

KENSINGTON BOOKS are published by

Kensington Publishing Corp.
119 West 40th Street
New York, NY 10018

All Kensington titles, imprints, and distributed lines are available at special quantity discounts for bulk purchases for sales promotion, premiums, fund-raising, educational, or institutional use.

Special book excerpts or customized printings can also be created to fit specific needs. For details, write or phone the office of the Kensington Sales Manager: Attn.: Sales Department. Kensington Publishing Corp., 119 West 40th Street, New York, NY 10018. Phone: 1-800-221-2647.

Kensington and the K logo Reg. U.S. Pat. & TM Off.

First Kensington Hardcover Edition: May 2019

ISBN-13: 978-1-4967-1473-2 (ebook)
ISBN-10: 1-4967-1473-3 (ebook)

ISBN-13: 978-1-4967-1472-5
ISBN-10: 1-4967-1472-5
First Kensington Trade Paperback Edition: April 2020

10 9 8 7 6 5 4 3 2 1

Printed in the United States of America

For the moms,

Harriet, Marianne, Susan, and Trudy

Acknowledgments

I had so much fun baking my way through this book. I hope one of the recipes will appeal to you.

As with every book, there were many people who helped me along the way. I owe special thanks to TiJuana Odum for her delicious and wonderfully easy chicken pot pie recipe.

Thanks also to Leslie Budewitz for her clever notion that we fall into two groups, the people of the pie and the clan of the cake. Hopefully both groups will enjoy this book.

Special thanks also go to Tary Haan for suggesting the lovely name Star-Spangled Pies.

As always, none of this would happen if it weren't for my editor, Wendy McCurdy, and her assistant, Norma Perez-Hernandez, who have been wonderful. I don't know what I would do without my agent, Jessica Faust, who is always there for me and regularly brightens my day.

Like Sophie, I am blessed to have such terrific friends. Nina, Reid, and Norwood are always just a text away.

And most of all, I have to thank my readers. I love all the wonderful e-mails you send. Thank you for being part of Sophie's gang.

Cast of Characters

Patsy Lee Presley — television star chef
Tommy Earl Felts — pastry chef
Roger MacKenzie — pastry chef and PiePalooza coordinator
Brock Anderson — Patsy Lee's assistant
Honey Armbruster — home cook and Patsy Lee's fan
Peter Presley — Patsy Lee's ex-husband
Remy Tarwick — bartender at The Laughing Hound
Willa Staminski — pastry chef
Dooley Stokes — entomologist
Nellie Stokes — pastry chef
Ali Stokes — Dooley and Nellie's daughter

Sophie and Friends
Sophie Winston
Nina Reid Norwood
Officer Wong
Bernie Frei
Mars Winston (Sophie's ex-husband)
Natasha
Detective Wolf Fleishman

Chapter 1

Dear Sophie,
My new mother-in-law wins the local pie contest every year. The recipe for her piecrust is top secret, and his family makes a huge fuss about it. She and her husband are coming to visit my hubby and me for the first time. Hubby says a pie is obligatory. Each of her other daughters-in-law bakes a pie for her visit. I'm terrified! What do I do?
Newlywed in Coward, South Carolina

Dear Newlywed,
Bake a cake. There's no point in competing with her, and a cake will last longer than a pie, anyway. If someone comments on the missing pie, tell your mother-in-law that you're eager to learn how she bakes her wonderful pies that everyone raves about.

Sophie

Daisy, my hound mix, stopped walking abruptly. I thought she had picked up the scent of a squirrel in the night air, but then I heard rustling in the bushes. In a split second, I was face-to-face with Patsy Lee Presley, and both of us screamed like we were under attack. Daisy barked, which added to the drama.

Wide-eyed, as though she were horrified, Patsy Lee took off running like a woman in her fifties who didn't get much exercise.

My heart still pounding, I sucked in a deep breath. It wasn't long ago that someone had meant to harm me. I guessed I was still wary and a little jittery. The truth was that the streets of Old Town, Alexandria, Virginia, were safe at night. I often walked Daisy after dark, enjoying the lights glowing in the windows of the historical homes that lined the streets.

Now that the momentary shock was over, I wasn't certain it had been Patsy Lee. I had never met her before, but I had seen her on TV many times. Patsy Lee Presley was the current darling of the TV cooking world with the number one show. Sweet as the pies she baked, she was slightly chubby, and watching her show was like a visit from a favorite doting aunt. Patsy Lee was due to be in Old Town on Friday for the pie festival, so it could have been her. But what was she doing hiding in bushes and running around like she was afraid?

I looked back in the direction she had gone, but she had disappeared. Whoever that woman was, I hoped she had the good sense to call the police if she was in trouble.

The next morning I told Nina Reid Norwood and Officer Wong about it while we rolled out dough in Tommy Earl Felts's class on pie baking. Nina, my best friend and across-the-street neighbor, unwisely added too many drops of water to her dough. I watched as it became sticky and unmanageable, but decided it wasn't my place to say anything. After all, Tommy was teaching the class.

Nina frowned at me. "Why isn't your dough sticking to your hands like mine?"

Wong glanced at her. "Mercy, Nina! Dip your hands in the flour, honey."

Wong focused on her own dough, which looked perfect to me.

"I'll check the log to see if anyone called in last night," she said. "It was probably some married woman sneaking home after a rendezvous with a boyfriend. Not to put Patsy Lee down, but a lot of women still wear their hair real big like she does. It could have been someone else."

Tommy Earl approached our group. "Bless your sorry little heart, Nina." Tommy gazed at the sticky lump in front of her, and patted her on the back. "Why don't you go to the mixer and try again? I don't think that's salvageable."

Tommy nodded approvingly at my pie dough. "Did I hear you talking about Patsy Lee?"

"I thought I saw her in Old Town last night. Do you know her?" I asked.

He snorted. "I taught her everything she knows."

"You did not," Wong scolded him. "On the show Patsy Lee is always talking about her grandmother, from whom she learned how to cook and bake. She was just a tiny thing when she started cooking. So young that she had to stand on a chair to reach the countertop to work next to her meemaw."

Tommy laughed aloud. "Is that the story she spins? Have you ever seen this meemaw on her show?"

"Good grief, Tommy," said Wong. "Patsy Lee is in her forties. Meemaw would probably be in her eighties."

Tommy lowered his voice and said, "Patsy Lee is so far into her forties that she has rolled over into her fifties. And

Meemaw doesn't come on the show because she has a receding hairline, a five o'clock shadow, and her legs are too fat to wear a skirt."

Tommy had done a fairly good job of describing himself. I couldn't help grinning.

Wong's eyes narrowed. "Are you saying there is no Meemaw?"

"I guess she had a couple of grannies, most people do." He shrugged. "But when *I* met Patsy Lee, she couldn't crack an egg without breaking the yolk."

Tommy moved on, pausing to talk to Nina about the dough she was carrying back to our workstation. She sidled in next to me and plunked her dough on the table.

"The secret to a perfect piecrust"—Tommy paused to build up suspense—"is vodka. I find drinking it helps *me*, but a splash in your dough will prevent too much gluten formation. There are other important factors, like keeping the ingredients as cold as possible, but the vodka is helpful because it makes the crust flaky."

Nina licked the spoon she had been dipping into the lemon filling for her lemon meringue pie.

"You won't have any filling left for your pie," I whispered.

"That's okay. You didn't think I was actually going to bake anything, did you?" she whispered back to me.

Officer Wong shot us a dirty look. "Shh!"

Nina had made fun of me for participating in the class. I had baked plenty of pies in my life, but piecrusts could be tricky. Tommy was a pro, and I figured I would pick up some tips. He baked pies for a living and sold them at Sweet as Pie on King Street in Old Town, Alexandria. Rumor had it that people drove an hour across greater metropolitan Washington, DC, just to buy Tommy's pies. At Thanksgiving and Christmas, they had to be preordered because he couldn't fill all the requests.

He roamed the room as he spoke. The buttons on his short-sleeved white chef's jacket strained a bit against the pressure of his stomach. I could relate. I had my own difficulties maintaining the weight I would like to be.

Wong giggled when he stopped to praise her dough. "I'm so thrilled to be in your class. My grandmother was an expert pie baker. I wish I had paid attention to her techniques."

Was she flirting with him?

Just as he had described, his hair had begun to recede, but he was taking it in stride and wore it brushed back off his face. He smiled at her and the little crinkles at the outer edges of his brown eyes deepened.

African-American Wong, who attributed her name to the wrong husband by a long shot, wasn't wearing her police uniform today. Her hair waved to just below her ears in a cut that was shorter in the back and longer in the front. One sassy curl dropped on her forehead.

I looked a little closer. She had taken a lot of care with her makeup today. The buttons on her shirt strained a bit, not unlike those on Tommy's jacket. The two of them could be cute together. Nina nudged me, and I suspected she was thinking the same thing.

While the pies baked, Tommy drifted through the room, engaging all his students. When he reached Nina, he asked, "Is it true that you're judging the pie-baking contest?"

Nina turned as red as the cherry filling I had cooked for my pie. "That's why I'm here. I thought I should have a feel for all the work that goes into baking a pie."

Tommy stared at her and appeared confused.

"She has an amazing palate," I offered.

Wong looked over at us. "What's that supposed to mean? I like food, too, but nobody asked me to judge anything."

"I mean that Nina has the ability to taste flavors that

the rest of us miss entirely or barely notice. If someone in this class sliced her fruit on a cutting board that was used to mince garlic last night and wasn't thoroughly washed afterward, Nina would still taste the garlic when she ate the fruit."

"I've seen contests like that. They blindfold people to see who can recognize the flavors or textures," said Tommy. "Well, Ms. Nina Reid Norwood, I apologize for doubting you. I guess there's more than one way to judge a pie."

"I hope you entered in the professional category," I said.

"You bet. I can't talk about it in front of a judge, though." Tommy winked at us.

"You're so cute. But it's not a problem," Nina assured him. "The pies won't have any names on them. It will be a blind tasting."

Tommy smiled. "Good to hear. I wouldn't want to be disqualified." He moved on to the next group.

An hour later everyone except Nina went home with a pie. The class was a small part of the Old Town Pie Festival, which was scheduled to commence in earnest the following day.

Nina offered to carry my pie as we neared my house. She took deep breaths. "Do you think there are calories in what a person sniffs?"

"I'm almost positive there are. I know I weigh more every time I leave a bakery."

As we approached my house, we saw a man peering in the window of my kitchen door. He cupped his hands around his eyes and leaned against the glass to see better. I could hear Daisy barking inside the house.

Chapter 2

Dear Natasha,
My daughter loves to bake fruit pies and we love to
eat them. But she makes such a mess of my oven! I
have to clean it every single time she bakes because
the bubbling juices always run over the pie pan.
        Fastidious in Elderberry Pond, Pennsylvania

Dear Fastidious,
Tell your daughter I said to always place a rimmed
baking sheet underneath the pie to catch any juices.
Problem solved!

                                        Natasha

"I've got your back," muttered Nina. "I'm dialing 911 now, just in case."

The man must have heard us approaching. He pulled away from the door and flushed with embarrassment at being caught.

"Put your phone away, Nina. I know him."

"Which one?" she asked.

"What?"

She pointed at a man who sprinted around the corner and disappeared.

"Who was that?" I asked.

"I didn't get a good look at him."

We walked toward my kitchen door.

Roger MacKenzie was wearing his trademark bow tie with a seersucker suit and looked completely comfortable in spite of the sweltering summer temperature.

"Roger, did you see a guy hanging around here?"

"Have you got yourself an admirer, Sophie?" he teased.

"Seriously. You didn't see anyone?"

"Darlin', I have got a lot on my mind. I can't say I saw a soul. But I'm sure glad that you're home. Disaster has befallen me." He clasped his hands over his chest as though our mere appearance had solved all his problems.

I had a hunch I knew what they concerned. Roger was a pastry chef who was sponsoring a weeklong PiePalooza event for home cooks and pie fans. But Roger wasn't an event planner, and while he had done a lot of things right, he had also been overwhelmed by the amount of work and planning that went into an event. Pie fans from around the country had signed up for the baking classes he offered. Over the last six months Roger had called me to ask questions. In the beginning I heard from him once a week. The number of calls increased with his level of anxiety as the date of his event grew closer. For the last month, he had phoned me daily.

He sucked in a deep breath, and touched the spots just over his eyebrows with three fingers of each hand as though he was doing some kind of relaxation technique. "Amy Wellington Smith has shingles." He lowered his hands and reached out to Nina. "Roger MacKenzie, pleased to make your acquaintance. Do you think shingles is a reasonable excuse? Twenty-four people have signed up for her class, Taming Beastly Berries. I think she should slap on some thick foundation and fulfill her obligation to her students."

He ran out of breath and stared at the two of us. I had a very bad feeling that he wanted me to agree with him.

I unlocked the door and invited him into my kitchen, where Daisy pranced with glee at our return, her long ears flapping. "From what I hear, shingles can be very painful. We have some excellent pie bakers in Old Town. Maybe one of them could fill in for her," I suggested, watching Nina set the pie on top of the island in my kitchen. She glanced at me and pulled a knife out of the drawer.

"It needs to set up first," I said. "Otherwise the filling will run all over."

Nina frowned at me, but she promptly refrigerated the pie.

"Have any of *them* written a book on pie baking?" Roger asked rather haughtily.

He had high expectations. "Patsy Lee Presley is in town—"

He cut me off. "She's already scheduled to teach Avoiding the Shame of a Shrinking Crust, on Tuesday, and Blackbottom Pie Doesn't Mean Burned, on Thursday. Amy Wellington Smith's class was also on Tuesday, at the same time as Patsy Lee's."

"What about Tommy Earl?" asked Nina. "I can vouch for him. He's an excellent teacher."

Roger's lips pulled tight. "Ohhh, I don't think so. His pies are delicious, I'll grant you that. But Tommy Earl is notoriously unreliable. Such a pity. He's so talented, but I know better than to hire him. I wish Nellie Stokes were available. That woman knows how to bake!"

"What's wrong with Tommy Earl?" asked Nina.

Roger didn't say a word, but he cupped his hand as though he were holding a glass and tipped it toward his mouth.

"Are you sure?" I asked. It wasn't as though I spent a

lot of time with Tommy Earl, but I had ordered plenty of pies from him for events and he had never let me down. "I've never had a problem with him."

"Trust me on this," grumbled Roger. "It's well-known in baking circles. Ask anyone in the business. He must have some great employees who cover for him at his shop. Sophie"—Roger gazed at me with sad eyes—"can't you help me out? Could you teach the classes?"

"Me? Good heavens. I just took one of Tommy Earl's classes. I'm not a pie pro by any stretch of the imagination. Not even a little bit. And I haven't published a cookbook." Whew. That would get me off the hook for sure.

But Nina exclaimed, "You should! I would buy it."

She wasn't helping. "Why don't you come to the Old Town Pie Festival tomorrow? A lot of professional pie bakers will be entering their pies in the contests there."

"I would sleep better if I had someone scheduled in the slot for Tuesday." He eyed me again.

Well, there was nothing I could do about that.

Nina said, "I find melatonin helps me."

I bit my lip to keep from giggling. "I'll keep an eye out for an appropriate baker tomorrow."

Roger no longer looked quite so crisp. He thanked us before leaving and dragged away like a disappointed child. I let Daisy out in my fenced backyard.

When I returned, Nina asked, "Can we try your pie now?"

"Not unless you want to see the Horror of the Runny Filling play out right here in my kitchen."

"Why do pies take so long?"

Her question was rhetorical. Nina knew that fillings had to set, although she probably wouldn't have cared. She would have scooped up the oozing filling with a soupspoon and declared it delicious.

"Besides," I said, "don't you think we'd better check on

Bernie? The pie festival is a big undertaking. He could probably use some extra hands."

When Daisy returned, she was panting and headed straight to the water bowl. I added a couple of ice cubes to her water to make it super cold. Her nose wet, she sprawled on the floor as if she was trying to cool off. The August heat was brutal, but the weather was supposed to cool off dramatically for the weekend.

I didn't feel guilty about leaving her at home when we stepped out into the humid heat again. We had only trudged one block when I asked, "How would you feel about an iced coffee or tea?"

Nina moaned. "Anything with ice in it would be welcome."

We stopped at Moos & Brews, relieved to be in the air-conditioned café while we ordered.

Nina checked the time. "Ugh. I am officially over the hill. I'm too old to drink real coffee after noon. I'll have a decaf iced caramel latte."

I ordered a plain iced coffee with a scoop of vanilla ice cream, which I knew would melt into my coffee in less than a minute once we were outside.

We were slurping the remains through biodegradable paper straws as we approached the park, where banners for the Old Town Pie Festival already fluttered in the gentle breeze.

"Francie is going to be mad that she missed this."

My elderly neighbor was a hoot, and had she been home, she would surely have attended the pie festival. "I don't think she'll be too upset. I'm sure she's having fun with her sister. How many women their age go on an African safari to photograph animals?"

So many people surrounded Bernie that he was barely visible. He had been the best man at my wedding. Bernie's sandy hair was perpetually mussed, and his nose had a kink in it where it had been broken, possibly twice. Footloose, Bernie had traveled the world before settling in Old Town, Alexandria, Virginia, and taking on the management of a restaurant for an absentee owner. To our astonishment, he had a flair for the business and The Laughing Hound had become one of Old Town's most popular eateries.

But today, mellow Bernie was being yelled at by one of our friends.

"For your information"—Natasha pulled her shoulders back and held her chin high—"I grew up in the country, and no one knows pies like country cooks. And why are *you* in charge of the festival, anyway? English people don't know anything about pies."

Bernie had listened politely right up until she said that part about the Brits.

In contrast to Bernie's just-rolled-out-of-bed mussed hair, not a single hair on Natasha's head dared stray out of place. She wore an admittedly elegant cream-colored suit in spite of the ninety-five-degree weather and unbearable humidity. Natasha fancied herself the Martha of the South— except she wasn't. Knowing her penchant for wreaking havoc, and given the chaos she caused the previous year, Bernie, who was in charge of the pie festival this year, had pointedly omitted Natasha from the event arrangements.

The two of them didn't get along at all. Natasha resented Bernie for not bowing to Her Highness's whims, and Bernie was unimpressed by Natasha's constant self-serving demands. A confrontation had been inevitable. I had expected kindhearted Bernie to relent, but then Natasha had to go and offend the Brits. I held my breath.

Chapter 3

Dear Sophie,
My family loves apple pie better than any other
dessert. I bake it all the time, but I always have an
air gap between the apples and the crust. What am
I doing wrong?
  McIntosh Mom in Apple Valley, North Carolina

Dear McIntosh Mom,
You're probably making your pie dough with short-
ening. Switch to an all-butter pie dough, which is
softer and will do a better job of sinking with the
apples as they cook. In addition, slice the apples as
thin as possible. And I'm sorry to tell you that
McIntosh apples are not your friend in a pie be-
cause they shrink more than most apples.

  Sophie

"Pies were well-known in England, as far back as the twelfth century," said Bernie in the English accent that made him sound like an authority on every subject. "Who do you think brought pies to America?" His voice sounded softer and conciliatory when he said, "Natasha, we've already been through this." He walked over to her and spoke in a low voice so as not to embarrass her, which I thought very kind. "We settled this weeks ago. We have already selected our judges. Do I really have to remind you that your entry last year sent the judges to the emergency room?" Smiling broadly and speaking louder again, Bernie pointed at me. "Sophie isn't entering the pie-baking contests, either."

Natasha glanced at me over her shoulder. "Well, I understand *that*. She's a home cook, not a chef. It would only be an embarrassment to her."

Nina whispered, "Are you going to let her get away with that?"

Actually, I was. She had just embarrassed herself by intimating that she was a chef, which she wasn't. Neither one of us was professionally trained to cook or bake. We wrote competing columns about entertaining, cooking, and all things related to lifestyle, but we had different approaches. I kept things simple while Natasha loved complex projects and keeping up with the latest trends.

I had known Natasha since we were kids growing up in the same small town where we competed at everything except the beauty contests that she loved. She might have a local TV show and fans, but I knew that underneath that perfect figure and coif, Natasha was an insecure mess, still searching for the father who abandoned her when she was a kid. True, she might have been waiting in the wings to nab my ex-husband when we divorced, but they had since separated. While my ex appeared to be thriving, Natasha seemed lost, grasping at anything she thought would propel her to the stardom that she craved.

None of that justified her ugly remarks about me, but I had grown largely immune to them. Natasha always thought she knew best and imagined that it was noble of her to improve the rest of us by imparting her wisdom.

"You're being completely unfair to ban me from the contest. Honey Armbruster is entering," Natasha said with disdain. "And she can't cook her way out of . . . out of a take-out bag."

"Look, Natasha," said Bernie. "You know the problem. I'm sorry, but your performance last year prohibits you from entering again."

"How was I supposed to know that a ghost pepper would burn their tongues? People eat them all the time. Besides, I'm not cooking with peppers at all anymore. They're passé. No one is interested in peppers. You should know that, Bernie. Everyone's into activated charcoal now."

I had a feeling the judges would be glad they didn't have to eat a pie made with charcoal.

Bernie just stared at her. "No."

"Then make me a judge. I know more about baking and flavor combinations than anyone else in Old Town."

"I've had so many great people volunteer to help out that I don't have any positions left to fill. Especially not judge slots."

"Hey, y'all! Patsy Lee is here." The singsong Southern voice rang out behind me. I turned to see Patsy Lee Presley, the woman with the number one cooking show in the country—and the woman who had been on the run in the street last night.

The sun gleamed on her light brown hair, which was blown out into a shoulder length fluff and sprayed into a helmet as immoveable as Natasha's. She strode into our midst with an air of entitlement. She wore a turquoise shift-style dress with a V-neck that showed off her ample cleavage. A strand of giant pearls lay against her tanned skin and a chunky gold bracelet encircled her right wrist.

The sun glinted off the diamond bezel on her watch, which sat prominently on her left arm.

To Natasha, she said, "Now, darlin', who are you?"

I expected Natasha to wither into a fan girl moment when she realized who was addressing her, but she simply said, "Natasha."

Patsy Lee waited a second longer, then raised her eyebrows when no surname was forthcoming. "Not *the* Natasha?"

Natasha beamed. "Why, yes." She smiled broadly as if unable to contain her excitement.

"Sugah," said Patsy Lee, "that explains everything. They didn't want you showin' up little ole me."

It was brilliant. She was one shrewd woman to have assessed the situation so quickly. Patsy Lee couldn't have said anything that would have pleased Natasha more.

Natasha touched the sides of her face with her fingers. "Oh, my word. You're right. Why didn't I see that? Of course, we're both TV stars, so we're really on a par."

"All the more reason. They probably didn't want you to step on my toes."

"We're like sisters," gushed Natasha. "You must join me for dinner one night while you're gracing our fair city."

I glanced at Bernie. He caught my look and discreetly waved his hand as if to say *not to worry.*

Patsy Lee smiled at her. "I would *love* that. You just get in touch with Brock here. He handles everything for me." She gestured toward an exceedingly beautiful young man, who stood a step behind her.

The person who coined the phrase *tall, dark, and handsome* must have known someone like Brock. His jet-black hair waved gently. I suspected he always needed a shave. His dark eyes were lively and sharp, like an owl that was taking everything in. His broad smile seemed very natural. He was a good twenty years younger than Patsy Lee.

Brock immediately latched onto Natasha. "Let's step over here and see when you're available." He steered Natasha away, but she was beaming. It was almost as though she didn't realize that he was moving her away from Patsy Lee.

Bernie introduced Nina and me to Patsy Lee and apologized for the little confrontation with Natasha.

Patsy Lee's gaze lingered on me for longer than normal, bolstering my belief that it had indeed been her in the bushes last night.

"Thank you so much for invitin' me, Bernie. I am honored to be back in Old Town. I miss livin' here. It feels like comin' home. And I can't wait to dig into those pies."

When someone else asked him a question, and he turned away for a moment, Patsy Lee asked me, "Who was that woman?"

"Natasha?" I asked.

She blinked hard. "Sweetheart, I understood her name. What I want to know is who she is."

Momentarily taken aback, I said, "She has a local cable-TV show about all things domestic."

Patsy Lee nodded her head. "I should have known. There's one in every town, and they're all trying to beat me at my game. Brock," she called.

The crowd had grown considerably, and I noticed that many of them focused on Patsy Lee. We watched as Brock finished up with Natasha and ambled toward us.

"I am not available to dine with Natasha." She turned her attention back to me, but said over her shoulder, "Or to do anything else, either."

Brock murmured discreetly, "A wise move. Trouble at noon and three o'clock." Brock held out his hand to me. "Brock Anderson."

I smiled at him and shook his hand. "Sophie Winston."

He nodded and introduced himself to Nina.

Patsy Lee glanced in the directions he had indicated and took a deep breath. "What about the guy in the suit?"

"He's not interested in you. He's watching Sophie."

"What?" I was alarmed by the mere suggestion. "How do you know that?"

"It's my job," said Brock.

I scanned the crowd for a man in a suit and spotted him right away.

"Is he the man who had sprinted around the corner?" asked Nina.

"He looks vaguely familiar, but I can't place him." Had he followed Nina and me here? He was lean. Maybe even too lean. He deflected his gaze when he saw me looking at him.

I wondered where he had been the night before when Patsy Lee was creeping around in the dark. What if Brock was wrong? What if he was the one Patsy Lee had been running from?

"Used to be I loved comin' to the South," said Patsy Lee. "It just feels like home, you know? As long as I live, I'll always feel like a transplant in New York. Don't get me wrong, there's a lot to like about New York City, but it's no place for a Southern flower. Lately, though, every time I venture southward, a ghost from my past floats back up again to torment me."

People were milling all around us. I had no idea who she was talking about.

Brock asked, "Shall I run interference?"

Patsy Lee shifted the V-neck of her dress and shimmied like she was trying to adjust her Spanx. "He'll just chase me around until I talk to him. Might as well get it over with. But I'll sign something for Honey first. For once she didn't have to travel to see me. I do love my fans." She shot Brock a look, and I realized that he steered Nina away from us.

"I believe we met last night," said Patsy Lee.

New York hadn't taken the South out of her accent. I nodded. "I thought that was you."

She adjusted the hefty bracelet and spoke very softly. "If you don't mind, I'd rather no one knew about that little incident. I was just surprised to see you there in the bushes."

I probably should have let it pass. It really didn't matter, but I was concerned about her. "It seemed to me that *you* were the one hiding in the bushes."

She took one step back and assessed me. "When you get to the top of your field, everyone wants to take you down. They look for any tiny chink to blow into a huge scandal. They sneak around and hold their breath, just waitin' for you to misspeak. I'm sure you understand."

I didn't. She had deftly sidestepped the issue of hiding in the bushes.

"It was lovely meetin' you, Sophie. I may call on you if I need somethin'. I hope that's okay."

"Of course, it is. Just let me know if I can be of assistance." No sooner were the words out of my mouth than I wondered if it had been wise of me to offer to help her. As she hurried off, once again opening her arms and calling out, "Patsy Lee is here!" I glanced at Brock. Heaven knew what kind of instructions she might give him about me. While I had initially thought her kind words that had placated Natasha were very smart, I wasn't sure what to think of her now. I had never seen someone give instructions to an assistant that were the equivalent of hanging out a DO NOT DISTURB sign. Maybe that was how all celebrities managed their lives. I had no idea.

A man with chestnut hair, which was shot through with silver, watched Patsy Lee. He wore a button-down blue plaid shirt, with aviator sunglasses tucked into a breast pocket. Smiling, he strode in my direction while Patsy Lee signed a book for Honey Armbruster, a domestic diva with boundless energy and according to rumor, an amicable divorce.

If gossip was to be believed, Honey demanded a list of the birthdays of students in her children's classes and brought homemade cupcakes to school for each child's birthday. And they weren't just simple cupcakes. They had themes tailored to the child's interests, like a favorite Disney character or a sport. Each year, Honey arranged a children's choir to sing at the hospital and senior center at the holidays. And at this time of summer, the front steps of her house overflowed with cascading flowers, all in various shades of pink.

Patsy Lee chattered nonstop with Honey, who clung to her every word and responded as though this was the highest point of her life.

Brock checked his Apple watch and moved in. "Excuse me, Ms. Presley, but people are waiting."

On cue, Patsy Lee exclaimed, "I wish we had time for a cup of coffee. I always love seeing you, but it's never long enough, darlin'."

Patsy moved on to the other person Brock had referred to as *trouble*—the man with the aviator sunglasses tucked into his shirt. His clothing and overall style marked him as a country fellow, more at home in a field or forest than on a city street. The portly man wore jeans at least two sizes too small for him. They were far too tight to sit at his waist and were tightly cinched by a belt below his belly. An eagle with his wings extended as though taking flight embellished the giant silver buckle.

"Hello, Peter dear." Patsy Lee reached out for a hug as though she were pleased to see him.

Brock discreetly moved away from them and sidled up to me.

I glanced at him, and he mouthed barely audible words, "Ex-husband, Peter Presley."

I could imagine them as a couple. The way she smiled at him didn't make me think Peter was really trouble like Brock had said. I was still good friends with my own ex-husband. Maybe Patsy Lee was, too.

Bernie called to me. I gave Brock a little wave and joined a group that was arguing about where to place the tent for meeting Patsy Lee Presley. I agreed with Bernie's vision that Patsy Lee should be in the center of things.

"We're lucky that it will be cooler tomorrow," said Bernie. "Tables for the nonprofessional bakers' and the young bakers' pies to Patsy Lee's right. Tables for the professional-baking competition to the left. That way there won't be any confusion between those baked by home cooks and those baked by professionals. Patsy Lee can hold court in the middle."

"The microphone will be in Patsy Lee's tent?" I asked.

"Excellent," said Bernie. "When she's through signing, we'll take the books off the table and showcase some pies on it during the judging."

Bernie whispered his thanks to me for backing him up.

"In the afternoon, after the judging, will the same tables be set for the pie-eating contests?" I asked.

"That's the plan. And vendors will be selling pies around the outer edges under their own tents."

"Sounds like you have it under control."

"Mostly. Have you ever heard of The Upper Crust?" asked Bernie. "It's a last-minute entry in the professional pie category."

"Never heard of it."

"That's what worries me. No one is familiar with it."

Chapter 4

Dear Sophie,
How do people make those beautiful piecrust
edges? I've been trying for years and they always
look mangled.
Desperate Daughter in Doughboy, Nebraska

Dear Desperate,
Believe it or not, I find it easiest to use the second
joint in my fingers. Use one finger on one hand and
push the dough through two fingers of the other
hand. If that doesn't work, make a rope with left-
over dough and use that as your edge. It's always
lovely!
Sophie

"Maybe The Upper Crust is in Maryland or farther south in Virginia," I suggested. "Did you put any location restrictions on the professional entries?"

"Live and learn. Maybe I should have. But this is the only entry from someone I've never heard of." Bernie grinned at me. "Maybe that bakery will have the best pie."

"Is there anything I can do for you?" I asked.

"Not at the moment. You're still coming to dinner for Patsy Lee and her entourage at The Laughing Hound tonight. Right?"

"I wouldn't miss it."

Shortly before six o'clock, I zipped up a plain fit-and-flare dress, which was the dark purple color of eggplant. I felt compelled to dress it up with a necklace of twisted pearls and mini amethyst chunks. A pair of dangling amethyst-and-pearl earrings completed the look. I knew it would have been more stylish to wear high heels, but I settled for gold sandals with sensible cushy soles so I wouldn't trip on the uneven brick sidewalks.

I fed a can of turkey and gizzards to Mochie, my Ocicat, who was supposed to have spots but had bull's-eyes on his sides instead. He wasn't impressed. Daisy, however, snarfed her dinner of barley, ground turkey, peas, and carrots.

I grabbed a little gold cross-body purse and stepped outside my kitchen door. I looked around before closing it, just to be sure the strange man wasn't outside waiting for me. I didn't see him and wondered if his presence earlier had just been a weird coincidence. Feeling better, I locked the door and headed for Nina's house. She was already waiting at the sidewalk in a turquoise sheath printed with large white flowers.

"Do you think the guy who was watching you at the park today was the dark shadow who sprinted away earlier?" asked Nina.

"Maybe. He seemed familiar to me. Anyway, let me know if you notice anyone."

"Have you done something wicked?" she teased.

"Yes. I wouldn't let you cut the pie before it set up."

Nina laughed, but I noticed that she turned around and

looked behind us. "What do you make of Patsy Lee?" she asked.

"I'm not sure. She seems nice enough, but—"

"I know! She's a little bit odd, isn't she? And that Brock guy! He's yummy to look at, but do you really think she needs a bodyguard?"

"She lives a lifestyle that we can't even imagine. But I'll admit I got a chill when I thought that guy was watching us today. Maybe there are people who hang on to her, and he has to keep them away." I didn't mention that it was *definitely* Patsy Lee who had crashed through the bushes the other night, but I wondered where Brock had been? Had she ditched him?

At The Laughing Hound we waved at the busy hostess and went straight to the private patio, where Patsy Lee and entourage were already mingling and sampling Parmesan *tuiles* with fresh tomatoes, figs with bacon, and shrimp toasts.

Diamonds flashed on Patsy Lee's fingers as she made the rounds holding a Sazerac in her hand. She tilted her head and tossed the drink back as if she was used to drinking.

I nursed my vodka tonic and looked forward to a tall glass of iced tea. It was a beautiful summer evening, early enough for the sun to be out, but late enough for the humidity to have abated. I gazed at the clear sky. Maybe the weatherman had been right about a break from the oppressive heat.

A raised voice at the door that led from the patio into the restaurant captured my attention. I edged over to see Peter Presley, Patsy Lee's ex-husband. His fleshy face had turned purple with fury. "But I'm Patsy Lee's plus-one. Her husband, for heaven's sake."

A burly waiter with a shaved head, who usually worked at the bar, had nodded and smiled at Nina and me when we walked out on the terrace. Bernie must have posted him as a bouncer.

He consulted a sheet of paper and said very calmly, "I'm sorry, sir. You are not on the guest list this evening. Perhaps you would care to dine on the front patio. I can recommend our barbecued baby back ribs."

Peter's nostrils flared. "But I'm with Patsy Lee's party. Listen, buster, you're going to be in big trouble when Patsy Lee finds out that you gave me the heave-ho."

"I'm sorry, sir. Surely, you understand. There are a lot of people who would like to sneak in to meet Ms. Presley. I have to go by the list."

"You will pay for this." Peter's tone was controlled but menacing. "I will not be treated like some stranger off the street." He turned abruptly and, in his haste, nearly toppled a waitress carrying a tray. The chilling tinkle of clinking glasses filled the air as the tray tilted and they swept together.

The waiter lunged forward like he was doing some kind of deep knee bend. Like Superman, he held out one hand. With his fingers poised upward, he caught the bottom of the tray just in time and righted it.

The waitress blushed as though he had kissed her.

He just smiled and said, "You'd better refill all those drinks. There's no telling what sloshed into other glasses."

She hurried away, and I said, "That was a great catch."

"Thanks. I've seen you around here. You're a friend of Bernie's, right?" He held out his hand to me. "Remy Tarwick."

I shook his hand. "Sophie Winston. You handled Peter very well."

He shrugged. "I used to be a bouncer. That fellow was easy. Might be difficult when he's not sober. Is he really her husband?"

"Ex-husband."

His eyebrows shot up. "So he lied to me to get in." Shaking his head, he said, "You never know who might cause trouble and exes are the worst."

A woman ambled up to him, so I gave him a wave and mingled on the terrace, where no one appeared to have noticed Peter's rejection. Patsy Lee and her entourage chatted and laughed. Bernie had been wise to provide a private place for Patsy Lee to relax without people asking for autographs or snapping photos.

Bernie had arranged the tables in a square, which I thought brilliant. No one sat on the inside, so it felt as though we were all sharing the meal not just with those beside us, but also with those across from us. A white cloth covered the tables and each place setting had its own grass-green cloth under the service platter, hanging down as long as the white tablecloth. Trendy pear-shaped lightbulbs hung over us, giving the patio an informal yet festive feel. As the sun began to set, a server came around to take drink orders for dinner. She poured white and red wine for most. I stayed with unsweetened iced tea.

Nina whispered, "You're missing out by not drinking the wine that was chosen for these dishes."

Maybe she was right, but the presence of the *dark shadow*, as Nina had called him, drove me to keep my wits about me.

The appetizer consisted of two teeny potato pancakes topped with sour cream, sliced salmon, and a garnish of caviar. I felt thoroughly spoiled. But the tender crab ravioli with a heavenly hollandaise sauce, which came next, was even more delicious. I would have been very happy to simply eat more of it for my dinner. But the waiters soon whisked our plates away and replaced them with sliced duck breast served with a bourbon-laced peach sauce,

roasted asparagus, and creamy Parmesan duchess potatoes.

Needless to say, the food was the biggest topic of conversation. Bernie's chef had outdone himself.

By the time the dessert arrived, I had relaxed enough
about the dark shadow to want to taste a cream-pie after-
dinner drink, created just for the pie festival.

We were all wondering if a pie would be served for
dessert when Willa Staminski, The Laughing Hound's pastry chef, strode in carrying an ice-cream pie with chocolate
sauce drizzled on top.

Willa wore her nutmeg-colored hair short and messy.
She was pale enough to be a natural blonde, with a sprinkling of freckles across the bridge of her nose.

I was always impressed by dessert chefs like Willa who
maintained a slim figure. I didn't know how they did that.
I would be tasting and eating all day.

The patio was alive with laughter at the wise and hu-
morous choice, since an ice-cream pie definitely wouldn't
be entered in the contest. The judges would be eating a lot
of pies the next day and probably appreciated a bit of ice
cream instead.

A waiter followed Willa with a tray of dessert plates
containing slices of the ice-cream pie.

Patsy Lee's mouth fell open. She stood up and cried out,
"Willa Staminski, as I live and breathe!"

Willa set the pie on the table and readily embraced
Patsy Lee. The two hugged for a long moment.

"I just can't believe this," said Patsy Lee. "It has to be
the highlight of my visit to Old Town. It's been years since
we saw each other."

It seemed to me that Willa was a little more restrained. I
didn't know her well. Maybe Willa was just naturally reserved and didn't show her feelings as much as Patsy Lee,

who tended to be effervescent or at least pretended to be excited.

"How do you know each other?" asked Nina.

"We go way back," said Patsy Lee. "Besties, I think the kids call it now. Willa, honey, we have got to find some time to get together and catch up while I'm in town. Give your number to Brock and he'll set it up. It's so good seein' you!"

With that, Patsy Lee sat down, emptied her wineglass, and started on her after-dinner drink. "Somebody pass me a piece of that pie. Willa is an amazing chef. I bet it's delicious!"

After everyone left, Nina and I lingered a bit to chat with Bernie and make sure he didn't need a hand with anything. An hour later we headed home.

We had only walked a couple of blocks when we spied Patsy Lee.

Chapter 5

Dear Sophie,
I need to bake a pie for my book club. I'm a com-
plete dolt with pie dough, but they'll know if I use
one from the store. I'm terrified. Who said easy as
pie? It isn't easy at all!
Panicking in Pie, West Virginia

Dear Panicking,
Make a graham cracker crust. You can just press it
in place! No rolling or fussing with dough required.
Sophie

She glanced around furtively. There were plenty of lights
from stores and restaurants, but she must not have seen
us, which made me wonder just whom she was looking
for. A man, perhaps? Was that the reason she didn't notice
us? She was looking for a man?

Nina elbowed me. We fell in step about half a block behind Patsy Lee. We hadn't even reached the end of the
block when Nina and I shared a look. We weren't the only

ones casually strolling behind Patsy Lee. Brock was tailing her, too.

"There's something up with that woman," whispered Nina. "Did you notice how unenthusiastic her bestie was? You'd better be excited to see me if we're ever apart for several years."

"I thought Willa might be the type that doesn't show her emotions."

"Hah! She was showing emotions all right. Either they didn't part on good terms or they weren't besties at all."

Patsy Lee made an abrupt turn to the right. Nina and I dodged traffic to cross King Street and catch up. By the time we reached the corner where she had turned, Patsy Lee was out of sight. Brock, however, stood in a dark patch on the sidewalk, just across from a small cream-colored town house. The light to the left of the front door shone a beam on a tasteful wreath and a flower box at the window that was full of coral impatiens.

The barest hint of a light shimmered through the downstairs curtain, but a light flicked on upstairs. Despite the fact that a gauzy white curtain hung in the window, there was no mistaking the fact that two people were in the room.

Nina sidled up to Brock. "Who's she with?"

Brock's eyebrows rose in surprise. "What are you doing here?"

"We were on our way home. So who is he?" Nina persisted.

I nudged Nina and murmured, "It's not any of our business."

Brock eyed us. "Maybe not, but sometimes you have to take care of people so they don't get into trouble. For the record I don't know who he is. He was already in the house when Patsy Lee arrived."

"Are you supposed to wait out here all night?" I asked. That sounded like a miserable job.

"I'm not supposed to know she's in there. She told me she was turning in for the night."

I couldn't help laughing softly. "She snuck out on you! Maybe we should leave and let her have her privacy."

"You two go ahead." Brock rubbed the top of his head. "I don't know what to do. She pays me to look out for her. Now I'm in a quandary. If I hadn't been down the hall getting ice, I never would have noticed her leaving our hotel. I'd be back in bed, having a drink and watching a *Big Bang Theory* rerun. But I followed her, so maybe I ought to stick around."

"She might be there all night," Nina cautioned.

I groaned. "What's wrong with you two? Brock, if she had wanted you to stand guard, she would have told you. But she didn't say a thing, right? The mere fact that she slipped out quietly without telling you indicates that she didn't want you to be here. If I were in her shoes, I'd be mighty mad if I knew people were gathering on the sidewalk to discuss my private business."

"That certainly applies to the two of us," Nina agreed.

"From what I can tell," I said, "Patsy Lee doesn't get much private time. I can't imagine living that way. It's like she's in a fishbowl with everyone watching. It would drive me nuts if people observed my every little move. C'mon, Nina. Let's scram."

"As much as I'd love to know who it is she's with, I think that's the right thing to do. You coming, Brock?" asked Nina.

He nodded. "You ladies are exactly right."

The three of us strolled back to King Street, where we said good night and split up. Nina and I headed home.

"You think he's doubling back?" asked Nina.

"We'll know tomorrow morning when he looks dead tired."

Nina peeled off to her house, but I stood silently on the sidewalk for a moment, peering into the dark just to be sure the dark shadow wasn't hanging around. When I didn't see him, I went home to Daisy and Mochie.

In the morning, I took Daisy for a stroll before breakfast. I felt obligated to be at the pie festival early, in case Bernie needed a hand.

I shivered a little as we walked down to the park, where vendors were already setting up their tents. Everyone had been right about a wave of cool air coming through.

Thanks to my job as an event planner, I had done business with local bakeries and recognized some of the people who worked at them. A few stopped setting up long enough to say hi and pet Daisy, but others clearly needed a second mug of coffee before they could function.

It probably wasn't right of me, but on the way back, Daisy and I strolled by the house where Brock had seen Patsy Lee the night before. After all, we had to walk somewhere.

The house was quite small, but it was a darling place in a prime location. People hurried by, a few undoubtedly heading to work on a Saturday morning. There was no sign of Patsy Lee, of course, which was just as well. I hoped Brock had gotten some sleep.

I stopped by the take-out window of Big Daddy's Bakery for some fresh pancetta and Gruyère croissants to enjoy with eggs for breakfast. Unless I missed my guess, Nina would be over shortly to join me.

On our way home Daisy and I passed the mansion where Bernie lived. My ex-husband, Mars, had moved in with him after leaving Natasha.

Mars bounded out on the front porch. "Soph!" He opened the door and shouted inside, "Sophie's out here."

A political consultant, Mars looked as clean cut as most of his ambitious clients.

I released Daisy's leash so she could scamper up the stairs to him. Neither Mars nor I could bear to give her up in our divorce, so we had worked out a custody schedule. She wriggled all over as he petted her.

"Bernie's been looking for you."

I checked my pocket. "Forgot my phone. Sorry about that. What's up?"

Bernie rushed out on the porch, looking more disheveled than usual. He raked a hand through his hair. "I'm so glad you turned up. What a morning! For a while there we thought Patsy Lee had gone missing."

I suspected I knew why that might have happened, but decided it was best not to mention where Patsy Lee might have been. As long as she was back, everything was fine.

Bernie loped down the stairs to the sidewalk. "I hate to impose, especially since you're already in charge of the pie-eating contests, but the guy who was supposed to accept pies from the professional bakers called in sick—"

"No problem." I patted his shoulder. "That sounds like fun. I bet Nina will help, too."

"No!" Bernie waved his hands crosswise. "She's a judge and can't know who submitted the pies."

"Good point. I forgot about that."

"Does that mean I can have Daisy this weekend?" asked Mars. "She'll be stuck in the house all day today, anyway, if you're at the pie festival."

My initial instinct was to say *no*, but he was right. Daisy would have more fun spending the day with Mars. "Sure." I handed the leash to Mars and knelt to give Daisy a hug. I looked into her sweet brown eyes. "You two have fun."

I snuck one croissant out of the bag from Big Daddy's and handed the rest over to Mars. "Maybe you and Nina can share these."

To Bernie, I said, "I'll grab a shower and some breakfast and meet you at the festival."

I hurried home and hopped in the shower, then searched my closet for a sleeveless cotton dress. The plain salmon-colored dress fit loosely, which came as a pleasant surprise. I added simple hoop earrings and slipped on cushy white sandals. I pulled my hair back and up into a loose French twist because I would be handling food. I didn't want to risk shedding onto a pie!

There was no way I would be able to function unless I drank a mug of hot tea before I left. I took a few minutes to boil water and pour it over an Irish Breakfast tea bag. I added a little sugar and a splash of milk.

Mochie waited by his empty food bowl, patiently watching me. When I didn't respond quickly enough to the silent messages he was sending me, his paw slid under the edge of the bowl. He knew banging his bowl would get my attention! Laughing, I rushed over with a fresh bowl and filled it with Tasty Tuna, which he seemed to like. I kept him company while I ate my croissant and downed the tea.

Mochie moseyed over to his favorite spot in the bay window, which faced the street. Sunbeams weren't hitting it yet, but passing people and lively squirrels were already providing entertainment. Mochie began to groom his face, and stopped, his right front paw midair, when a squirrel dared to look in the window at him.

I locked up and set off for the festival. The park already buzzed with activity. Throngs of people milled among the vendors' tents, buying pie for breakfast. Moos & Brews was having a busy morning. It seemed like almost everyone was carrying coffee cups with their logo of a cute cow head.

Bernie handed me preprinted sheets that listed the people who had entered the contest, the name of the bakery or restaurant they worked at, and the type of pie being submitted. All I had to do was give each pie a number and mark it on the sheet. That sounded easy enough.

"You'll be the only one who knows which pie belongs to which person," said Bernie, handing me a box of gloves.

"That's a lot of power," I teased.

"I have total faith that you will not use your powers for evil." Bernie winked at me. "Now, if we don't lose Patsy Lee again"—he glanced at his watch—"and she turns up on time, we should be good to go. Be sure to use those food-prep gloves. I don't want anyone handling food without them."

Not two minutes later the bakers began delivering pies to me. Dutifully wearing the food-prep gloves, I gave them numbers and arranged them on the table according to the type of pie. Most were sweet, like chocolate meringue pie and peach bourbon pie. But some of the bakers had gone with savory pies. I hoped I would get to taste chicken Florentine pie, but I had my doubts about spaghetti pie.

I was giving a pie a number when I heard, "Hi, y'all! Patsy Lee is here!"

I glanced over at her and picked up on the relief on Bernie's face.

Daisy showed up next, and delicately took the ribbon decorating the pie table in her mouth. "Is that a threat?" I asked her. "If I don't sneak you a slice of pie, then you'll pull on that ribbon?"

She wagged her tail as though she understood and posed for a newspaper photographer.

"There you are," said Mars.

"I told you Daisy would lead us to Sophie," said Nina.

"Daisy, can you lead Mars and Nina to buy tape so I

can attach the numbers to the bottoms of the pie pans?" That way a stiff breeze wouldn't accidently mix them up.

Nina nodded. "A good move. I guess this wind is bringing in the change in weather."

Roger approached the check-in table with a pie in hand.

"Roger Mackenzie," he said formally, speaking as though I didn't know him.

He wore a bold blue golf shirt that brought out the azure in his eyes against skin so pale I knew he wasn't an outdoorsy type.

I laughed and played along. "Sophie Winston. What kind of pie are you entering in the contest?"

"Full Moon Pie."

"Moon Pie? Like the cookies filled with marshmallow?"

"Sort of along those lines."

"That sounds good!" I paused. I didn't think he was working at a bakery. I decided I had to treat him just like everyone else. "What's the name of your business?"

"The Upper Crust."

I didn't expect that. "Oh! We were just discussing your bakery. Where is it located? I'll have to drop by."

"It's opening in October. We were hoping a win might get us some publicity."

If nothing else, the interesting flavor combination might get them some mentions in the local press. "Good luck!" I handed him a blue tag that said *Professional Pie #15* and walked over to the table of sweet pies, where I placed it in the middle.

When I returned, I saw that Roger had ambled over to the table next to me, where Patsy Lee reigned. He stood a few feet away and watched her as though he was too shy to approach. I noticed that in between chatting with eager fans, she caught a glimpse of him. She showed no reaction, but her glance lingered on him briefly.

Tommy Earl snapped his fingers at me. "Sophie!"

"Sorry."

He pulled on food-prep gloves to remove his pie from a box. "Are you watching Patsy Lee or Roger?"

"Both," I admitted sheepishly. "Do you know Roger? He's about to become your competition."

"Hardly. Can't say I'm too worried about him." Tommy Earl leaned forward and whispered, "Keep your distance. Roger's known for inappropriate advances. Can't get a job anywhere. He's ruined his reputation and no one is willing to take a chance on him."

"Thanks for the warning." I looked at the pie Tommy Earl was handing me. Without any doubt it was the most gorgeous pie I had ever seen. Dough leaves lay on the edge all the way around. The middle bore the traditional criss-crossed pastry in a most unconventional way. The ribbons of pastry dough were different widths and some were even braided. On top of that, Tommy had artistically added pastry flowers in different shapes and sizes. It didn't have to taste good, I would give it a blue ribbon for sheer beauty!

"Darlin's," I heard Patsy Lee drawl. "I'm desperately in need of coffee. Brock?"

He gave her a thumbs-up. "I'm on it." Brock turned to me. "Where's the closest place with great java?"

"I'm partial to Moos and Brews. It's two blocks in that direction." I pointed to be sure he understood.

"Back in a flash. Can I get you anything?"

"That's very thoughtful. Actually, I would love an iced coffee." I offered him cash, but he waved it away.

Mars delivered the tape I had requested.

By the time I was through taping the numbers onto the bottoms of the pie plates, Brock had returned. He handed me the iced coffee I had requested.

I sipped through the straw immediately. "Thanks, Brock. This hits the spot. It's great."

"Hey, Sophie!" Bernie pointed to a line of pie-bearing chefs.

I got back to work, handing out numbers, placing the pies, and wishing *good luck* to each baker.

Patsy Lee declared, "I need to stretch my legs! Y'all pardon me for a bit."

She walked over behind me. In the tiniest voice that I could barely hear, she said, "Bernie tells me you solve mysteries."

"Not exactly."

"I need your help. I have a little problem. Your tact in the matter the other night leads me to believe that I can count on you to be discreet."

"I think you're under the wrong impression. I've solved a few murders—"

"Sugah, I need someone to do somethin' very private for me. Someone who can keep a secret. Lunch today at Bernie's restaurant? He has guaranteed me a private dining room so we can talk."

What could I say? The least I could do was listen to her. Maybe I could even point her in the right direction to get whatever help she needed. After all, she had been running from someone. "Okay."

"Thank you, Sophie. Now, I'm off to see if Brock has cleared the ladies' room for me." She waved her hands under her chin. "I swear this humidity is about to do me in. And I think the food at that diner this morning isn't sitting well with me." She toddled off in search of Brock.

I continued to take in pies, but my mind was on Patsy Lee. She returned to her position at the book-signing table and winked at me.

After a submission of chicken pot pie from Star-Spangled Pies, I looked up to see the man Brock had pointed out the day before. Was he the dark shadow?

He stood in the crowd with a young girl. Now that he

was closer, I recognized him. Most weekday mornings when I was filling the kettle with water for tea, I saw him through the window over my sink. He strode by on the sidewalk on the other side of the street, never smiling, always carrying a dark brown leather briefcase. He had a preference for dark gray suits. His loafers were generally scuffed and comfortably worn. He wasn't part of the local gala scene or I would have noticed him at some of my events.

I was still a little bit creeped out by him, but as I watched, he took on a harmless and kind appearance. He patiently coaxed the girl to submit a pie. He placed a bony hand behind her back as if he wanted to propel her toward the youth table.

The girl was darling. Her hair was cut short, just long enough to cover her ears. A rose-colored headband pulled it off her round face. She had a summer tan, which made her blue eyes even more prominent. She gazed at the junior pie submission table with a serious expression. The dark shadow whispered something to her. She took a deep breath and stepped across the grass slowly, walking as if she were headed to her doom.

Willa, the pastry chef from The Laughing Hound, strolled over to me. "Hi, Sophie." She studied each pie.

"Hi. No pie to enter?" I asked.

Willa smiled. "Bernie said it wouldn't be fair for us to enter, since he's in charge this year. I'm one of the judges this time. It's kind of fun to be a bystander. Did you notice this pie with the tiny strips of dough on top twisting around in a giant circle? It's a work of art. It must have taken an hour to get them all perfect like that."

"There's one with roses and leaves that's equally amazing."

Willa clucked in dismay. "Will you look at this one? That's from a form. You press it into the dough and it cuts the shapes. Patsy Lee will recognize that in a minute."

"It's pretty, though."

She glanced at me. "It's probably Tommy Earl's pie. He's known for shortcuts. That kind of trick belongs in the home baker category, not the professional one."

I knew it wasn't Tommy Earl's pie. It took every ounce of forbearance I could muster not to defend him. There were a lot of other pies, so telling her that one wasn't Tommy Earl's wouldn't be the equivalent of pointing his out to her. Nevertheless, it was supposed to be entirely anonymous. I had to keep it to myself.

At that moment Roger walked by.

"Perfect timing," I said, and quickly introduced Willa to Roger.

He gasped. "Willa!" He reached out to hug her. "It's been so long. What are you doing these days?"

"I'm the pastry chef at The Laughing Hound."

"Oh, my gosh! I've had your pie! Of course, I've eaten every pie offered in Old Town. But yours are simply outstanding."

Another baker walked up to me with a pie, so I excused myself, but I could hear Roger telling Willa about his PiePalooza event.

The hour flew by as last-minute bakers arrived, one still painting finishing touches on his pie as I checked him in.

Willa returned to examine the pies on the table again.

"Something wrong, or are you eager to start judging?"

"Did I leave my coffee here? I've lost it somewhere."

"Sorry, but I haven't seen it. I would have noticed it on the table with the pies."

I reviewed my list and noted that all the entries were present. When I looked up, Bernie stepped in front of the microphone to introduce Patsy Lee, who was seated behind him.

Chapter 6

Dear Sophie,
We're having a pie-throwing event at my school to
raise money for a class trip. What's the best kind of
pie to throw?
            Messy Mona in Sweets Corner, Massachusetts

Dear Messy Mona,
The obvious answer would be the kind of pie the
victim likes. But generally I think that a cream pie
with a meringue or whipped-cream topping would
be more gentle against the face. Definitely avoid
double-crust pies!

                                    Sophie

Bernie tapped the microphone. "Thank you for coming to Old Town's Pie Festival! We shall kick off the festivities by judging pies in three categories: professional, home baker, and junior, which means the baker is under the age of fourteen. After each pie is judged, the remainder will be cut into sample bites for you to try. But it's not over after the judges award the ribbons! Then the serious pie eating will commence with the pie-eating contest!"

The crowd applauded and cheered.

"But first," Bernie continued, "the star of our show, everyone's favorite pie baker, one of our own who used to be a resident of Old Town, the fabulous queen of cooking shows, Patsy Lee Presley!" Applauding, Bernie stepped away from the microphone to make room for Patsy Lee.

The number of people in attendance astonished me. Of course, I was looking forward to trying some of the pies, too. Apparently, I wasn't alone.

Many people clutched Patsy Lee's latest cookbook, *Sweetie Pie: Recipes from Patsy Lee's Kitchen*. She obviously had a devoted following.

Patsy Lee stood up and slowly walked the few steps to the microphone to speak. A selection of stunningly beautiful pies provided by vendors graced the table in front of her, with copies of her latest books standing in a semicircle behind them.

I suspected she had applied her makeup with cameras in mind. Her eyes were artfully lined to be prominent but ladylike. Her foundation was packed on like mud, but would look perfect in photos and on the news. If there were flaws on her skin, no one would be the wiser.

She had worn the big pearls and bracelet again, this time with a sleeveless dress in shades of lime and turquoise.

The temperature was unusually pleasant so it was surprising that beads of sweat were starting to erupt into tiny craters in the impeccable makeup on her forehead. Was she shy about making live appearances?

I wondered if Tommy had been correct about her age. She didn't look over fifty. In fact, I would have guessed her to be in her midforties, which wasn't easy to pull off in person.

She wobbled a touch and braced herself against the table

when she said brightly, "Hey, y'all! Patsy Lee is here!" She paused and swallowed hard. "I am so honored—"

Patsy swayed and took a deep breath. She placed a hand on her collarbone and seemed to be gathering herself. Ever the pro, she forced a smile. "I am so honored to be here. Y'all know there's nothin' I love better'n a homemade pie 'cept maybe my fans!"

With that, Patsy Lee pitched forward and fell onto the vendors' pie display on the table face-first. The motion of her body pitched the table forward. The microphone squealed and howled as it crashed to the ground. The beautiful pies around her slid off, smashing on the grass, and poor dignified Patsy Lee Presley lay at an angle on the toppled table, her face in a pie and her legs in the air.

A moment of silence followed as everyone absorbed what had happened.

As Bernie and I rushed to her rescue, screams and wailing began.

"Nina! Call 911," I shouted.

It didn't look good for Patsy Lee. She had landed with her face smack in a butterscotch cream pie. I slid my arm under hers and lifted, with Bernie doing the same on her other side. I could hear cameras snapping photos.

Brock scooted a chair behind her. We sat her down. Her eyes were closed and butterscotch filling clung to her skin. But her head rolled back and to the right as though she had no control over it anymore.

My heart skipped beats. This wasn't good at all. I seized some pie festival napkins and poured ice water on them. As gently as possible, I wiped the creamy pie off her face and tried to use my body to block onlookers from snapping more photos.

Bernie was feeling her neck for a pulse. When he looked up at me, I could see horror in his eyes.

Officer Wong and my former beau Wolf Fleishman, who

worked in the criminal investigative division of the Alexandria Police, must have been in the crowd because they arrived immediately. They transferred her to the ground so Patsy Lee lay on her back and then they started chest compressions.

Brock hovered behind them. He knelt by Patsy Lee's head. "Patsy Lee! Come on. You can do this, Patsy Lee."

Peter Presley watched anxiously a foot from her feet. Willa stood beside him, looking every bit as worried as Peter.

Three emergency medical technicians arrived and took over for Wong and Wolf. They asked Brock to move back to give them room.

"She was sick this morning," he said.

The third EMT delicately coaxed him up and away from Patsy Lee. "What time was that?"

Wolf and Wong sidled up to them. I snuck along and stood behind them, eavesdropping.

Brock glanced at Patsy Lee. "About an hour ago. She went to the ladies' room half an hour before that, too. I don't know if she was sick then, but she was definitely retching the second time."

"Had she eaten any of the pies?" asked Wolf.

"No. She's supposed to be a judge, but the judging hadn't started. We ate breakfast at Aunt Rosie's Diner. By the time we got here, we were all parched. Patsy Lee sent me for coffee"—Brock stopped and gestured toward me—"which I bought at Moos and Brews."

"Why are you pointing toward Sophie?" asked Wolf. "Did she go with you?"

"She recommended Moos and Brews," said Brock.

They all looked at me, so I nodded. But I was a little worried. If something was wrong with the coffee, I would be feeling sick soon.

Nina grabbed my arm. "Bernie wants you," she hissed.

"Now?"

"Yes. Hurry!"

Reluctant as I was to leave, I followed Nina through the crowd. A van with the logo of The Laughing Hound pulled up on the road next to the park, with bartender Remy driving.

Bernie was in full control, directing Remy and another employee to remove each pie and load it into the van.

"What are you doing?" I asked.

"Patsy's not going to make it," he whispered. "We've got to refrigerate these pies."

"She's going to die? How do you know that?"

"Because I couldn't get a pulse. I don't think they'll be able to revive her. And even if they do, we still need to cool these pies so no one else will get sick. It's just a matter of time before Wolf throws crime scene tape around the entire park."

I watched as Remy picked up a pie, his large hands visible through the food-preparation gloves he wore. The carefully placed number that marked it flapped loose. I envisioned the nightmare ahead—a pie that won, but had the wrong number attached. That could happen so easily if we were sloppy. I hoped the tape would stick well.

"Maybe we should call off the festival," said Nina.

Bernie nodded. "I thought about that. But we've got all these pies, and people are coming from all over the place. We can't let them down, not to mention the vendors."

"The show must go on," muttered Remy as he grabbed two pies with their numbers.

I felt terrible. Patsy was dying and all around her life went on. I gazed at the people roaming the park and looking at pies. Most of them probably didn't even realize that a woman lay dead or dying mere feet away from them.

Bernie slung an arm around my shoulders. "I know, Soph. I feel the same way."

I heard doors close behind me. Bernie and I rushed back, but Wong held out her hand to stop us from entering the area where Patsy Lee had been. We watched as the ambulance pulled away.

"Is she . . . ?" I asked.

"I can't believe this," said Wong. "I'm such a big fan of Patsy Lee's. I never dreamed I would be stringing crime scene tape where she had been sitting."

"So she's dead?"

"They'll probably call it dead on arrival at the hospital. Good thing Wolf was here. He's looking for you."

"Which one of us?" I asked.

"Both of you. He's over by the pies where she fell. Just stay out of the crime scene."

"Why are you calling it a crime scene? She probably had a stroke or something," said Bernie.

"We don't know what happened to her. That's why we have to do it. The medical examiner might find something no one noticed, but then it would be too late to come back and collect evidence. Hundreds of people would have trampled through the area."

People were treading over the area as she spoke. Wong made perfect sense. But it would impede the festival. What was I thinking? Patsy's death put a huge damper on it! Nothing could be worse than that.

Bernie and I stayed outside of the yellow tape as we followed it to Wolf. He calmly examined the once-beautiful pies that slid off the table Patsy Lee had fallen onto.

Sunlight glinted on the silver that crept into Wolf's dark brown hair. He wore jeans and a light blue button-down shirt with the cuffs rolled back. "Bernie, you were the closest to her. What did you see?" he asked.

"Not much. She seemed a little unsteady, then she fell forward."

"Did you notice anything out of the ordinary earlier?"

Bernie groaned. "I wish I had. Not that it would have changed anything. If she had looked very ill, I think Brock and her crew would have taken her to the emergency room. I was busy with people, making sure everything was running smoothly. I had no idea Patsy Lee wasn't feeling well."

"How about you, Sophie?"

"I was off to the side. All I noticed were the beads of sweat on her forehead. I thought it was odd because it's not particularly hot today. She started to speak, repeated herself like she had lost her train of thought, and then she pitched forward. But, Wolf, I spoke to her and she said her stomach was upset. Probably from breakfast."

He scowled. "Thanks, Sophie."

"Wolf, the night before last I was walking Daisy after dark and Patsy Lee darted out of the bushes and ran away like she thought someone was chasing her. She asked me not to say anything, but now . . . Now I wish I had."

Wolf cocked his head sympathetically. "Don't blame yourself. You didn't know what would happen." He took a deep breath and gazed around the park. "Is there any-place we can move the pie festival to?"

Never in my life had I seen Bernie look so panicked. "I hope you're joking."

"What if we ask everyone to clear out for one hour?" I asked. "I know it doesn't seem like much time, but . . ." I gazed at the expanse of grass. "Bring in half a dozen cops and they'll have it checked out in no time." As I spoke, I knew it was unlikely.

"Your faith in the speed with which that can be accom-plished is endearing," said Wolf. "But you've given me an idea. Wong!"

She walked over to us.

"See if you can get the recruits out here," said Wolf.

Wong grinned. "This is the perfect time for them to learn how to do a grid search."

"We'll do our best," said Wolf. "A couple of hours, maybe? Bernie, does that work for you?"

"Do I have any other choices?"

I groaned aloud. "It's not ideal, but having the star attraction keel over dead isn't exactly wonderful, either."

Wolf looked over the top of my head. "And here come the press. That's all we need."

"Wong"—Wolf pointed toward the TV vans arriving on the street—"see if you can head them off. Sophie, Bernie, get the vendors out of here. No packing up their tents. Just move everyone out."

Wolf picked up the microphone and tapped on it. The high-pitched squeals drew the attention of the crowd. "Ladies and gentlemen, this is the Alexandria Police. Due to circumstances beyond our control we have to ask you to leave the park for a short time. That includes the vendors and all participants. As soon as we're done, the festival will resume. You can anticipate that it will take a few hours. This would be a good time to grab lunch at one of our fine restaurants. Thank you for your cooperation."

A buzz ran through the crowd. The vendors were irate and I couldn't blame them. They had to fit their pies into coolers quickly and trust that no one would meddle with their setups.

It turned out that Bernie and I were pretty good sheepdogs. Or maybe word had spread about Patsy Lee's condition and that was the reason most of them were cooperative, even if they weren't happy about it.

In my hurry to clear everyone out, I forgot about Patsy Lee's friends—until I found Willa staring at the spot where

Patsy Lee had been sitting. Willa seemed rooted to the ground. Tears rolled down her face, but she made no effort to wipe them away.

I touched her arm gently. "Willa? Are you okay?"

Her voice raspy, she said, "We were best friends once. There was a time when we were almost inseparable. I was so busy being angry with her that I'd forgotten about the good times we had. And now it's too late."

"I'm so sorry, Willa." I could see Wolf signaling me to get her out of there. "Honey, we need to move across the street. The police have to make sure there was no foul play."

Willa finally changed her focus from the spot where Patsy Lee had taken her last breath to my face. "Nooo," she breathed. Her head hung down and she sobbed aloud. "I wish . . . I wish she had never . . . changed."

"Willa, we have to go," I coaxed.

She staggered across the street as though she could barely function. "Peter. Where is Peter?"

I spied him in the crowd on the sidewalk, talking with members of Patsy Lee's entourage. I propelled her toward him. Peter opened his arms and embraced her. The two of them cried together, Willa sobbing so hard that her shoulders shook.

Someone at the police station must have worked wonders because by the time I found Bernie, the park practically crawled with police recruits.

Nina caught up to us. "I can't believe this is happening. Wolf questioned me, but while I was talking to him, someone came up and said he had Patsy Lee's fall on video. And you won't believe who it was!"

I took a wild stab. "Natasha?"

Bernie hissed, "Natasha?" He scanned the crowd. "Notable by her absence. What is she up to now?"

"You *did* ban her," Nina said.

"I had to," Bernie protested. "I am not the one who baked a pie with such outrageously hot peppers that the judges needed hospitalization. So who took the video?"

"The dark shadow!" Nina said in a loud whisper.

Chapter 7

Dear Natasha,
You're always so elegant and never flustered on
your show. I wish I could be more like you. I have
to bake several pies for a local event. Can I make
the pie dough in advance and freeze it in aluminum
pans so I'm not trying to do everything in one day?
Overwhelmed Wife in Chocolate Bayou, Texas

Dear Overwhelmed Wife,
Would you want to eat frozen pie dough? I think
not. Don't embarrass yourself by showing up with
inferior pies.

Natasha

It was exceptionally bad timing. Cicely Comstock, a re-
porter whom I recognized from the local news, obviously
had no compunction about barging in on our conversation.
"Who is that? Did he murder Patsy Lee?"

The three of us stared at her in surprise.

Nina recovered first. She held out her hand. "Nina Reid

Norwood. He's been following Sophie. He turns up everywhere she goes."

"Has he been following Patsy Lee?"

"Not that I know of."

"How long has he been following her?"

Now Nina seemed a little miffed. "He's been following *Sophie* for a couple of days."

Bernie looked as appalled as if she had slapped him. "You didn't tell me anything about this. Does Wolf know?"

I wasn't sure how to respond. I had been a little creeped out by the guy, until I saw him with the girl today. It wasn't so much the way he looked, but the fact that he appeared to be watching me. On the other hand, we didn't really know that he was following me.

"I saw him at the pie festival," I said. "He was with a very sweet little girl who was entering a pie. He didn't even look at me. Maybe we were wrong about him. And, for your information, Bernie, Wolf does not know, nor does he need to know. To be honest, I'm not certain that he's following me at all, though he did seem to be lurking on our street the other day."

At that moment Mars joined our little group. "I've been looking for you guys. Patsy Lee has hypokalemia."

Cicely's gaze snapped to him. "What's that?"

Speaking with hesitation, Mars said, "It's an electrolyte imbalance. Not enough potassium."

"What would cause that?" she asked.

"Any number of things."

"Is she dead?" asked Cicely.

Mars's eyes widened. Poor Mars looked uncomfortable and a little bit bewildered.

I tilted my head and motioned subtly with my hand for us to move away from her. We took a few steps. I was relieved to see her asking someone else questions.

"I used to like her when I saw her on the local news,"

whispered Nina. "But she's like a coyote, roaming around and waiting to see what she can pounce on."

"Sophie, point this dark shadow guy out to me when you see him again." Bernie scowled at me. "I don't like someone following you."

Nina giggled. "Don't worry, Bernie. He's so skinny that Sophie could overpower him."

I glared at her. She didn't need to go putting thoughts like that in his head. "So, Mars, what does that mean about Patsy Lee?"

"Her cells weren't working correctly. It's especially important in the heart."

"She had a heart attack?" asked Bernie.

"I don't know about that, but low potassium can lead to heart arrhythmia."

"Poor Patsy Lee. She reached the top and now she won't be around to enjoy all that success she worked so hard for," I said.

"Maybe you should postpone the pie festival until tomorrow," Nina suggested.

Bernie sighed. "I fear that would be a disaster. A lot of people came a good distance. I'm not sure they would bother to return. We could post about it on social media, but I don't know if that would suffice to bring everyone out again. I'll give Wolf until one o'clock. If he doesn't release the vendor area by then, I'll see what we can do about a one-day delay."

"How about some lunch while we wait?" I asked. "I'm parched and I left my iced coffee in the crime scene zone."

Bernie stared at me. "Okay. Maybe we'll see this Dark Shadow fellow."

We headed for Moos & Brews, which I was certain would be swamped. But when we arrived, the doors were locked and a big handwritten sign was taped to the inside of the glass door: *Temporarily Closed. Please check back.*

"They ran out of coffee!" Nina exclaimed.

"I don't think so." I pointed at the people inside. "They're not drinking coffee."

Nina peered inside. "Cops?"

"The last thing Patsy Lee was known to consume was coffee from Moos and Brews. They shut it down fast!" I gulped and concentrated on my own stomach. I felt okay. I looked around. "I bet they shut down the diner where she ate breakfast, too." Was it selfish of me to hope that was where Patsy Lee ate whatever made her sick? Had I consumed the same thing? It was a scary thought. I wondered if anyone else had fallen ill. Moos and Brews had sold a lot of coffee to people attending the pie festival.

We moved on to Le Sandwich, where we bought turkey heros to take out, and I splurged on a strawberry milk shake. After all, it would probably be good to drink milk to coat my stomach. Just in case. I hadn't had one since I was a kid. It was so thick, I couldn't even sip it through the straw on the way back to the park.

There wasn't anyplace to sit on the sidewalks across the street from the park. We found a tree a good bit farther down that was outside of the yellow crime-scene tape, and we ate in its shade, watching the police recruits line up and walk in a tight row, examining the ground. I suspected that anything they found would be from the crowd and not helpful, but who knew? Maybe they would find something with DNA on it that would later match a suspect and indicate his or her presence. I guessed an attorney could argue that it had been there for days. Still, as Wong had pointed out, it was now or never for collecting evidence.

At twelve forty-five Wolf crossed the street to us. "Sorry to have to do that, Bernie. I'm keeping the center where Patsy Lee sat cordoned off, and I'd appreciate your assistance in making sure people stay out of there so it won't be further contaminated. But you can let the vendors back in and continue with the pie festival."

"Can you bring the microphone out to me so we can use it?" asked Bernie.

"Sure. No problem. Thanks for cooperating." Wolf smiled at him.

"Any news about Patsy Lee?" I asked.

"They tell me it's all over the news that she died. I haven't heard anything official."

We dumped our wrappers in the trash and hurried back into the park. While Bernie hit the microphone and announced that the pie festival was back on, Nina and I rearranged tables so the focus wouldn't be on the site of Patsy Lee's death. Wong enlisted the aid of police recruits in removing the crime scene tape, which surrounded the park.

People flooded back in. I had been afraid that many would lose interest and leave, but there was no sign of that.

Nina whispered, "I think people came to see the scene of the crime."

I cringed at the thought. But when I gazed over at the area that had been cordoned off, tears sprang to my eyes. People were leaving flowers there in memory of Patsy Lee. One fellow even brought a pie and set it next to a framed photograph of her.

Bernie hurried over to us. "I hate to sound so insensitive, but we're shy one judge. We only have Nina and Willa."

"Mars?" I suggested.

Bernie wrinkled his nose. "Wouldn't it be better to use someone who has some degree of expertise? *Sophie?*"

"I can't judge. I know who brought the pies."

At that exact moment Natasha strode in, looking cool

and, while I hated to admit it, rather stunning. She wore a robin's-egg blue pantsuit, with a widely spaced black window-pane pattern on it. Her sandals and purse were black like the buttons on the suit jacket and her oversized hat. She wore large sunglasses.

"How can she stand long sleeves and trousers in warm weather?" asked Nina.

In a polite monotone Bernie said, "I don't believe there's much under the jacket."

He was right. While nothing racy was showing, she didn't appear to be wearing a blouse.

"No." Bernie said it softly but emphatically. "No! I am not inviting her to judge."

"Tommy Earl would be perfect, but he submitted a pie." I stopped short of mentioning how beautiful it was because I didn't want to influence Nina. "What about Patsy Lee's ex-husband? Think he might do it in her honor?"

"Do you know how to reach him?" asked Bernie.

"I bet Brock does." It wasn't until I uttered Brock's name that I remembered Patsy Lee's rendezvous the night before. I excused myself and hurried toward Wolf, who stood just outside the area that was still surrounded by crime scene tape.

"Wolf, this might not be important at all, and maybe Brock already mentioned it, but Patsy Lee met with some-one at a town house last night. Evidently, she didn't want Brock to know about it, but he caught her sneaking out after she said she was hitting the sack."

"That's interesting. Thanks, Sophie. Do you know which house it was?"

I nodded. "I walked by it this morning with Daisy."

"The next time you're over that way, it would be helpful if you got the address."

"Sure. I'd be happy to do that. One other thing." I felt awful betraying Patsy Lee's confidence, but given the circumstances, I guessed it didn't really matter anymore. "Patsy Lee asked me to have lunch with her privately. She had some kind of problem that she wanted me to help her with."

Wolf looked at me blankly. "What kind of problem? Are we talking wardrobe, recipes, or murder?"

"I honestly don't know. She said something about a possible murder—if she didn't solve the problem—but I took that as just an expression."

"She didn't give you a clue?"

"Honestly, she didn't. But something was bothering her."

"Thanks, Sophie. I don't really know what we're dealing with yet. We'll know more once the coroner's report is in. She could have died of natural causes."

I turned away, but he nabbed my arm. "Do me a favor and don't mention anything about her nocturnal adventure last night to anyone. Okay?"

"Nina was there, too. I'll let her know."

"Good grief." Wolf massaged his brow with his hand. "I hope she hasn't blabbed about it yet."

I scurried over to Nina. "Wolf wants us to keep the information about Patsy Lee's excursion last night under wraps. No telling anyone."

Her eyes widened.

"You haven't mentioned it to anyone?" I cringed in anticipation of her answer.

"Only Bernie . . ."

I sucked in air and let out a sigh of relief. Bernie was a decent and pretty discreet fellow. I gazed around for him. He was on his phone. I made a beeline for him.

He hung up his phone and smiled at me. "Peter Presley was a great suggestion. He sounds quite broken up about Patsy Lee's death, but he's very amenable to filling in for her. Said it would give him something else to think about and take his mind off losing Patsy. He's on his way."

"Great! Uh, Bernie? Wolf has asked that we not mention anything about Patsy Lee's rendezvous last night."

"Makes sense. No problem, Sophie. I haven't said a thing. Poor Patsy Lee. She couldn't even meet with a friend without people gossiping about it."

I let out a deep breath of air. "Time to unload the pies?"

"I'm way ahead of you. Remy and Mars are unloading them as we speak."

"Mars?"

I spied him carrying pies from the truck and ran over to him. "Where's Daisy?"

"Relax, Sophie. While you were working this morning, we went to the dog park. She's at home, stretched out on the floor and fast asleep in the air conditioning. You'd better get these pies arranged for the judging."

I was trying to remember which pies were savory and which were sweet, without checking each one specifically. Some were easy to identify, but I finally had to consult my chart. I didn't want them mixed up. It wouldn't be fair if the judges hit a garlic cheddar pie in between a raspberry pie and a peanut butter pie.

Peter Presley arrived promptly.

I introduced myself to him. "I'm so very sorry for your loss. It was a shock to all of us."

"That's mighty kind of you, Sophie. I lost *my* Patsy Lee a long time ago. I guess I always hoped she might come back to me. What happened today was all the harder because that door slammed shut on me forever. I'm just glad that I could be here for her today."

Bernie announced that the judging was about to commence. To my surprise the crowd on the plaza quieted down. Were they hoping to hear the comments the judges were making?

The three judges considered the amateurs' pies first. When they had made their decisions and moved on to the pies by professional bakers, I cut the amateurs' pies in pieces, as small as I could, and placed them on tiny tasting plates for the public.

I could hear Willa insisting that the pie with a top crust made through the use of a form could not win. "A professional baker should know how to work artfully with the dough," she insisted. "Besides, the flavors are questionable. I'm not even sure what it's supposed to be."

They moved on to the next pie.

"Peter, what's wrong?" asked Nina.

He stood staring at a pie as if paralyzed. "Did Patsy Lee bake a pie to enter?"

"Of course not," said Willa. "She was a judge."

"Well, this is Patsy Lee's pie. It looks just exactly like it." He took a bite and shook his head. "I'll be! It tastes exactly like her pie, too. I know this pie like I know the back of my own hand. No question about it."

I edged closer to them to see which pie he was talking about.

Chapter 8

Dear Sophie,
What is mincemeat pie? My husband says it's
chopped-up meat. I say it's a nut pie. Dinner at
my favorite restaurant is riding on this.
                    Hopeful Wife in Buttermilk, Kansas

Dear Hopeful Wife,
Originally, mincemeat contained beef, suet, or veni-
son, which was mixed with sugar and alcohol to
help preserve it. Today it's more commonly a com-
bination of dried fruit, spices, brandy or spirits, and
sometimes the more adventurous still add suet.
                                          Sophie

The pie in question had meringue piped on top instead of mounded. A smooth thick band of chocolate, probably pudding, ran underneath it dotted with something white. I couldn't quite tell what it was. Marshmallow, maybe? I wondered what would happen if one poured warm pudding on marshmallows. I might have to try that.

Peter took another bite. "There's whisky in this. I'm tellin' you, ladies, it's Patsy Lee's recipe."

They huddled together, but I couldn't hear their discussion. They moved on and sampled the rest of the pies.

They had a suspiciously long discussion before they announced the winners.

Finally Willa took the microphone. "Like me, I'm sure many of you were friends and fans of Patsy Lee Presley. I would be remiss not to mention Patsy Lee. I feel confident in saying that she would love nothing more than to be here with you right now. She was a dear friend of mine for many years. I'm reeling from her loss. To be honest with you, it was the very last thing in the world I ever expected today. But I know one thing for sure, Patsy Lee would have been the first to say that the festival must go on."

The audience applauded in a respectfully subdued manner.

"The moment you've been waiting for is here," said Willa. "I have to tell you that each and every pie was absolutely delicious. There wasn't a single pie that we wouldn't have been delighted to eat. These were very difficult decisions. I'm thrilled that you will be able to sample some of the pies yourselves to see which one would have been your winner."

Willa yielded the microphone to Nina, who handed out ribbons to the winners in the home baker category. I was very happy to see awards for youngest and oldest contestants where it didn't matter what their pies looked like or how they tasted. The ninety-one-year-old grandmother of ten and the six-year-old girl both received excited applause and whistles from the crowd. Nina went on to award ribbons for the prettiest pie and best piecrust.

When she announced the winner of the best pie by a baker under the age of fourteen, a little boy ran up to claim a trophy. I gazed at the crowd in search of Dark Shadow and the little girl. He patted her shoulder gently. With a stoic expression she watched the winner take a bow.

"And now," said Nina, "the coveted prize for overall best pie in the home baker category! Honey Armbruster!"

Patsy Lee's fan—and Old Town domestic diva—Honey ran up to the microphone like she thought she was getting an Academy Award. She sobbed as she spoke. "I wasn't sure I would be here this afternoon. I am utterly bereft at the loss of the greatest person I have ever known. Patsy Lee wasn't just a sweet and thoughtful person, she was the guiding influence in my life and in the lives of so many others. I'm especially proud to have won today in her honor. I feel like she's smiling down at me. . . ."

Her voice broke up and she handed the microphone over to Peter before rushing off.

He sniffled for a moment before he started. "I knew Patsy Lee way before y'all did. Back in the day she tried her recipes out on me." He patted his belly. "Which is how I got to look this way. I wish Patsy Lee could be here herself to feel your love and admiration. She was a remarkable woman. I, uh, I'm glad I could be here for her. And now, with no further delay, ladies and gentlemen, the moment you've been waiting for. The prize for most beautiful pie goes to Tommy Earl!"

The crowd cheered and applauded.

Tommy ambled toward Peter.

Peter wasn't through, though. "And the prize for tastiest pie goes to Tommy Earl! And"—he paused for a moment to heighten the drama—"the prize for best overall pie by a professional goes to"—he paused for seconds that felt longer—"Tommy Earl!"

Tommy grinned and was proudly accepting his ribbons when someone shouted, "It was rigged!"

Everyone turned to look at the person in the crowd who made that claim.

My knees went weak when I saw that it was Natasha. Bernie had been right all along. She was up to something.

Tommy froze as though he didn't know what to do. He looked at Natasha, wide-eyed.

What was she thinking? She hadn't entered the competition. She hadn't tasted the pies. Why would she be so unkind and disruptive? To get revenge on Bernie for not including her in the festival? I sighed, and made my way through the gathered people to Natasha, who stood next to Roger.

"What are you doing?" I hissed.

"He always wins."

"Did you see his pie? It was a masterpiece."

"I know for a fact that there were better pies."

"You couldn't possibly know that. You haven't tasted them. And you didn't even submit a pie. Why would you care?"

Roger started to inch away from her.

Natasha folded her arms over her chest.

"Look," I said, "let Tommy have his day in the sun and maybe you can compete in another pie festival."

"I contest the outcome of this contest," Natasha announced loudly.

Oy. Why didn't she realize that she upset everyone when she acted this way? "You behave yourself!" I hissed. "You're always preaching etiquette and good manners. This is completely out of line and inappropriate."

She gasped and clasped one hand over her mouth.

Roger glanced at me from the corner of his eye, his head down like a small child who had been caught misbehaving. What was going on with him?

Bernie arrived, his face flaming. "Could we speak privately?"

Natasha started to follow us, her head held high. But she reached back and grabbed Roger by the arm to tug him along.

As we paraded to the front, just ten feet away from the microphone, we passed the dark shadow and my breath caught in my throat.

We gathered in a small cluster with the judges and Tommy.

Bernie, who seldom lost his temper, spoke in an even but decidedly irritated tone. "What's this about, Natasha?"

"The other pies didn't have a chance. It was fixed for Tommy."

Tommy snorted. "You think I bribed the judges or something? Get over it, Natasha."

"I will not. My pie should have won."

I unfolded the list of pies I'd been carrying around. "Your name isn't on here, and I think I would know if you had handed me a pie."

Roger's face was red as an overripe tomato, and suddenly I realized why Natasha's name wasn't on the list. "The Moon Pie that Roger entered—that was your pie?"

Chapter 9

Dear Sophie,
I see other moms bake the cutest pies for special events. They're decorated with flowers, turkeys, leaves, and zoo animals. Am I the only one who isn't artistic? How do they do that?
No Van Gogh in Hungry Hollow, Pennsylvania

Dear No Van Gogh,
There's a very easy little trick—use a cookie cutter! You can cut out shapes for vents in a double-crust pie or add shapes to the top of a pie.
Sophie

Peter Presley pointed at Natasha. "You? You're the one who made that pie?"

Natasha's lips grew tight. I suspected she was preparing herself for a fight. "Yes. I baked the pie. Bernie wouldn't allow me to submit an entry. I had to do it under Roger's name."

I expected Peter to blow up about Natasha using Patsy Lee's recipe, but he was surprisingly calm.

"Well, well, well," he said. "Sugah, you didn't win because that was Patsy Lee's recipe. Didn't you think she would recognize her own pie?"

Natasha jerked her sunglasses off, turned her head, and glared at Roger so hard, I thought he might feel the burn.

"I cannot believe you, Natasha." Bernie shook his head in dismay and waved his hands. "I knew you'd pull some kind of stunt. So that's that. Tommy is the winner. End of story."

"I demand a bake-off," Natasha said calmly.

Tommy leaned toward her. "You're on!"

Bernie held up his palms. "I will have nothing to do with that." He ran up to the microphone and declared, "Tommy Earl is our winner! Ladies and gentlemen, we now invite you to taste the pies. We're handing out tickets, free of charge for tastes of two pies of your choice. Once you have tried two pies, you may get back in line for more tickets and sample as often as you like until they are all gone. Enjoy, everybody!"

I was relieved that was over. Nina tugged at my sleeve and nodded in Peter's direction.

He hadn't taken his eyes off Natasha.

Willa smiled and gazed right at Peter. "I could use a good cup of coffee after all that pie. Who's in?"

"I am!" said Nina. "I'm parched. Peter?"

"Sorry. I'm filling in for Patsy Lee as the official judge of the pie-eating contest."

Nina shot me a look as she walked away. I knew what she had noted. Peter had homed in on Natasha like a hummingbird on sugar water. I couldn't help wondering if he was flirting with her.

My current beau, Alex German, strolled up to me, rubbing his palms with glee. Former military, he still had incredible posture. His dark chocolate hair was neatly trimmed. He wore white shorts with a navy short-sleeved golf shirt.

That was about as casual as he got. "Where do I go for the pie-eating contest?"

That wasn't like the Alex I knew at all. "You're joking."

"Absolutely not. I love pie."

Really? Neat and proper Alex was about to be snarfing a messy pie? "This I've got to see. Good luck!"

I excused myself and hurried over to the tables where the pie samples had been consumed. There wasn't a single piece left. But there were plenty of crumbs.

I hastily cleaned off the tables, while Remy lined up chairs behind the tables for the pie-eating contestants.

I hustled over to the microphone. "Welcome to the official pie-eating contest! We have several tables set up. No registration is necessary. If you have always wanted to try, come on up and join us. We have several of these fantastic awards to hand out to the winners." I held up trophies topped with plastic slices of pie. "There will be one adult winner and one winner between the ages of five and twelve. Participants will eat in the traditional method with their hands behind their backs. Any sign of illness is an immediate disqualification. Parents must sign a waiver for children under eighteen to participate. Come on up and join the fun! Our official judge today is none other than Peter Presley! He will determine who eats the most pies in the allotted time. In the event of a tie, Peter, at his discretion, will choose the winner based on who is wearing the most pie and the biggest smile."

Minutes later the tables were packed with contestants. I remained at the microphone. "Peter, are we ready?"

He gave me a thumbs-up.

"We'll start with the children's contest. Moms and dads, please remain close by. Everyone cheer for your favorite contestant! And . . . go!"

Bernie stood beside me with a stopwatch. We didn't want anyone to get sick, especially not children.

The crowd yelled encouragement. One skinny little fellow devoured pies at an amazing speed. If I were a betting person, I'd have put my money on him. Most of the kids had whipped cream and butterscotch cream pie filling from their foreheads to their chins.

When Bernie blew a whistle signaling the end of the contest, Peter walked over to the skinny boy and raised his right hand.

"What's your name, son?" asked Bernie.

"Paul Evanright."

Bernie coaxed him up to the microphone and handed him a sixteen-inch-tall trophy bearing a plastic slice of strawberry pie with whipped cream on the top.

The crowd cheered and Paul's grin was priceless. His proud daddy exclaimed, "I got it all on video. You'll go viral!"

"And now for the adult contest. Ready, everyone? Go!"

I leaned forward a bit to watch staid, tidy Alex. He had no problem dipping his face into the pie. Remy handed him another one!

One by one the participants stopped eating. Two of them paused, but kept taking a bite or two as if they didn't want to give up.

When Bernie blew the whistle, there was only one guy with his face in a pie—Alex. He lifted his head and looked around.

Peter walked over to Alex, raised his hand, and said, "That was amazing. And you're not even tubby like me."

Alex bounded up to the microphone and gave me a big smooch, taking care to rub some chocolate cream pie filling and whipped cream in my face in the process. That brought more cheers and laughter from the audience.

I handed him the trophy. "Ladies and gentlemen, our winner is Old Town's own Alex German. Who knew he had this kind of skill?"

Bernie took the microphone and made a few remarks, telling everyone the vendors would still be around for a few hours and that he would announce the winners of free pies at four in the afternoon.

I was through with my duties. A good thing, too, since half my face was covered with sticky, sugary chocolate and cream. I eyed Alex. "How did you learn to do that? You chowed down longer than guys who are twice your girth."

He raised an eyebrow. "I had a sordid past that I haven't told you about. Let's just say this isn't the first eating contest I've entered. But it was more fun. It's much harder to eat a lot of hot dogs or burritos."

"Do you have any other secrets I should know about?"

He grinned. "None that I'm telling you."

I didn't like the sound of that, but I suspected he was just teasing me.

Wolf walked over to us. "You two really need to learn about using napkins." He motioned to us and to Bernie.

We followed him away from the microphone and the crowds of people.

I wiped my face with paper napkins but they didn't help much.

"It's going to be on the news tonight, and if I know Old Town's rumor mill, it won't be long before inaccurate information spreads. We'll know more after the autopsy, but it now appears that Patsy Lee died of an overdose of caffeine."

Alex frowned at Wolf. "How does that happen? Was she drinking those super-caffeinated beverages?"

"Just coffee," I said.

Wolf shook his head. "It was something more than regular coffee. Even the caffeinated drinks shouldn't have affected her this much. Sophie, could I have a word with you in private?"

"Sure."

Bernie and Alex took the hint and stepped away.

"You said Patsy Lee was at a house with someone last night. Can you get me the address pronto? I'd like to speak with the person who was with her."

"Of course. I'll go right now and call you with the address."

"Thanks."

When Wolf walked away, Bernie and Alex descended upon me, asking what he had wanted.

Wolf wouldn't have asked privately unless he wanted it kept quiet. Bernie already knew, but Alex didn't. Besides, it was the perfect time for me to give Alex a little taste of his own medicine. "I, too, have secrets!"

I hurried away before they could rib me about it. Besides, the sweet pie filling on my face was beginning to itch, and I was eager to wash it off. I paused at the little house where Patsy Lee had been and texted the address to Wolf.

Mochie greeted me at the door. "Were you lonely without Daisy?" I asked.

He purred, rubbed his head against my hand, and then rushed toward his empty food bowl, raised it, and let it clank on the counter.

"You little rascal. All you want is more to eat." I spooned Savory Salmon into his bowl. The sweet fellow purred while he ate.

After a much-needed shower, I poured myself a glass of iced peach tea and retreated to the computer in my little home office to Google the address of the house where Patsy had been the night before. I was hoping to identify the owner, too. To my annoyance ads popped up for vacation rentals and short-term accommodations. Apparently, I had to go to the courthouse to get the name of the owner, but one site identified them as $B^{*****}d$ $F^{**}i$ and $M^{******}l$ $W^{*****}n$.

I stared at those initials for a long moment. They looked way too familiar to me. I reasoned that there were a lot of short surnames that started with *F.* But the longer I looked at them, the more I thought they might be Bernard Frei and Marshall Winston.

Chapter 10

Dear Natasha,
I love lattice top pies. Do I divide the dough in half
to make them? Or do I just use scraps?
New Baker in Cherry Grove Beach, South Carolina

Dear New Baker,
Never use scraps! Make a double-crust pie dough
and reserve 1/3 for the lattice.

Natasha

My hair was still wet when I crossed the street to Bernie's house. He would still be at the pie festival, but chances were good that Mars was home.

I knocked on the door and heard Daisy whining.

Mars swung the door open, and Daisy bounded out to kiss me.

"You're not picking her up already, are you?" Mars looked distressed.

"You poor little doggy," I said to Daisy, stroking her soft head. "Everyone wants you! Actually, I thought I might take her home with me, but I really came over to ask you a question. What do you know about a cute little two-bedroom house just off King Street that—"

Mars burst out laughing. "Bernie wins." He motioned me inside the cool mansion and ushered me to the family room, where he had been watching golf on TV. "Another week and I'd have won."

I perched on the seat of a plush leather chair. "What are you talking about?"

"Bernie and I bet on how long it would take you to figure out that we had bought that place. Bernie said it would be less than two weeks, and here you are."

"That's embarrassing. Am I *that* nosy?"

"How did you find out?" asked Mars with the most annoying grin on his face.

I stared at him. I knew Mars better than I knew just about anybody. He still looked great and kept himself in moderately good shape. Half the women in Old Town were chasing him. But somehow I couldn't see him having an affair with Patsy Lee. Curiously, I couldn't picture her with Bernie, either. "Did you or Bernie know Patsy Lee when she lived in Old Town?"

Mars quit smiling. "Can I get you a cold drink? Maybe an aspirin? Were you out in the sun too long today?"

"I'm fine. Why are you dodging my question?"

"Sophie," he said gently, craning his neck to peer at me more closely, "we were talking about the house Bernie and I bought and you jumped to the subject of Patsy Lee."

He didn't know about Patsy Lee being at his house? I could see the concern on his face. I thought he would have come clean if he had met with her there. "Just this morning no one could find Patsy Lee." As I spoke, it dawned on me that if Mars and Bernie owned the house, and one of them had been with her, they would have known where Patsy Lee was. Maybe it was a rental? Now I was confused. "Did Patsy Lee rent it from you?"

Mars stared at me without blinking. A smile spread slowly across his face. "That old dog! Patsy Lee was at our new house?"

I cocked my head. "Who's the old dog?"

"We bought the house as an investment, thinking we would rent it out, but then Bernie talked to some guy who's making a bundle with short-term rentals over the Internet. It's easy to do, and given the cost of hotel rooms and rentals in Old Town, it's an interesting prospect. So we thought we'd give it a try."

"Who rented it this weekend?" I held my breath.

"Patsy Lee's ex-husband, Peter. He lives farther south, a couple of hours away, and he didn't want to drive back and forth."

"And he needed a private place to meet with Patsy Lee," I added.

"Gotta give the guy credit. Sometimes old loves don't wither away."

I shot Mars a doubtful look. "Do you think Peter murdered her?"

"Whoa! Aren't you jumping to conclusions?"

"She died of caffeine poisoning."

"She could have done that to herself. Maybe she was tired and she went overboard with caffeinated drinks. You know she must maintain a hectic schedule."

"Brock! He would know if that was her habit. That guy kept an eye on her every minute. Mars," I said, "Brock was the one who brought coffee to Patsy Lee. And to me, too."

Mars scowled at me. "You're too inclined to jump to murder. She probably overdosed on something she thought would give her energy."

"Then why is Wolf asking for the address of your rental house?"

Mars paled. "That does point to Peter. Maybe Wolf is being cautious, just in case. He's that kind of guy."

I hoped Mars was right.

"So Bernie says some creep is following you around."

I tried to be nonchalant about it and flipped my hand at him. "I'm not one hundred percent sure. But he was hanging around outside my house the other day. He walks along our street every morning on his way to work."

Mars squinted at me. "The skinny guy with the briefcase?"

"Do you know him?"

"Bernie does. He's married to a chef or something. Bernie knows all the great chefs and cooks in town because of The Laughing Hound. He says he needs to stay on top of the food business in Old Town."

"That makes sense. I'm beginning to think he wasn't following me, anyway. Maybe he just happened to be in the neighborhood. But he did take off around the corner when we spotted him. . . ."

"You win. Daisy can go home with you."

I hadn't talked about the dark shadow for that reason, but I was happy to take her home.

That night I turned out the lights and went to bed early. I was exhausted after the long day and Patsy Lee's death. From my bed I could see pink streaks in the sky as the sun set, indicating good weather for the next day. I drifted off until Daisy nudged me.

"Don't tell me you have to go out," I grumbled. I turned over, but she persisted by sticking her cold nose under my blanket and prodding me. "Okay, okay." My eyes closed, I sat up and swung my legs over the side of the bed.

Only then did I hear someone knocking on the door. Adrenaline kicked in. My eyes opened wide. This couldn't be good. I threw on a bathrobe and stumbled down the stairs as fast as I could go.

I flicked on the outside light. When I peered through the peephole, I couldn't see anyone. *Uh-oh.*

I gazed at Daisy, who didn't seem concerned. She looked at me expectantly as though she was wondering why I didn't open the door.

"Who is it?" I called.

A small voice responded, "Aly Stokes."

Chapter 11

Dear Sophie,
I found my grandmother's recipe for apple pie. At the end, it simply says egg wash. What is that?
    Granddaughter in Apple Canyon Lake, Illinois

Dear Granddaughter,
An egg wash is an egg, egg yolk, or egg white that is beaten with a small amount of water, cream, or milk and brushed over the top of a pie to give it a shine. Some people like to sprinkle coarse sugar on top of it for added sweetness.

    Sophie

I checked the peephole again and tried to look downward. Was that a little head?

With a sigh I unlocked the door and opened it. Sure enough, a little girl stood there. In fact, I thought it was the same one I had seen at the pie contest.

"Are you Sophie Winston?" she asked.

I peered into the darkness behind her, hoping she wasn't bait to get me to open the door. "Come inside, Aly."

I felt relieved when she entered the house and I could lock the door behind her. Daisy was busy licking Aly's face. That was one vote of approval.

I turned on the lights and ushered her into the kitchen. Unlike me, she wasn't wearing sleep attire. Little Aly wore baby blue shorts and a matching white short-sleeved shirt with blue polka dots. A white headband held her hair back out of her face. She carried a beige canvas bag with a huge artistically swirled letter *A* on each side.

"Would you like a glass of milk and a slice of pie?" I asked.

She turned clear blue eyes toward me. "I'm here on business."

I smiled at her. "You can still eat."

She nodded. "Okay. My mom is a pie baker. What kind is it?"

"Cherry."

"Sounds good. Mom used to bake a lot of pies for us."

Oh no, I hoped this precious little girl hadn't already lost her mother. "May I ask how old you are?"

"I turned twelve last month."

"Would you prefer milk or tea?"

"Milk, please. I think it goes better with cherry."

That surprised me. She sat calmly and stroked Mochie.

I went ahead and cut three slices of pie. I wasn't the only nosy person in the neighborhood.

Sure enough, as I was setting the plates on the table, Nina showed up at my kitchen door.

I opened it to admit Nina. She was breathless from dashing across the street. "I saw your light . . ." She stopped when she spied Aly. "I see you have company."

I introduced the two of them. As I had expected, Nina helped herself to a glass of wine while I delivered the milk and tea to the table.

I sat down on the banquette. "How can I help you, Aly?"

"May we speak privately?"

Nina blurted, "I'm her assistant."

That was a blatant lie. I wasn't sure what to say so she could save face, but I figured it didn't matter, anyway. Besides, I had a hunch it was about her entry in the pie contest. Nina had been a judge, so she might be in a much better position to explain why Aly's pie didn't win.

I leaned back, cradling the mug of tea in my hands and waiting for Aly to speak.

"This is pretty good," she said. "I entered a pie in the contest, but it didn't win."

Nina's eyes went wide with discomfort.

"But that's not why I'm here," Aly continued. "I go to the library a lot after school. There's an older kid there, Gavin Haberman, and he told me about you." She drank some milk and delicately dabbed her mouth with a napkin. "His dad was murdered."

Dread welled up in me. "Your mother was murdered?"

In a matter-of-fact voice, Aly said, "She's in prison for murder."

Nina choked on her wine.

Aly glanced at Nina. "I thought maybe you could help her get out."

Nina choked again.

"I don't know what Gavin told you, but honey, I'm not a lawyer. I don't know how to get someone out of jail."

Aly tilted her head. "I thought you solve murders."

I nodded. "I have solved a few—"

Aly sat up straighter. "That's what I need. Someone to prove my mom didn't do it."

My heart broke for this serious little girl. Had I seen her smile even once? I didn't think so.

"Who was killed?" asked Nina.

Aly was mature beyond her years. She didn't cry. Her voice didn't even crack. "Grainger Gibbard."

Nina gasped, which didn't help the situation. But I hadn't expected that answer, either.

Sergeant Frank Gibbard and his son, Grainger, had opened Star-Spangled Pies in Old Town a few years back. The family was well-known, not because of the restaurant but thanks to Frank's twelve children.

I didn't know any of the family members personally, although I had eaten in their restaurant on occasion. The sergeant had a reputation for a short temper but the food was good. It seemed like Gibbards were everywhere in Old Town. His daughter sat on the city council, and his youngest son was a popular local artist. When one of their vast clan met his end in an alley behind the family restaurant, the killer was arrested within hours. That must have been Aly's mom.

"Wasn't that a few years ago?" I asked.

Aly nodded. "She went to prison five years, three months, and four days ago."

"That's awfully precise," I observed.

"I mark it on a calendar every day so I won't forget her. She's going to be there for the rest of her life. And that means for the rest of my life I won't have my mom."

"Does your father know you're here?" I asked.

I saw the first flicker of guilt in her eyes. "No. Please don't call him. He thinks I'm in bed. We don't live very far from here. I promise I'll go straight home when we're through."

I couldn't imagine having such a serious and sensible child. Maybe when your mom went to jail for murder, you had to grow up fast.

Aly pulled a stack of papers out of the canvas bag and placed them on the table. Looking me straight in the eyes, she said, "She didn't do it."

I felt fairly certain that every child would want to believe that about a parent convicted of murder. I wasn't sure what to say to her. I feared that her mom had actually killed Grainger. Even if she hadn't, years had passed since Grainger was killed. It was unlikely that we would manage to stumble upon anything that would exonerate Aly's mom.

As though she could sense my reluctance, she pulled a photograph out of the stack of papers. "This is my mom, Nellie."

Nina leaned in for a better look.

Nellie could easily have been one of our friends. She was laughing in the photograph and cuddling a much younger and smiling Aly at the beach. Nellie wore her sandy hair shoulder length, exactly like Aly. I had to think that was intentional. It was Aly's way of clinging to her mom. In the photo they wore matching blue sundresses and Aly's headband sported a blue bow. If I had to guess, I would have said Nellie streaked her hair to hide the gray. Her wrists were tiny, she was definitely petite, and there was something about the raw joy on her face that spoke to me. I liked Nellie immediately.

What if Aly was right? What if Nellie was innocent?

Could I leave this woman unjustly incarcerated for the rest of her life?

Chapter 12

Dear Natasha,
My mother always makes pies in glass pie dishes
and they just look awful on the table. I say she
should use a pie dish that isn't see-through if she's
going to bring the pie to the table. Can you back
me up on this? She'll listen to you.
                    Disgusted in Lardintown, Pennsylvania

Dear Disgusted,
If your mother watches my show, she should know
that one only brings a pie to the table in a beautiful
ceramic or porcelain pie dish. If she bakes in a
glass dish, she should plate the pie before it makes
an appearance on the table.
                                        Natasha

I looked up at Aly, who was watching me. I thought she
might be holding her breath. I reached across the table
for her small hand. "I can't promise you anything, Aly. I
can tell you've been through a lot. You seem very mature,

so I'm going to be as honest as I can with you. This is a long shot. Do you know what that means?"

Aly nodded, but I felt her fingers squeeze mine tighter.

"Honey, it's highly unlikely that we'll be able to find out anything that would get your mom out of jail. Neither Nina nor I are lawyers. We're not detectives or cops. We're just a couple of nosy ladies."

Aly still didn't smile, but she squeezed my hand. "I like nosy ladies." She released my hand and looked down at the table. "Besides, you're all I have."

"Can we walk you home?" I asked. "I'm pretty sure Daisy needs to go outside," I lied.

"Okay. Can I hold her leash?"

"Sure!" I slid Daisy's halter over her head and handed the leash to Aly. I locked the door, pocketed the key, and the four of us walked along the sidewalk in the quiet night.

Aly lived a mere four blocks away. I knew which house was hers before we reached it because every light in the house was on.

"I have a feeling your dad is looking for you," I said.

"I left a note." She said it calmly as if that was surely sufficient.

The kid amazed me. I grinned at Nina.

When we walked up to the front door of a small Federal-style house, Aly turned the knob and stepped inside. Nina, Daisy, and I waited outside to make sure everything was okay.

"Alyson Frederika Stokes! Where have you been? I was about to call the police."

"You know you can't do that," Aly said in a serene voice. "Besides, I left a note."

The man pulled a piece of notebook paper from his

pocket and read aloud, "*Have gone to get Mom out of the slammer* is not adequate. Where were you?"

She tugged him by the hand toward the door.

Nina nudged me and whispered, "The dark shadow!"

"It's okay," I whispered back. "At least I think so."

Her father came to the door. His pale face flushed plum red at the sight of us. "You're Sophie Winston!" He gazed at his daughter. "Aly, what did you do?"

"Sophie is going to fix everything."

I was horrified. "That's not quite what I said."

"Please come in." The dark shadow peered outside and hurried to close the door. He gestured toward the living room. "Won't you have a seat?"

Their living room had been painted a creamy peach color, which served as a nice background for a cushy dark green sofa and peach chairs with hunter green pillows.

The dark shadow drew the curtains closed as fast as he could. He perched on the edge of the sofa. "I'm Dooley Stokes. Obviously, you have met my precocious daughter, Aly. I apologize if she troubled you."

"Not at all," I assured him. "She's a charming young lady."

Aly turned a smug, satisfied face to her father.

"Aly, it's time for bed."

"But, Dad . . . !"

"Go ahead. I'd like to speak to these ladies."

There was no mistaking her annoyance with being sent out of the room, but she did as she was told, pausing for just a moment to look at Nina and me. "Thank you. *Pleeeease* help my mom."

She scampered up the stairs. We heard a door open and close. From my position in the living room, I suspected I was the only one who could see her sitting on the top stair to listen in. I tried not to grin. I had done the same thing as a kid.

Dooley moved awkwardly, like a colt that hadn't gotten its legs yet. Tall and slender, he eyed us nervously. "I'm a little ashamed that it took my daughter to reach out to you. I've been trying to work up the nerve to speak with you."

"That's why you've been stalking Sophie," said Nina.

"Oh no! That wasn't my intention at all. I'm sorry. I don't usually follow people. I had no idea I was scaring you. Please don't think I'm a stalker. I just couldn't get up my nerve to talk with you. I'm desperate and this is way out of my comfort zone. You're a stranger, yet I'm coming to you for help."

Nina's eyes brightened at the word *desperate*. I wasn't so sure I shared her enthusiasm.

"I guess Aly told you about my wife. Actually, my ex-wife. She's in prison for murder." Dooley looked away, his eyes brimming with tears. "They gave her life in prison without parole."

I had a vague recollection of reading about the murder, but I wanted to hear what he had to say.

"I'm terribly sorry, Mr. Stokes. I told Aly that we would do what we could, but you ought to hire a professional. People mistakenly think I solve murders, but I'm actually an event planner who got lucky a couple of times."

He gripped the arm of the sofa as though he hoped it would give him strength. His eyes were so sad that I wanted to look away but couldn't.

"Please call me Dooley. If you only knew Nellie, you would understand that she couldn't have murdered Grainger. Bernie will back me up on that."

"Bernie Frei?"

"He's a friend of yours, right? He knows Nellie."

Nina and I exchanged a glance as it dawned on me that Roger had mentioned a Nellie Stokes.

"She's the kindest person I have ever known," said Dooley. "There has been a terrible miscarriage of justice."

"Most people aren't quite so fond of their ex-spouses," Nina observed with a hint of sarcasm.

I shot her a look. Mars and I were still friends.

Nina flicked her hand at me. "You don't count. You and Mars aren't normal."

Mr. Stokes appeared hopeful. "You were married? And you still love each other?"

I began to explain, "Well—"

But Dooley assumed what he wanted and kept talking. "Then perhaps you *can* understand. Nellie was my first love. To be honest, she is my only love." He heaved a shuddering sigh. "She left me for someone else. A grave error, as it turned out. And now, Aly and I are her only hope."

Dooley wiped away tears under his eyes with the backs of his hands. "No one else cares about Nellie locked away in a cold little cell while the real killer gets away with an atrocious murder. Except for Aly and me, the world has forgotten about Nellie. It's as though everyone else on the entire planet was okay with her incarceration. They didn't care who it was, as long as someone went to jail."

I still wasn't placing Nellie. It seemed like I would have heard more about the crime. Even though Old Town was next to Washington, DC, it was a small community and murder was big news.

"I fear someone used her in a nefarious way."

Nina sat up, her mouth gaping. "You think she was framed?"

I held out my hands, palms up. "Dooley, you and Aly have my deepest sympathy. But it sounds like you need a private detective. This is way out of my league."

He stared at the coffee table, his shoulders sagging. When he looked up, I swear his lower eyelids drooped like a sad bloodhound's. He reached his hands toward me, almost like a person in the desert reaching for water. "Please? I already hired a private detective. He took my money and produced no results. Nothing. It was a total waste. I'm sorry to say that I can't afford another one. Though in all honesty, even if I could, I don't know that I would trust another private detective." His voice dropped to a mere whisper. "I mortgaged this house to the hilt, sold my car, and spent every cent I had for Nellie's legal defense. There's nothing left. I . . . I was told you work for free?"

His pale face flushed crimson and I could tell it pained him to have to ask for help.

Nina looked at me, her eyes wide.

While I *had* solved a few murders, I wasn't a professional. I might even muck things up instead of making them better. Not to mention that it all happened so long ago. There certainly wouldn't be any evidence lying around. All I could go by was what people told me. Memories weren't always reliable and had probably warped a bit since the actual murder. But I had promised Aly I would try.

I studied Dooley silently. He was definitely stressed. His breath came fast and in short bursts, like a panting dog. I wondered if he had blood pressure problems.

What if Nellie were my sister? Or what if I landed behind bars for a murder I hadn't committed? I hoped Mars might move heaven and earth for me if that happened. But in all honesty, I didn't think I would be able to accomplish much in this instance.

"What about Nellie's lawyers?" I asked. "Aren't they doing anything on her behalf?"

"The standard appeal for ineffective counsel was filed, but that wasn't successful. I have no one to turn to. I wouldn't be begging you if I wasn't at the end of the line. I just can't bear the calendar days sweeping by while poor, sweet Nellie wastes away."

I had already promised Aly. I wasn't about to let her go through more of her life without her mother. Not if I could help it.

Maybe I wouldn't be able to spring Nellie. Maybe Nellie *had* committed the crime. But I knew two things—I couldn't let Aly down, and I couldn't bear to live my life, having fun, even just waking up in the morning and seeing the sun shine, with the knowledge that Nellie might have been wrongly incarcerated and that I hadn't bothered to try to help.

"Dooley," I said, "I don't want you to have high hopes. It's unlikely that we'll discover anything helpful. A lot of time has passed and that will make it more difficult."

My words of caution clearly meant nothing to him. His face lit up. The hangdog look vanished. "Thank you! I can't even begin to express my gratitude."

He rose and fetched a document from a desk. Handing it to me, he said, "The great news is that Nellie was temporarily transferred back to the Alexandria detention center. You won't have to go far to meet her. Here is all my contact information. Do you think you'll be able to see her tomorrow?"

Nina nodded her head. I reached out my hand to stop her from making promises we couldn't keep. "Tomorrow is Sunday. I don't even know if the detention center is open on Sundays."

He froze as though I had tossed an icy drink on him. "But it is!"

He was so anxious that I wondered if I was making a mistake. He wanted Nellie released and that was something I probably couldn't accomplish. "I'll do my best."

He loosened up. "If Nellie were here, she would have baked a pie to enter in the festival. Aly wanted to honor her mom by baking one."

"Nellie was a good baker?"

He cocked his head as if surprised by my question. "Nellie is the best pastry and dessert chef in the United States."

His response took me aback. "Her name doesn't ring any bells with me."

"Star-Spangled Pies took all the credit. Nellie worked very quietly in the back, preparing their wonderful desserts."

"Where do you work, Dooley?" asked Nina. "Are you a chef, too?"

"Good heavens, no. I wouldn't know where to start. I've lost forty pounds since Nellie left me. I'm an entomologist at the Smithsonian museum."

Nina wrinkled her nose at him. "Bugs?"

"The United States Insect Collection is the second largest in the world!" he declared proudly. Dooley's eyes widened and he was suddenly animated. "Did you know that no matter how much you clean your house or where you live, whether in the jungle, the forest, or a city, you still have approximately the same number of insects in your home?" He sat back and lamented, "Of course, if we lived in a jungle, the insects would be far more interesting."

Noting Nina's disgust, he turned to me. "Inmates are allowed only two visits a week, so Aly and I won't go to see Nellie until after you do. It's far more important that you have a chance to meet her and get the story from her."

I received his message loud and clear—*Hurry up and visit her so Dooley and Aly could see their beloved Nellie.*

He got to his feet. "Nellie always called me her praying mantis because I have such long thin arms and legs."

"And what did you call her?" I asked.

"My ladybug."

He stood up and opened the door for us.

"One last question before we go," I said. "You said Nellie left you for someone else. Who did Nellie leave you for?"

Nina and I stepped outside and turned around to face him as he said, "Grainger Gibbard."

Chapter 13

Dear Natasha,
I baked a blackberry pie following your recipe pre-
cisely. It was awful! Shudder! It was so sour that
we could hardly stand it.
Still Puckering in Blackberry City, West Virginia

Dear Still Puckering,
The first rule of baking any fruit pie is to taste your
fruit. Berries are notorious for being surprisingly
sour, but even apricots and peaches vary in sweet-
ness. Always adjust the sugar to the sweetness (or
lack thereof) of your fruit.

Natasha

To say I was stunned would have been an understate-
ment. Nellie left Dooley for Grainger, who was her boss,
and then murdered him? I couldn't help thinking it might
have been Dooley who murdered Grainger and couldn't live
with the guilt of knowing that Nellie was paying the price
for his crime.

Nina and I strolled along the sidewalk, with Daisy lead-
ing the way.

"Maybe I shouldn't have said we would look into it."

Nina cleared her throat. "Funny how neither one of
them mentioned that little detail. Makes a person wonder
what else they omitted. On the other hand, if you were accused of murdering Alex, I bet Mars would do everything
in his power to help you."

"Fortunately, I'm not inclined to kill anyone. Do you
think Dooley killed Grainger and that's why he feels so
miserable about Nellie landing in prison?"

Nina winced. "It hadn't occurred to me until Dooley mentioned her victim. But that would explain his panic about
Nellie spending the rest of her life in prison. I thought he was
too crazy about her for someone who got dumped!"

"But if that were the case, and I were in his shoes, I
don't know if I would ask anyone to look into it. If Dooley
murdered Grainger, then he knows that the trail will lead
back to him. It would be easier to just confess."

Nina held out her hand for the paper Dooley had handed
me. "He's meticulous." Nina paused under a streetlight to
read it. "It's the visiting schedule. Prisoners have to make
arrangements in advance for a visit. But"—she grinned at
me and then paraphrased—"an exception can be made by
the watch commander. Think Wolf could pull some strings?"

"Maybe. I'll give him a call in the morning."

We said good night and went to our respective homes. I
had been exhausted, but now I was too agitated to sleep. I
heated some milk and poured in a splash of coffee liqueur
to flavor it. Daisy and Mochie followed me into the sunroom. Daisy curled up on the loveseat next to me and
paced her head in my lap, which didn't leave any room
for Mochie. He didn't seem miffed, though. He promptly
jumped onto the back of the loveseat. I could hear him

purring behind me. I didn't turn on any lights while I thought about Aly.

Nellie should have been my primary concern, but it was Aly who broke my heart. At this point she had lived almost half of her life without her mother. Dooley was clearly doing a great job of raising her. She was bright and appeared to be well adjusted, even if she never smiled.

In the morning I phoned Wolf Fleishman on the outside chance he could get us in. I didn't expect him to take my call, since he was probably busy with Patsy Lee's death, but he answered right away.

"Hi, Sophie. Thanks for that address."

When I explained what I wanted, Wolf was silent for a long moment. "Nellie Stokes? Sophie, that's a closed case."

"Do you know anything about Grainger's murder?"

"A little. It wasn't my case. Kenner handled it."

Chill bumps raised on my arms. I hadn't heard Kenner's name in a long time. He'd been awful to me. I knew exactly how he must have treated Nellie. As far as I was concerned, it was all the more reason to look into her case. "Any chance you can get me in to see her?"

He was silent again. I knew better than to keep chattering or pleading my case. Wolf was thinking. "Okay. I'll call you back."

I let Daisy out in the backyard. A familiar banging sound came from the kitchen. I hurried back. As I expected, Mochie was picking up the side of his empty dish and letting it drop on the counter with a clank to let me know it was time for breakfast.

I laughed at him. "I wouldn't have forgotten you. How does Pumpkin Tuna sound?" I poured it into a clean dish and set it before him. He ate it with gusto.

I fixed Daisy's breakfast and placed it on the floor, then finally put the kettle on for tea.

When I opened the door for Daisy, she bounded in with Nina right behind her. Daisy ignored me entirely and raced to her breakfast.

"Did you hear from Wolf yet?"

"I called him. But it could take days for him to make arrangements. Don't hold your breath."

The phone rang just as I said that. Wolf said, "They can fit you in this morning if you can be there by ten."

"Wow! Thanks for pulling strings, Wolf."

"No biggie. The watch commander is an old friend of mine."

"Any news about Patsy Lee?" I asked.

"I'm guessing you know by now who owns that house," he responded.

"I do."

"I'll stop by later today if I have time. I'm hoping we'll get Patsy Lee's autopsy results soon."

He hung up, leaving me mystified. It was nice of him to make the arrangement for us to see Nellie, but he'd left me with a slightly bad taste in my mouth about the little house where Patsy Lee had been the night before her death.

Nina handed me a mug of tea.

"We're on at ten o'clock."

She smiled smugly. "I thought so. Wolf knows everyone. To save time, we can have pie for breakfast."

Nina was the most adaptable person I knew. I couldn't help laughing. I cut each of us a slice of pie.

Nina flicked on the news just in time for us to see Cicely Comstock standing in front of the park. "News of Patsy Lee Presley's untimely murder has swept the nation. From New York to Los Angeles, Patsy Lee's devoted followers are weeping and hitting social media with their loving stories about her. Right behind me, you can see people gathering near the spot where she took her last breaths. There has been a steady parade of people bearing flowers, gifts, and, of course, pies. Police have been exceptionally close-mouthed about Patsy Lee's death. They have not yet confirmed the rumor sweeping Old Town that Patsy was being followed by the Dark Shadow, an as-yet-unidentified man known to lurk around Patsy Lee, possibly a deranged fan."

Nina's mouth fell open. "That's pure craziness! Cicely overheard us talking about something else entirely and has twisted it to apply to Patsy Lee."

"Can you believe her? I'm calling Wolf to let him know what happened. Otherwise the cops will be chasing someone who doesn't exist."

Unfortunately, Wolf didn't answer his telephone. I figured he was back at work. I left a very clear message. "The Dark Shadow does not exist. Cicely misunderstood something. Call me when you get a chance, and I'll explain."

In the time it took for me to leave a message, Nina had managed to snarf a piece of pie and start on a second slice. Minutes later she hurried home to change clothes.

At nine forty I backed my hybrid SUV out of the garage and picked up Nina in front of her house. Traffic was scarce in Old Town at that hour on Sunday morning.

We drove past the cemetery and out toward Mill Road. It only took ten minutes to get there.

A sheriff's deputy escorted us to a private visiting room with one table and three chairs. Nellie was already seated. The deputy remained in the room with us. I knew she was a convicted murderer, but I had a hard time imagining her lunging at us.

I wouldn't have recognized Nellie from her photo. I had been right about the blond streaks in her hair. It had grown out gray and the cute cut in the photo was long gone. She was tiny. I was only five feet tall, but she was so delicate I felt like I could blow her over with a good sneeze. The lines in her face showed the stress of imprisonment. Still, a spark of hope flickered in her eyes when she saw Nina and me.

"Hi," she said. "Thank you for coming." She squinted at me. "I feel like I know you?"

I held out my hand to her. "Sophie Winston. We live on the same street, but different blocks."

She shook my hand and then Nina's. "I've probably walked by your houses a million times. No wonder you seem familiar. Old Town seems like such a small place but between the residents, and the tourists, and the people who drive in to work every day and then go home somewhere else, the population is pretty big."

We sat down, and I said, "Aly misses you, and Dooley is very concerned about you."

The edges of her mouth turned down and she studied her hands. For a long moment I thought I had begun our little talk the wrong way.

"I can't even say Aly's name without crying." Her forehead wrinkled up. She balled one hand into a fist and clutched it with the other hand. She took several deep breaths. "Dooley says you can help me, and I appreciate you coming, but I'm afraid that I'm a lost cause." She closed her eyes, and took a deep breath before opening them. "When you're in prison, the one thing you have a lot of time to do is think. Dooley isn't the most exciting man on the planet, that's for sure. But if I hadn't left him, I wouldn't be sitting here now."

"What do you mean?" asked Nina.

"I would have changed jobs and left Grainger. If I had been smarter and stayed with Dooley instead of falling for Grainger, I never would have been blamed for his death because I wouldn't have been in the alley that night."

"Why don't you tell us what happened?" I asked.

Her shoulders and entire chest rose when she took a

deep breath of air. "I worked for Grainger Gibbard, making desserts at Star-Spangled Pies. I had known him for years. He was an extremely accomplished pastry chef, but was spending more of his time managing the restaurant. Grainger would come in the back and talk with me, pitching in and doing what he loved, rolling out pastry or making dough. And fool that I was, I fell for him. Please don't think that I'm a terrible person. It just happened. Grainger was everything that Dooley wasn't. It's hard to explain. Dooley is kind and thoughtful. He's comfortable, like an old sofa. Heaven forgive me for saying this, but he's dull."

Nellie sighed. Speaking slowly, she said, "He's just so dull! Dooley is a creature of habit. Every day is like every other day. Of course, now I miss that! I'd love to sit out in our backyard while Dooley inspects plants for bugs. He's something of a gardener because he wants plants to attract unusual insects. I know that sounds boring. It is! But what I wouldn't give to go back to that life. You don't realize how good your life is until it's gone and you live in a cell."

Nellie glanced over at the guard before continuing. "Grainger was the polar opposite of Dooley. He was clever and witty. You never knew what interesting thing he might do next. He wasn't wild—I don't want you to think that. He was exciting. Grainger was full of ideas and fun to be with. Then one day I arrived at work before dawn. I was always the first one in to get everything started, and I found Grainger lying in the alley."

I sensed Nina getting ready to speak and shot her a quick look. I wanted Nellie to ramble and tell us everything without us steering her words or thoughts, at least in the beginning.

Nellie blinked hard. "It was horrible. I've been through some trying times, but nothing was as bad as that morning. It was still dark out and a single lightbulb illuminated the alley behind the restaurant. I actually tripped over

Grainger. I didn't see him sprawled on the ground. I fell over him. All I knew was that my hands were wet and that someone was lying on the ground. They say my screams woke some of the people in town houses behind the restaurant. They called the police, who found me on my knees, beating Grainger on his chest."

"Why were you beating him?" asked Nina.

"CPR! By that time I had realized it was Grainger, and I was trying to restart his heart."

Nina glanced at me. "But you don't beat someone when you're doing CPR."

"You do when a heart won't start! I thought he needed a shock, a defibrillator. All I had were my two hands, so I was trying to get it beating again. The police interpreted it differently."

"I heard Kenner was on your case," I said.

Nellie shivered. "The mere thought of that man makes my blood run cold. He was horrible. He decided I had killed Grainger and there was no convincing him otherwise. I was doomed from the start."

"How was Grainger killed?" I asked.

"He was poisoned and then stabbed. It had to be by someone who could bake because Grainger ate strawberry-rhubarb pie made with the leaves of the rhubarb plant. They never found the pie, but they discovered it during the autopsy. I guess he didn't die fast enough, so the person stabbed him, too. I'm no shrink, but someone would have had to be very angry to stab him after poisoning him."

As gently as I could, I asked, "Were you upset with Grainger? Had he broken off your relationship?"

"Not at all. Grainger and I were getting very serious. We had talked about marriage. I knew it would be hard on"—she paused and swallowed hard—"Aly. But other kids do fine with divorced parents. And she thought Grainger was cool. He was very sweet with her."

I looked Nellie in the eyes. "I know this will be hard for you, but I have to ask you this. Do you think Dooley might have murdered Grainger?"

"That's what my lawyers thought. Honestly, I can't imagine Dooley having the grit to do something like that. He's such a timid person."

Even timid people could be pushed to the edge. Jealousy was a powerful motivator.

"Dooley told you I left him?" she asked.

I nodded.

"Did he tell you why?"

"He said you left him for Grainger."

Nellie studied her hands. "He likes to omit the real reason."

Chapter 14

Dear Natasha,
I'm so impressed by the pie dough you make on your show. I struggle with pie dough. Can you share some tips that I can try when my dough won't cooperate?
                                          Dough Dunce in Tipton, Oklahoma

Dear Dough Dunce,
When you've made a mess of your dough, there's nothing you can do except start over.
                                                                    Natasha

"Dooley doesn't like to talk about what led to our divorce. He's fine with letting people think it was all my fault. You see, Dooley was having an affair."

Nina and I exchanged a glance. The odds of Dooley having an affair were almost as remote as little Aly murdering Grainger. "With whom?"

"He never told me. He denies it to this day. But I knew. Someone was blackmailing him. I found a letter."

Dooley had said that he was out of money because of legal fees and the private investigator he'd hired to pursue

Nellie's case. But that might be another reason he was low on funds. Could he still be paying someone to keep quiet? Or was it moot now that Nellie knew the truth?

Nellie's eyes glistened with tears. "Dooley is a decent guy. Not the most handsome. He'll never be a movie star, and he'll never be wealthy, but he's kind and gentle. The last thing I ever expected was that he would cheat on me. I was so foolish. I guess it can happen to anyone. When I found the letter, I was in shock. The person was demanding thousands of dollars. I think Dooley would have done anything to keep it quiet. He didn't want me to know about it. He was right to be worried about me finding out. It destroyed our marriage. He never even told me who she was. Maybe that was the honorable thing to do. I'm still not sure about that. If I knew, would it have made a difference? Would I have stayed with him? At least I would have known who my competition was. In the end I had to leave him. How could I trust him anymore?"

"Did you find out who was blackmailing Dooley?" asked Nina. "That might lead us to his mistress."

"No. I felt so betrayed. And when Dooley denied everything and refused to tell me her name, I had to move on. How could I live that way?"

I was a little bit confused. "But you sound as if you would like to take Dooley back." I hastily added, "If you could."

"Oh, I would!" She looked from me to Nina. "No one else loves me enough to be trying to help me get out of here. Not any of my friends or my brother. Only Dooley and Aly! Everyone else has given up on me. Dooley may have had an affair, but that kind of devotion is rare. He would have to come clean to me, of course." She shook her head. "But I would be an idiot not to go back to him. No one will ever love me like he does."

"Was Grainger involved in an argument with anyone?" asked Nina.

"Not that I know of. I still think it had to be someone who bakes. Grainger would never have knowingly eaten rhubarb leaves. Everyone knows that they're toxic. In court a psychologist testified that the use of a knife often indicates rage and a personal connection to the victim."

Clearly, that didn't help Nellie's defense. "Did Grainger have an issue with any of the employees? Had he fired anyone?" I asked.

"There was a server's assistant, a busboy, who was fired. Gosh, I haven't thought about Remy in a long time. He was into bodybuilding and could easily have overpowered just about anyone."

Uh-oh. How many Remys could there be in Old Town in the food industry? "Remy Tarwick?" I asked.

"That's him! He got into a brawl with a customer. Remy deserved to be fired. You can't have that sort of thing going on in *any* business."

"Do you think he might have taken it out on Grainger?" asked Nina.

"He seemed like a nice guy up until that happened. I didn't know him well enough to assess his character." Nellie's face brightened. "No one ever mentioned him as a potential suspect. I think Kenner just homed in on me because I was there. But my presence was valid. I had to be at work to start baking."

"Is there anything else you would like to tell us? Anything you feel might have been overlooked?" I asked.

"The timeline doesn't work." Nellie spoke with full confidence. "The restaurant closes at two in the morning. By the time everyone is out and everything is cleaned up, it's at least two thirty or two forty-five. So I figure Grainger must have been attacked after he locked up for the night and was leaving, probably between two thirty and three in the morning. I tripped over him when I arrived at five thirty. That means he was out there for at least two and a half to three hours before I came along. It makes no sense whatsoever that I would have lurked in the alley, waiting for him to lock up the restaurant, so I could stab him. In the first place I couldn't have known if he was leaving with a bunch of people. He often did, although he was alone that night."

She paused as if to collect her thoughts. "It's remotely possible, of course, that Grainger's killer called him and made an arrangement to meet him there, but surely Grainger would have thought a meeting at that hour was peculiar and would have told him to come in during restaurant hours. That makes sense, doesn't it?"

Nina and I nodded.

"Secondly, if I had been waiting for him in the alley, then I would have known he was there, and I wouldn't have tripped over him. Nor would I have tried to revive him. If I had meant to kill him, I would have done it on a day when I had an alibi or on a day when I was off so someone else would have found him. I certainly wouldn't have taken a chance at pretending that I was trying to re-suscitate him."

"No alibi?" Nina asked. "Nothing at all?"

"Are you kidding? I used to get up just before five in the morning, hop in the shower, and rush to work. I had left Dooley and was living in a tiny apartment with Aly. But it was a night when Aly was with Dooley, so I was home alone. It's not like there's a lot going on in Old Town at that hour. Sure, there are always a few early birds out on the street, but I wasn't paying attention. I don't know who might have been out there. I was thinking about work, not about providing an alibi for myself. Who would have ever thought I would need one? The way I see it, when Grainger was murdered, I was at home deep asleep."

"So the case against you was based on what the police saw when they arrived on the scene?" I wondered if she had touched the knife before she tried to resuscitate him. In an effort to not sound accusatory, I simply asked, "Were there fingerprints on the knife?"

"The knife was never found. There's another glitch in their theory. They maintained that I baked him the pie, watched him eat it, and then when he didn't die, I followed him out into the alley and stabbed him. Then, they said, I unlocked the door and went inside the restaurant, where I washed the knife and returned it to its rightful place before the police arrived." Nellie shook her head. "There are ridiculous holes in their story! They crafted it to suit the scenario they wanted to believe."

I felt certain they would have collected knives from the restaurant and tested them for blood. It was notoriously difficult to wash off.

"I don't know what Dooley told you about Nina and me." I tried to smile at her. "We're not trained investigators. Not by a long shot. We have solved a few murders, but they have generally been around the time of the incident, not years later. I don't know if we can help you at all."

Nina's eyes grew large, and I could see that she was afraid of what I might say.

"But we'll look into it."

"Oh, thank you! Thank you so much. You're my only hope."

We said goodbye and assured her we would be in touch, probably with more questions.

We were silent in the car on our way home until Nina announced, "I believe her."

"If it hadn't been Kenner who was in charge of the investigation, I might have more doubts about Nellie's innocence." But I had dealt with the man. He was intimidating and manipulative. Besides, Nellie made some very good points. "Seriously, Nina, how many murderers would stop to wash the knife? You would have to be completely nuts and extremely comfortable that no one would discover you. Besides, if the knife was from the restaurant and replaced, that would indicate the killer was familiar with the restaurant."

"An employee," breathed Nina. "That should narrow down the list of suspects."

"Or a former employee," I pointed out. "Definitely someone he knew. I wonder if he would have tasted pie for a wannabe employee? Do restaurateurs do that? Presumably Grainger was about to lock up or had just locked up, so he would have had the key on him. Still, it would take some serious guts to sit there and watch him eat pie, then stab him, and go inside the restaurant to wash the knife and put it away. Besides, wouldn't the killer have been covered in blood spatter? The cops would know for sure if he had been inside."

"He probably would have left shoe tracks, too. Assuming Nellie's description is accurate, I can't imagine anyone managing to avoid stepping in blood."

Traffic had picked up considerably when we returned to Old Town. The Sunday brunch crowd had arrived and we moved at a crawl.

Nina gasped and her hand landed on my arm. "Oh, my word! Look who's having lunch together."

In the front window of a chic restaurant on King Street, Natasha gazed attentively at none other than Peter Presley.

"He couldn't take his eyes off of her yesterday," muttered Nina. "But he's not her type. She usually goes for slick guys, not the kind that look like they'd be more comfortable on a farm or in the woods."

"People change. Maybe she sees something in him that she's been missing in citified men."

"Does he have money?" asked Nina.

"I haven't the first notion. You think she only goes after men with fat wallets?"

"Maybe," said Nina. "Or maybe it only seems that way because she's still looking for her dad. It's too bad her father will never know how badly he scarred her by abandoning her and her mother."

At long last we rolled up to my garage and pulled inside. We entered the house through the back entrance and heard the doorbell ringing. I rushed through the foyer with Daisy ahead of me, and flung open the door.

Wolf stood outside, his face haggard from exhaustion. "Got a minute?" He petted Daisy, and picked up Mochie but skipped formal greetings otherwise and followed us into the kitchen. Still holding Mochie, he asked, "What do you know about the Dark Shadow?"

Nina snorted. "Can you believe that Cicely reported about him on TV? How desperate was she to make up something like that?"

Wolf frowned at her. "She must have picked it up somewhere."

"It was just a silly nickname," I explained. "Nellie Stoke's husband, Dooley, was hanging around. It turned out that he wanted to talk with me, but didn't have the guts to initiate a conversation. We were calling him the dark shadow because he had dodged around the corner like, well, a dark shadow. Cicely overheard us talking. It's all fine. We've met with Dooley. It had nothing to do with Patsy Lee."

"Dooley Stokes was your dark shadow?" Wolf rubbed his chin. "I see. It all fits together now. He's a bit of an odd duck."

It was my turn to be concerned. "What do you mean by that?"

"He's just a little different. I always feel like he's scared of me."

I took the opportunity to be nosy, hoping to sound very casual. "Was he a suspect in Grainger Gibbard's murder?"

"A person of interest," Wolf clarified. "Nellie and Dooley had just divorced. He had to be considered. Jealousy is a powerful motivator."

"So you do know something about it," I said.

Wolf shrugged. "Not much. It didn't take long to wrap it up. Nellie was arrested on the spot. As I recall, there was talk about her having some kind of episode at the time. That was why she couldn't remember stabbing Grainger, but felt great remorse afterward and was trying to revive him."

I didn't like the sound of that. "What if she didn't remember because she didn't do it?"

"Sophie, I'm not up on the details. I just remember that the jury didn't buy that explanation. The other reason I came by was to tell you that Patsy Lee's death was from caffeine powder. I know you were drinking coffee from Moos and Brews and I didn't want you to worry. In some cases caffeine powder is an intentional overdose, but there are also documented incidents in which someone consumed more of it than they intended and died as a result."

"Caffeine powder?" Nina shrieked. "Like instant coffee? I drink coffee all the time. Are you saying I could drink too much and keel over like Patsy Lee?"

Wolf shook his head. "No, no, no. Highly unlikely. Caffeine powder isn't like instant coffee. It's a crystalized form of caffeine. According to the medical examiner, it's highly concentrated. One teaspoon is the equivalent of drinking almost thirty cups of coffee at once. It's been banned by the FDA, but is still readily available."

I chose my words carefully. "So, most likely, Patsy Lee was tired and took powdered caffeine to give herself an energy boost?"

"Maybe." Wolf ran a hand through his hair. "We're going to have to figure out whether Patsy Lee ingested it intentionally, or whether someone spiked her food or drink. We didn't find any sign of it in her hotel room or luggage. If she was in the habit of using it, you'd think we would have found some there. At this point I have to treat her death as a homicide."

"You know that Brock brought her coffee," I reminded him.

Nina snapped her fingers. "He might have carried it around for her. He probably had all kinds of things she might need in a bag of some sort."

"We're aware of that. Brock definitely had the best opportunity of all to mix caffeine powder in her coffee before he handed it to her. But from what I gather, now that there's no Patsy Lee, Brock doesn't have a job."

"Good point." Nina nodded. "It would be contrary to his own best interests to do that intentionally."

"Do you have time for"—I'd almost offered him a cup of coffee—"some lunch?"

"I do!" Nina headed for the refrigerator, muttering, "I'm starved."

Wolf and I chuckled. He checked his watch. "Sure. I'm running on about two hours of sleep. I'd love a bite to eat."

Mochie accompanied us and snuggled with Wolf while I whipped up some ham and Asiago cheese sandwiches and popped them into the panini machine.

Nina was already slicing what was left of the pie. "Hmm, looks attractive. Filling is smooth and firm, but not gelatinous. This might be a winner."

"Now that you've been a pie judge, am I going to have to go through this every single time I serve pie?"

Nina held her head high. "I have *credentials*!"

I brought iced tea to the table while Nina, the new pie expert, placed a slice of pie in front of each of us.

Wolf ate a bite of his sandwich. "Just what I needed. So, did either of you see anything unusual yesterday? Did you see Patsy Lee or anyone mix something into her coffee? Did you see her in the ladies' room, doctoring her drink? Anything at all?"

"I hate to let you down," I said. "I was next to her in the morning, but I can't say I noticed anything strange. A lot of people clustered around her, and even more stood close by and just watched, like they were in awe of her star status."

"I arrived a little later," said Nina. "If I were you, I'd be taking a hard look at Brock. It seems like he's around her all the time."

"What about Peter Presley?" I asked. "After all, she was alone with him the night before she died. Maybe they had a spat."

Wolf nodded. "If you two hear any gossip, let me know. I hate to take off so soon, but I'd better get back to work."

I saw him to the door, glad that he'd stopped by and stayed for a bite.

He stepped outside and turned around. "Could I have a quick word with you?"

"Sure." I stepped outside.

Wolf pulled the door shut. "Is there anything you'd like to tell me about Patsy Lee?"

I blinked at him. "I think I've told you everything I know. She was hiding in the bushes and then seemed to be running from someone in the dark."

"But that wasn't the dark shadow?"

I shrugged. "I didn't see anyone else that night. I have no idea. Then yesterday she wanted to have lunch with me privately, but she didn't tell me what that was about."

"What were her exact words?"

I blew out a breath of air. "I don't know. She said because I hadn't blabbed about her hiding in the bushes she felt like she could trust me to be discreet about this other problem. Oh! I said that I had solved some murders and she responded that someone might be murdered if she didn't clear up her problem." I looked Wolf straight in the eyes. "At the time I thought that was a joke. You know, an exaggeration."

"But now?"

"Why are you questioning me like this? Obviously, in light of what happened, I wonder what she meant."

"Did she hire you to do anything for her?"

"You mean like an event?"

"Like anything. Anything at all."

"No."

"Did you sell her something?"

"Wolf! No. I barely knew the woman."

"Then why did she jot down your name and address on a piece of stationery in her hotel room?"

Chapter 15

Dear Sophie,
Our company is having a pie-eating contest at a
summer picnic for employees. I'm worried that my
idiot husband who loves to eat will gorge and get
sick. How do those skinny guys who win eating
contests do it?
*   Worried Wife in Grand Gorge, New York*

Dear Worried Wife,
Believe it or not, the people who are serious about
eating contests work out and practice eating large
quantities. They learn to pace themselves and drink
adequate water. It might be wise to put a limit on
how many pies a contestant can eat. Multiple win-
ners are always more fun, anyway.

*   Sophie*

I knew Wolf too well to imagine that he was joking. "I
have no idea. Maybe she planned to pay me a visit?"
"This isn't the time to be flip."
"Wolf! There are probably people all over Old Town

with your name written somewhere. You can't help that any more than I can."

"Why did she write a check to you?"

"She didn't."

"Sophie, I know that she did. And it was for a hefty amount."

"That's just bizarre." I ticked items off on my fingers as I spoke. "She didn't hire me for anything, she didn't owe me anything, and there was absolutely no reason for her to pay me a single cent. As far as I know, I met Patsy Lee for the first time in my life on Friday."

"You understand that this involves you in the case of her death."

His words slammed me like a punch in the gut. "I . . . I see why you might think so, but I have told you everything I know. Do you want to search my office for the check?"

"We may have to see your bank account."

"Wolf! She didn't give me any money. I don't know what you're suggesting, but it doesn't make any sense. I hardly know her. There isn't a reason in the world for her to write a check to me, and I know nothing about her death."

"If anything comes to you, let me know."

He sounded so serious. "Wolf!"

"I have to do my job, Soph. You know that." Wolf turned and started toward the sidewalk.

That news had drained me of energy. What could she have been thinking? And worse, why was Wolf treating me like I was hiding a secret?

Wolf stopped and looked back at me. "Be careful, okay?"

I tried to smile at him. At least he wasn't telling me to butt out and mind my own business. Maybe he had come to the realization that it was futile. Or maybe he thought I'd better figure out what that check was about.

I closed the door and returned to the kitchen, where Nina was reading some of the papers Aly had left for us.

"Here it is." She moved one finger along a page as she read. "A Dr. Klaus Brenner says a person can commit murder during an alcohol-induced blackout. But on cross-examination it's revealed that Nellie Stokes did not have alcohol in her system at the time of her arrest. Nellie's team had a Dr. Rufus Smythington testify, who insists that it's not a blackout, per se. It's called *dissociative rage* and the perpetrator doesn't recall his actions when they are over. He may, in fact, feel great remorse."

"It's odd that she didn't mention a blackout. Did Nellie take the stand?" I asked.

"Not that I can see."

"I guess they didn't want her insisting that she hadn't blacked out," I mused. "Is it just me or does it sound like Kenner and the prosecutors made up one theory, and Nellie's attorneys made up another theory, but no one was concerned about what actually happened that night?"

"Grainger's father testified that Nellie was obsessed with Grainger and was about to be fired because her behavior toward him was inappropriate and unprofessional."

"Ouch!" I picked up the dishes and glasses, then rinsed and placed them in the dishwasher. "So if I understand this correctly, the prosecution claimed that Nellie was chasing Grainger. Do you think she was delusional?"

"She doesn't strike me that way now," said Nina. "Of course, we're not shrinks."

"One of them was lying. Think we should have dinner at Star-Spangled Pies tonight?"

"Good evening, Sergeant Gibbard. So tell me, were you lying at the trial of your son's murderer?" Nina quipped.

"I hope we'll be more subtle than that!" I sat down at the table and told her about the check Patsy Lee had supposedly written. "It's so strange. All I can imagine is that she wanted to hire me for something."

"Brock. We need to talk with Brock," said Nina.

When she went home, I put Daisy's halter on her and went for a walk. We stopped by the florist and bought a single white rose, which I carried down to the park and added to the mound of gifts in Patsy Lee's honor.

Roger stood nearby, his mouth twitched up into a scowl. I walked over to him, wondering what had possessed him to team up with Natasha and enter a pie that Patsy Lee was known for. "Hi. Thanks for entering the contest."

"Sorry about the fuss. I didn't know Natasha would act like that. It didn't go as I had planned. It was, if you'll pardon my saying so, a pie in the face."

"That happens. Was it really Natasha who baked the pie?"

"She told me she couldn't enter, but she wanted to prove that she could win. I had no idea she was banned! She's not speaking to me anymore." He wrinkled his nose. "I guess she won't be opening the bakery with me, either. Figures. Every time Peter shows up everything goes haywire for me."

"Whose idea was it to use Patsy Lee's recipe?" I asked.

Roger's face was turning pink. Was he blushing or getting a sunburn on his pale skin?

"It's *not* Patsy Lee's recipe. You don't have to give me that look. I know what I'm talking about. It was *my* recipe, and Peter stole it from me."

"Surely, Patsy Lee made it her own? She must have made changes to it. Isn't that how recipes work? Everyone makes their own changes?"

"They didn't change a lousy thing. Nothing. I perfected that pie." Roger glanced at the memorial. "I'm sick to my very core that Patsy Lee died. I have rarely felt such grief.

But she was not the sweetheart everyone thinks. Look at them." He gestured toward two women who were weeping. "They completely bought into Patsy Lee's brand, which I prefer to call her schtick. Peter made her into a phony, from her dyed hair right down to her pedicured toes."

Chapter 16

Dear Natasha,
I have never baked a pie before. I'd like to impress
my boyfriend's parents. What is the easiest pie to
bake?
            Hoping to Awe Them in Yum Yum, Tennessee

Dear Hoping to Awe Them,
I recommend pumpkin or chocolate cream pie with
piped whipped cream. But bake a test pie first to
learn how to do it.
                                        Natasha

I couldn't help wondering if Roger was simply jealous. Was that why they said not to speak ill of the dead? It sounded petty? "She was very successful. That wasn't fake."

"I knew her back when she was a nobody like us. I liked that Patsy Lee. She was funny and . . . and real." Roger grunted unbecomingly. "How she won her first cooking competitions is beyond me. She couldn't bake. And she sure couldn't cook. Patsy Lee didn't know the difference between a simmer and a boil."

That jibed with what Tommy Earl had said. "She must have learned fast."

Roger shot me a look. "She cheated. Peter was a bad influence on her. They stole, lied, and conned their way to the top. You know why I wanted Natasha to enter my pie? Because I knew Patsy Lee would be a judge. I didn't care about winning or a trophy. I wanted Patsy Lee to taste that pie and look me in the eyes. She knew what she had done, and I wanted her to admit it."

He was some kind of angry. I didn't want to insult him by saying the wrong thing, but if you asked me, he seemed overly upset about one pie recipe.

"You see, if the pie won, I was going up to take that trophy, and my winning would mean she was admitting that *my* recipe was the best." He tapped his chest with his fingers. "If I didn't win, it would be because she knew it was her signature recipe and someone had baked it to trick her. *Me!*"

It sounded harmless enough, if a little absurd.

Roger's face contorted with anger. "You know, when you're a chef, the most important thing you have is your reputation. They didn't care who they stepped on and squashed to make it big. Patsy Lee had a crummy childhood. I mean the kind of misery that sends people to shrinks. They hid all that. *My* meemaw really did teach me how to cook. Peter stole that story straight from me, lying about Patsy Lee helping her meemaw. I wouldn't have had to invent a past. I don't have it in me to mistreat people the way they did. Gotta say, though, while I might sleep better at night because I'm a decent human being, it would have been nice to have the big house and the big bucks. Instead

I have to kowtow to hopeless wannabes like Natasha just to scrabble together enough funds to open a bakery."

I couldn't say what I was thinking. I was pretty sure that one stolen pie recipe and a story about Meemaw weren't what launched Patsy Lee on the road to fame and fortune. But I found it interesting that both Tommy Earl and Roger claimed the meemaw story. Besides, none of us knew what would have happened had we taken another path. He was envious—plain and simple. "I'm sorry," I murmured.

"Yeah. Me too. My life could have been very different. I can't help wondering if fate caught up to her. Maybe she finally stepped on the wrong person."

I watched Roger amble away, his hands in his pockets. I needed to tell Wolf about Roger. Maybe he thought he was taking fate into his own hands and poisoned Patsy Lee in the belief that she was stopping him from becoming a star. Or maybe he was deranged. Sometimes unhappy people tried to blame their failures on the successes of others. In any event I wouldn't dream of eating anything he baked!

Tommy Earl waved at me and hurried over. "Natasha is a friend of yours, right?"

"I've known her all my life."

"Buckle your seat belt, buttercup, because she's going to be the next Patsy Lee."

"I'm not following you."

"Peter Presley made Patsy Lee a star. If it hadn't been for Peter, Patsy Lee would be in the back of a restaurant or bakery like the rest of us. The man has got unbelievable marketing skills. I'm not saying they're all on the up-and-up, but he knows what he's doing."

"That's what Natasha has always wanted." I couldn't help grinning. "Can Peter really make that happen?"

"She has hooked her star to the correct chariot if that's what she wants."

I backed off my joy just a little bit. "When you say not on the up-and-up, do you mean things like stealing recipes?"

Tommy snickered. "There will be plenty of that. If you give her a recipe, be sure to leave out something important."

"Tommy Earl!" I scolded. "Don't tell me you really do that."

"We have all learned the hard way. Back in the day we were a pretty tight crew. Grainger Gibbard, Patsy Lee Presley, Roger MacKenzie, Willa Staminski, and I were all hired by Apex Pie. We churned out pies that went to grocery stores all over the eastern seaboard. Hundreds of them! You probably ate them all the time. It was like a pie sweatshop. But we had a good time and got to know one another very well. We were close friends then. Right up until Peter started watching cooking shows on TV."

I couldn't help being doubtful. "Come on. It's not that easy, or everyone would do it."

"Peter's pretty sharp. He knew Patsy couldn't cook. She could barely handle the work at Apex Pie, but she had a couple of things going for her. She was pretty in a down-home way. Know what I mean? Patsy Lee looked like a real person, not a model. She looked like everybody's aunt. And she had an outgoing personality that made people comfortable with her. When you met Patsy Lee, you felt like she'd been your friend your whole life."

That worried me for Natasha. She was beautiful, but more like a model than Patsy Lee. And she rarely made anyone feel comfortable. Actually, now that I thought about it, that was one of her biggest flaws. Natasha thought she was always right and that it was a kindness to correct everyone else, which made everyone feel awkward and embarrassed.

"I won't say there wasn't some luck involved, but Peter was brilliant."

"Yet they divorced," I observed.

"From what we gather, Patsy Lee got up on her high horse and started thinking she was a star. She didn't want to take directions from Peter anymore. He put everything he had into her career, and she rewarded him by hiring some fancy shark lawyer who left poor old Peter with just a few pennies jingling in his pocket. He went from Patsy Lee's manager and husband to . . . nothing."

I winced. That was probably the kind of gossip that would interest Wolf. "You said Grainger Gibbard was part of your group?"

Tommy smiled sadly. "Grainger was fun. I still have trouble imagining that he's not around anymore."

"Didn't Nellie Stokes work at Apex Pie, too?" I asked.

"Oh, wow. Haven't thought about her in a long time. Poor Nellie. I was stunned when she flipped out and killed Grainger. They had so much going for them."

His lips mashed together and he snorted. "How life changes. I was so angry with Grainger at the time. I had this idea for a TV show set in a pie bakery. The two of us were going to do it together. Then he stole the idea, set it in his restaurant, and dumped me. I never expected that from him. I was furious. And hurt, you know? Because we were friends up to that point. I never spoke with him again."

"Do you think she did it?"

"Oh yeah. The story goes that the jury was unanimous from the first vote, but they wanted lunch brought in so they discussed the case and voted again after they ate. I don't know what Nellie was thinking, but I can guarantee that Grainger didn't deserve what happened to him."

"Was Nellie part of your crew at Apex Pie?" I asked again.

"Did I leave her out? Freudian slip, I guess. I'll never be able to understand what possessed her that night."

Tommy checked his watch. "Better get home and shower. I've got a date tonight."

"Wong?" I asked.

"She told you?"

"Just a guess."

"There's a special dinner this evening for the people teaching classes at the PiePalooza. I thought Wong might enjoy it."

I knew I had seen a spark between them! I tried not to grin like a fool. But hadn't Roger said Tommy Earl was unreliable? "Are you teaching a class?"

"You didn't know? Roger said you recommended me after you took one of my classes."

"Wonderful!" But very, very odd. I guessed Roger had run out of choices. I struggled to change the subject. "Nina and I are going to Star-Spangled Pies tonight. Do you have any favorite dishes to recommend?"

"They have some young kid baking for them now." Tommy flapped his hand in a dismissive gesture. "It's not like it was when Nellie worked there. The turnover in that kitchen is constant. Every few months word goes out that they're looking for a new pastry chef. My guess is that the Sergeant is a tough guy to please. Let me know what you think about their food." He gave me a quick wave and hurried off to prepare for his date with Wong.

I stared at the impromptu memorial to Patsy Lee and wondered who was taking care of the funeral details now that she wasn't married. A handwritten letter set me straight—*I have all your pots and pans, as well as your cookbooks. Thank you for making me the baker I am today. I'll never forget you.*

Who was I kidding? Patsy Lee Presley wasn't just a person, she was a business. She had *people* who took care of details for her. Her friends were bitter about her success.

But I didn't doubt for a moment that their jealousy stemmed from their craving what she had achieved.

I walked home slowly, thinking about the pastry bakers who had begun together at Apex Pie. Two were dead and one was in prison. How many of them had there been? Tommy, Patsy Lee, Willa, Grainger, Roger, and Nellie. I counted six. Half of them came to terrible ends. What were the odds of that? Something wasn't right in the Apex Pie gang.

At six thirty I fed Mochie and slid Daisy's halter over her head. Star-Spangled Pies had a sizeable outdoor patio in the back of the restaurant where dogs were welcome.

I locked the kitchen door behind us. When we passed through the little gate that led to the street, Nina already waited on the sidewalk in front of her house. During the stroll down to Star-Spangled Pies, I told her about the Apex Pie group and the jealousy that ran deep there.

"Isn't it always that way?" she asked. "I would feel the same, especially if I were better at something and my inept friend became wealthy while I struggled. It's human nature."

"Would you be envious enough to kill your pal?" I asked as we walked up to the restaurant.

At that moment a man in a chef's jacket stormed out the door.

Chapter 17

Dear Natasha,
My mom says you can make a pot pie with frozen
puff pastry. Is that true? It seems easier than mak-
ing one from scratch.
                    Pot Pie Princess in Flower Pot, Arizona

Dear Pot Pie Princess,
I'm swooning from the vapors at the mere thought
of using frozen puff pastry. Make your own crust,
already!

                                        Natasha

Someone inside shouted ferociously.
Daisy balked and barked.

"It's okay," I assured her, though I wasn't at all sure that was the case.

The shouting continued while we walked around the side of the restaurant to the outdoor dining tables. Almost all the diners, now wide-eyed, had stopped eating and were listening intently.

Only Willa was composed and continued eating her dinner. She spied us and waved her hand. "Come join me!"

When we sat down, Willa patted Daisy. "I hate to eat alone. Besides, I've been dying to ask Nina something. Do you think the little boy who won the junior division of the pie contest had help from his parents?"

Nina gasped. "Oh no! You think they cheated?"

"We'll never know unless they blab, but I've been thinking about it and that pie was far too advanced for someone his age," whispered Willa. "It was the best pie in the youth category, but when I saw that little guy accepting the trophy, I just had a hunch he wasn't the one who baked it."

"Aww," Nina moaned. "That's unfortunate for the other children. But how would you know unless they baked the pies in a public forum?"

Willa nodded. "It doesn't really matter, anyway. I just wondered if I was the only person who suspected more than a little help from his mom and dad. Maybe I'm wrong and he's a pie savant!"

"Who's doing all that yelling inside the restaurant?" asked Nina.

Willa responded calmly, as though it were common. "The Sergeant. He's not the best manager. He's been yelling since Grainger died, and probably before that. Grainger's sister Greta took over, but she doesn't know beans about restaurant management. She's a nice woman, but the Sergeant keeps interfering and firing people."

"You seem so calm about it," I observed.

Willa's laugh was warm and hearty. "I worked here for a few months after Grainger's death. When the Sergeant yells, it reminds me how good I have it at The Laughing Hound. I can't imagine Bernie losing his temper like that."

I opened the menu and said, "Neither can I. He gets an-

THE DIVA SWEETENS THE PIE   125

noyed with Natasha, but I don't believe I have ever heard Bernie scream like that."

"I've been here before, but I've never heard any screaming. How's the chicken pot pie?" asked Nina.

"Used to be the best in town when Nellie worked here. It's still good, but the crust isn't as delicate."

A woman wearing her hair in a long ponytail arrived at our table. "Willa!" she cried. "I didn't know you were here." The woman sat down with us. "Would you come back and work for us again?"

Willa introduced Nina and me to Greta Gibbard. Greta was very gracious, but immediately turned her attention back to Willa. "I'll pay you twice what Bernie is paying you."

Willa cocked her head. "Very tempting. But no amount of money would bring me back here."

Greta slumped in her chair. "I don't know how Grainger managed Dad. He tries to run this place like a boot camp."

"You can't get him to stay home?" asked Nina.

Greta winced. "My mom doesn't want him there. Thank goodness we've maintained a reputation for good food. But every time Dad erupts and fires someone, we lose diners. I can't blame them, really. Who needs an old grouch yelling when they go out to eat? Do either one of you bake?"

"Sophie does!" offered Nina.

"Sorry, I'm not a pastry chef, and I have a job."

Greta rose. "If you hear of anyone who is looking, send him or her my way."

I thought of Roger. If I saw him, I'd let him know. He had wanted a bakery of his own, but maybe in the meantime he'd be content here. We placed our orders and Greta retreated to the kitchen.

Nina lowered her voice when she said, "My family is so

quiet. I can't imagine putting up with a dad who yells like that."

"If he would limit himself to that kind of behavior at home," said Willa, "I could deal with it. But the old man has a volatile temper."

Surely, the Sergeant hadn't killed his own son? "Did you work here when Grainger was managing the place?"

"Nope." Willa shook her head. "I came on board the week after he was murdered. Nellie had been the pastry chef up until then. They were closed for several days before and after the funeral, and that's when I was hired."

"By the Sergeant?" I asked.

"He seemed so nice during the interview. Greta is right, he tries to run the place military style, but that just causes people to quit."

"You must have heard a lot of gossip," said Nina.

"About Grainger? That was all anyone could talk about." She clammed up when a waiter arrived with our food.

He placed pot pies on the table for us, then knelt to Daisy and said, "This is our chicken pie for doggies." He placed a bowl of food and another of water in front of her. "No crust and no onions," he said for our benefit before he walked away.

Daisy plunged her nose into the bowl and ate with gusto.

Willa dug into her pie. "Mmm. There's a nice touch of thyme, and I love the way they sliced the carrots. When they dice them, I always wonder if they were frozen."

Nina eyed her. Leaning toward Willa, she said, "I heard that Nellie and Grainger were engaged."

"I don't think it had gone that far. The Sergeant thought Nellie wasn't good enough for Grainger. Apparently, he was upset that she had left her husband. I remember him saying it would be one thing if Nellie were a widow, but if a woman left one husband, she would leave the next one, too. All nonsense, of course, but he's old school and has some crazy ideas. Rumor had it that Nellie wouldn't have been working here at all if it weren't for Grainger. The other employees said he was completely besotted with her."

"Then why would she have murdered him?" I took another bite of the savory pie.

Willa shrugged. "It has never made any sense to me. He adored her, and she was crazy for him. What could he possibly have done to make her that angry?"

"Did Nellie have a temper?" I asked. "Was she the kind of person who might flip out if Grainger broke up with her?"

"Nellie?" Willa sipped a glass of white wine. "That's rich. Nellie would walk a mile out of her way to avoid a confrontation. Now, Patsy Lee, she was another story. She stood up for herself."

Patsy Lee? It was an odd jump from Nellie to Patsy Lee. "Was Patsy Lee around Old Town at the time Grainger was murdered?"

Nina's fork clattered to her plate. "Are you suggesting that Patsy Lee murdered Grainger?"

I had been *trying* to be subtle.

Willa's lips drew tight. "I don't know why she would have murdered Grainger, but she was in and out of town for a long time. I always suspected she had a honey down here in Old Town."

Now that it was out there, I might as well ask Willa more questions. I lowered my voice lest other diners overhear. "I've been hearing stories about Patsy Lee not knowing how to bake and miraculously becoming a star by stealing recipes and stories from her friends."

Willa groaned. "All true. She and Peter stopped at nothing in their quest for Patsy Lee to be a star."

Someone at another table looked over at us. I lowered my voice and shifted the conversation to another topic. "So you were Patsy Lee's best friend?"

"Oh, gosh, yes. We went way back. I was her maid of honor when she married Peter. She was"—she paused as if choosing her words carefully—"a different person then. She really was a country girl, more at home with horses and goats than anything else. She was sweet and honest, and I would have trusted her with my cat's life."

Nina frowned at her. "She changed when she became a star?"

Willa took a big swig from her wineglass. "The biggest mistake I made in my life was moving to New York to work for her. I left behind everything I loved just to help her. Five months later she canned me because I wasn't sophisticated enough for her anymore. You know, the sad thing is that I felt like the real Patsy Lee, the simple one whom I knew and loved, was still in there somewhere."

Willa sighed and picked at her dinner. "But now it's too late. Do you know why I came here to eat dinner tonight? Because this is where Patsy Lee and I had agreed to meet to catch up." Willa raised her wineglass. "To Patsy Lee, the woman I knew, not the star. May you rest in peace."

Nina and I joined in her toast. It was a melancholy moment. One I wouldn't soon forget.

Nina, Daisy, and I walked Willa to her condo after dinner. The sun had set and the day-tripping tourists had gone home to start the workweek fresh on Monday.

Willa lived in a redbrick house that had been divided into condominiums. She said good night, walked up the stairs to a grand glass door, and disappeared inside.

"Would you fire me?" asked Nina.

I laughed. "Would I hire you in the first place?"

"I knew there was something going on between them when they met at Bernie's the other night. Patsy Lee was excited to see Willa, but I'll never forget the wariness on Willa's face."

"None of them trusted Patsy Lee. It sounds like they all liked her in the beginning, but each one of them got burned by her in some way."

"She stepped on everyone's shoulders on her way up and never looked back."

Nina stopped in front of her house. "Do you think there's a connection between Patsy Lee's death and Grainger's murder?"

"I guess that's what we need to find out." I gave her a little wave and walked on. But before we crossed the street to our house, Daisy stopped cold. She lifted her muzzle and sniffed the air. Under the light of the streetlamp, I could see her nose twitching.

"Raccoon?" I asked.

A light breeze blew and I thought I saw someone dart into the dark of night. Daisy relaxed and crossed the street. Everything seemed fine at home. Nevertheless, I double-checked all the doors to be sure they were locked.

I wanted to curl up on the love seat in the glass-enclosed sunroom again that night, but the lights would expose me to the lurker—if there was one. Now that we knew Dooley wasn't a stalker, I thought that was behind me. Maybe it had just been my imagination that someone lurked in the dark.

I settled in the small den off the kitchen, where I could pull the curtains shut. Daisy jumped up on the sofa with me, and Mochie settled on the back of the sofa, his legs splayed like a wildcat on a branch.

There was a detail I was curious about and I hoped I might find it in the materials Aly had supplied to us. The transcript of Nellie's case was shorter than I expected. There was no mention at all of Dooley or any other potential murderer. In my opinion Nellie's attorneys had done a halfhearted job.

But I found the item I wanted to know about. Kenner had taken the stand, and the prosecutor asked if the murder weapon had been found.

"Poisonous rhubarb leaves were discovered during the autopsy. The knife wasn't on the ground in the vicinity of the kitchen, but when Sergeant Gibbard arrived and unlocked the restaurant door, there was a distinct odor of bleach. Clearly, the knife had been cleaned of blood and replaced where it belonged."

I scanned for the defense questions regarding the weapon. There were none, but in his closing statement, Nellie's attorney had argued that the prosecution had not been able to produce the murder weapon. The prosecution, on the other hand, argued that Nellie had taken the time to bleach any blood that she might have tracked into the kitchen when she cleaned the knife.

I sat back, listening to Mochie purr. If I had been on the jury, would I have bought that explanation? I didn't think so. Nellie had been more persuasive with her account of the timeline.

How could I find out what had been going on in Grainger's life back then? Was it possible that the same person had poisoned Patsy Lee? Maybe he or she had felt the attorneys' treatment of the knife issue had been a lucky break and returned to poison to get rid of Patsy Lee?

Monday morning brought crisp air, a reminder that fall would soon be upon us. When I took Daisy out for a morning walk, I scanned the street to be sure no one was hanging around. Everyone seemed to be on their way somewhere. Morning traffic passed slowly as if no one was eager to work in the last weeks of the summer.

Daisy and I were a block away from home when Dooley strode up to us and gave me an awkward hug.

"Thank you, Sophie. Nellie's spirits haven't been this high in years. Mine either. I'm counting on you to bring my sweet Nellie back to me."

While he talked, a sleek black limousine glided by us. We watched as it came to a halt on my block.

"You have some snazzy neighbors," said Dooley.

Chapter 18

Dear Sophie,
My mother-in-law's pie recipe begins with these
words, "Blind bake the shell." Help! What does
that mean?
                    Perplexed in Shell Island, South Carolina

Dear Perplexed,
It means you need to prebake the bottom crust of
the pie. Prick the dough with a fork, line it with
aluminum foil, and pour uncooked beans into it to
weigh it down. Bake about twelve minutes.
                                            Sophie

The driver stepped out and opened a back door. Natasha emerged from her house, gracefully walked down her front stairs, and entered the limo. The driver closed the door. The limo merged with traffic and rolled away.

Dooley checked his watch. "I'd better get to work."

"Me too."

Taking giant strides that made me think of Ichabod

Crane, Dooley was halfway down the next block before Daisy and I reached the cross street.

After our morning walk I made a big mug of tea for myself and popped a frozen bagel into the oven for my breakfast. Mochie sat next to his food bowl watching me. Daisy's eyes darted from the counter to the floor and back. She was telling me she wanted her breakfast. I fed Mochie and Daisy while the bagel came back to life.

It was hard to focus on work. I made phone calls and booked some venues a year and a half in advance for upcoming conferences. But Nellie and Patsy Lee continued to haunt me.

At lunchtime I took a walk down to Alex's office. I could see him through the big plate-glass window in his reception area. He had furnished the office in a classic style with Oriental rugs and antique furniture. On a pedestal in the corner a bronze statue depicted Lady Justice in a blindfold and holding scales. His administrative assistant, seated at her desk, was on the phone.

I walked in quietly, lest I interrupt something. It sounded like they were trying to locate a client.

Alex slid his arm around me and kissed me on the cheek.

His assistant hung up the phone. "Hi, Sophie. No luck, Alex. No one has seen him."

Alex clutched his head. "What does he think he's doing?" To me, he said, "One of my clients didn't show for court this morning. We have no idea what happened to him. How about an iced coffee, Soph? I could use a little break."

"Sure." I asked if we could bring anything back for his assistant, but she had packed a lunch.

When we stepped outside, Alex headed toward Moos & Brews.

"Are you ready to drink their coffee?" I asked.

Alex shot me an amused look. "You mean because of

Patsy Lee's death? It had nothing to do with Moos and Brews. She added the powdered caffeine herself."

"How do you know that?"

"Simple logic. She had a brutal schedule and probably did it on a regular basis when she needed a boost. I'm sorry to say that we're all ingesting a little more caffeine than we probably should. My assistant drinks coffee all day except for the caffeine-laden energy drink she must have every day around three o'clock. She's not the only one. Everybody is overworked and overbooked. Besides, who would have wanted to kill Patsy Lee?"

I smirked. "Little do you know."

Alex moaned. "Don't tell me you think she was murdered?"

"Let's just say she wasn't as beloved as one might have thought. I'll have an iced mocha, please."

We paid for our cool drinks and giant fluffy ham biscuits that they made from scratch. Alex carried the drink tray, and I carried the sack of food. We wandered over to Market Square, where we perched on the edge of the fountain to eat. "So what do you know about Fribble and Dothford?"

"The law firm?" Alex handed me an iced coffee and took a sip of his. "Yuck. Wrong drink." He swapped his for mine.

I nodded. "Yes, the law firm."

With a serious look Alex said, "You know that one of the perks of dating a lawyer is free legal advice."

"Thank you! Good to know if I should run into trouble. So what do you know about those guys?"

He sipped his iced coffee while he thought. "I will simply remind you that someone is at the bottom of every graduating law school class."

"Ouch! That's brutal."

He raised his eyebrows. "Maybe so, but it's still true."

"So you're saying they're dolts."

"I don't believe I said that, nor did I use that word, but I wouldn't hire them to fetch my coffee. Why are you asking about them?"

"They represented Nellie Dooley."

Alex swallowed a bite of his ham biscuit and turned his head to stare at the fountain. "Grainger Gibbard's murder? That was years ago."

"Know anything about it?"

"Nope."

"Some help you are."

"You're so bored that you're digging up closed cases?" he asked.

"I'm not bored, and I'm not digging up anything. There are some people who don't believe that Nellie Stokes killed Grainger. Fribble and Dothford represented her. It's possible that she didn't get a decent defense. I know nothing about trials, but I suspect that I could have done a better job than they did."

Alex laughed. "I bet you could have."

"Nellie's ex-husband said they had already been through an appeal based on ineffective counsel—"

"But the conviction was affirmed." Alex completed the sentence for me. "It's a pretty high standard."

"They didn't put her on the stand to testify on her own behalf," I argued.

"That's not unusual. You take a big chance when the defendant testifies. A lot of people make things worse for themselves. It's a judgment call."

"You're not saying things I want to hear." I bit into my ham biscuit and savored the salty flavor of Virginia ham.

"Sophie, I know how you love to investigate. And I think I've been pretty indulgent about that. But this is a little bit different. The case was decided. It was appealed and affirmed. It's a done deal."

"Are you saying courts are never wrong?"

"Of course not. But now you're fighting the system."

"Maybe someone needs to in Nellie's case."

"Does it have to be you?"

"Alex! What happened to being entitled to free legal advice?"

"I meant for you." He wadded the paper that had wrapped his biscuit, shaped it into a ball, and pitched it into a trash can like a basketball. "And he scores!"

He was trying to lighten things up. I understood. I didn't like it, but I knew what he was doing.

"Look, Sophie. I don't want to fight over this. But I have serious reservations about you getting involved in a case that has already been tried."

I handed him the wrapper from my biscuit. He wadded it up and tossed it at the garbage can. It hit the edge and fell to the ground.

I walked over to it, picked it up, and threw it into the receptacle, along with my coffee cup. "I win."

Alex walked up beside me. "How would you feel if I got involved in event planning?"

"I'd think I would be holding your hand through the entire process the first few times." Just like I had been helping Roger.

"And we might be after the same clients?"

"Maybe . . ."

"What if I tread on the toes of your friends?"

"How would you do that?"

"I might use you as a reference. Or maybe I would steal clients from your buddies."

I raised my hands in the air. "I give. You could have just come right out and said that I might damage your reputation as a lawyer. I get it. You don't want to date someone who is a pest to the people in your field."

"That's a relief."

"I'm still going to look into Nellie's case because I promised someone very special that I would. But I'll be careful, and I won't embarrass you."

He eyed me. "I guess that's the best I can ask for?"

"Pretty much."

"Okay. Call me if you need me."

Ha! Did he not know me at all? After that little warning it would have to be an emergency of the highest order for me to go to him seeking help.

"Sophie," Alex said softly, "*if* you're right and Nellie was unjustly convicted, that would mean someone violent is still out there." He stopped walking and placed his hands on my shoulders. "You could be stepping into a hornet's nest. Think about it. What would you do if you had quietly gotten away with murder years ago and someone started poking around?"

His concern was sweet, but he wasn't telling me anything I didn't already know. "If that had been me, I would have gotten out of town while the getting was good. Whoever murdered Grainger is probably long gone, like your missing client."

Alex blinked rapidly. "I'd better get back to work."

I had to admit that there was a slightly bitter taste in my mouth when I left him at his office. Alex didn't want me involved. Legal matters were his territory, not mine. Even though I understood his desire to keep me out of his area of expertise, I wasn't pleased.

It even crossed my mind that this reluctance was exactly the reason I needed to help Nellie. Only an outsider would be willing to cut through the baloney to get to the truth. I didn't want to believe that was true, but I suspected Dooley was right. No one else cared. Even Alex tried to tell me they had their man, as it were, and the matter was closed.

I tried to put Alex out of my mind to focus on Nellie. It seemed to me that the key was Grainger. If I worked backward from the premise that Nellie didn't murder Grainger, then there was someone else who was angry with him. What had Grainger done?

I strolled down to Star-Spangled Pies. A sign on the door said CLOSED ON MONDAYS. A light flicked off inside the restaurant, but I couldn't see anyone through the windows.

I walked to the end of the block and doubled back through the alley to see the place where the murder had occurred.

It was a sad place to die. Garbage sat outside the backs of stores, waiting to be collected. A lone cat stared at me before jumping onto the top of a fence that separated the alley from houses. He disappeared over the other side. A few cars were parked in reserved spots.

I could imagine how desolate it probably felt at night. Looking up at the houses that backed to the fence, I saw a few rear windows. But leafy trees had grown tall, probably planted as a buffer between the homes and the business area. Unless someone happened to be awake and looking out a back window at the time Grainger left the restaurant, no one would have noticed anything. There must have been some loud arguing or screaming. Grainger would probably have called for help, wouldn't he? But maybe his pleas melded with the normal sounds of the night as bars and restaurants closed and employees left.

The gate to the back patio of Star-Spangled Pies banged open. A boxy man with tanned skin and white hair barged out yelling, "Eighteen hundred! Be ready."

A slender woman followed him at a relaxed pace. She flapped her hand at him dismissively.

As he hurried into a car, she noticed me in the alley. Without a word she made a subtle gesture with her hand that I took to mean I should stay where I was.

Chapter 19

Dear Sophie,
I'm in a complete panic. I promised to bring pie to
my bridge club (and they're very critical), but the
edge of my crust is an unsightly mess. What now?
                    In a Pickle in Goofy Ridge, Illinois

Dear In a Pickle,
Don't panic. If your piecrust isn't pretty, pipe
whipped cream around the edge for a quick fix.
                                              Sophie

The car sped through the alley away from me, moving much faster than it should have. The woman waited until it reached the street and turned left. Only then did she walk toward me.

"You're Sophie Winston."

"Yes." I met her halfway.

"I recognize you from the annual Hope gala."

The popular ball raised money for families of local children who were sick so their parents could focus on their kids getting better instead of the bills that were mounting.

I had been the event planner of the gala for the last few years. "Thank you for participating. It's one of my favorite charity events."

I felt a little bit guilty for not recognizing her, but I arranged a lot of events. Mostly I dealt with those in charge and didn't meet the attendees.

She held out her hand to me. "Martha Gibbard. My daughter told me you dined at the restaurant last night."

"I enjoyed it very much."

Martha looked back at the road where her husband's car had driven away. "Won't you come in and have a slice of pie with me? I missed lunch."

"I would love to." We walked through the gate, which she latched behind us from the inside.

"What's your favorite pie?" I asked.

"It's not even close. I'm afraid I'm a chocoholic. Chocolate cream pie with whipped cream on top just cannot be beat." There was a sparkle in her eyes when she said, "I hope there's one in the fridge!"

Martha unlocked the door and stepped inside. But I stopped and looked back. How stupid of me. I had forgotten about the patio when I thought about the killer washing the knife. Grainger's killer would have had to walk across the patio to unlock the door and wash off the knife. Nellie was right. There would have been blood somewhere.

The faint smell of bleach lingered in the kitchen.

I turned to find Martha gazing at me silently. She didn't wear much makeup. A touch of eye shadow, but nothing else.

"My hair went white when Grainger was murdered." She said it as a matter of fact, without emotion.

I closed the door. "I've heard of that happening after a big shock."

"Doesn't get much bigger than the shock of your child being killed. We stopped offering any kind of rhubarb pie after Grainger died. I won't have rhubarb in the house or the restaurant." She put on a kettle of water. "Are you a tea drinker?"

"I am."

"So am I. It's calming. All my children will tell you that the louder it got in our house, the more tea I drank."

"You have a lot of kids."

"It was tea or booze. I had an uncle who drank too much alcohol. It made him vicious. When you have a family member who overindulges, you think twice about drinking." She brought a sinfully luscious pie to a tiny table. Whipped cream was piped around the edge, but the chocolate center shone under the lights.

Martha sliced the pie and delivered mugs of tea to the table. We sat down and tasted the pie.

"No wonder this is your favorite. It's delicious!"

She sipped her tea. "Isn't chocolate marvelous? It's perfect any time of year and for any occasion." She gazed at me. "Are you looking into Grainger's death?"

I plunged a bite of pie into my mouth to buy time to think. Should I admit it?

"That was a silly question," she said. "You wouldn't have been in the alley otherwise."

She reached across the table and rested her hand on top of mine. "Nellie didn't murder Grainger."

I couldn't have been more surprised if she had thrown the pie in my face.

She pulled her hand back. "I'm so relieved that someone is finally trying to help that poor girl. She's not one of my children, but she was almost a member of our family. I lie awake at night thinking about her." Tears welled in her eyes. "I'm not a genius or anyone special, but I have a feel for people. I understand character. Not only didn't Nellie have a reason to kill Grainger, but she didn't have it in her. She's not that kind of person."

I'd heard that before. Anyone could be pushed over the edge if the circumstances were right. Like in self-defense, for instance. I didn't tell her that, though. I wanted her to keep talking.

"I noticed a faint scent of bleach when I walked in. As I recall, at the trial it was argued that the smell of bleach meant the killer had bleached the knife."

"Uttered by someone who isn't in the restaurant business. I guess most people come in when the ovens are on and scents of cinnamon or apples fill the air. But when we shut down at night, this place gets a thorough cleaning."

"What was going on in Grainger's life at that time?"

"He was negotiating to do a show. One of those reality things. They were going to call it *Star-Spangled Pies* and base it here at the restaurant. I remember Grainger telling me we had the perfect cast. His father was the crazy old man yelling all the time and wanting to fire people on a whim. His *long-suffering mother*—those were his words, not mine—and sweet Nellie would be in the back of the house, complaining about the old man. Nellie and Grainger's wedding would be one episode. I thought it was a great idea. If my husband saw how he looked when he wigged out, maybe he would tone it down. And his outbursts would be somehow easier for us to take if they were on film. We could justify everything he did as drama for the show."

"And how did your husband feel about that?"

"The Sergeant was vehemently against it."

"So he and Grainger were fighting about it?"

Her nostrils flared and she exhaled. "I loved my husband once and in some ways I suppose I still do. I loathe his outbursts. He won't get counseling, and he doesn't appear to grasp that his behavior is wrong. I know people chalk it up to his time in the military, but that's not the cause. He grew up with a father who was a bully. It's what he saw and learned as a child."

Martha paused and stared at her fork. "His brother was murdered at the age of eighteen. Even my husband believed that his father was guilty. But the case was never solved."

I stared at her, trying to comprehend their situation. It finally dawned on me why she was telling me all this. Even though we were alone, I whispered, "You think your husband murdered Grainger?"

Martha didn't burst into tears, as I expected. She drew herself up straight. "You can't tell anyone. He would kill me if he knew what I was saying to you right now. And I don't mean that in the trite sense of the phrase."

"Where is he?" I asked, worried that he might return.

"Playing golf with buddies. He won't be back for hours."

"But I'm under the impression that the killer was a baker. Or at least someone who could bake a strawberry-rhubarb pie."

"It would have been very easy for him. He had access to everything he needed, *except* the poisonous leaves, right here in the restaurant. My husband may be loud and bossy, but he's capable of baking a pie."

"Was your husband ever a suspect in Grainger's death?"

"I don't believe so. The investigator, Kenner, treated him with utmost respect."

"He would. They're the same type. Weren't you home with your husband that night? You would have known if he had gone out."

"Our daughter Matilda had just given birth to her first child. I was staying with her to give her a hand."

"So he definitely had the opportunity. But would he really have murdered Grainger over a TV show?"

A sigh rippled out of her mouth. "There was a confrontation between my husband and our youngest son, Logan. He'd been working at the restaurant as a waiter and he loathed it."

"Logan is the artist?"

"Yes." A smile flickered on her lips. "The Sergeant doesn't think much of art as a career. Logan announced that he was quitting his job here and there was a confrontation between him and his father. Grainger stood up for Logan. I was so proud of him for that. Logan stormed out with Grainger protecting him. Logan and his dad haven't spoken a word since."

"But Logan is wildly successful! People talk about his paintings all the time."

"Isn't it wonderful? The Sergeant still talks about his art as trash."

"But that's not a reason to murder Grainger. I understand he disliked Nellie? Would he have framed her?"

"Poor Nellie. Do you know her? She's kind and sweet and I would have been proud to have her as a daughter-in-law. But my husband had this strange notion in his head that she was beneath Grainger. I never understood it. We didn't come from fancy families. Sometimes I wonder if he feels the restaurant escalated him to a higher social position. Did he think of it as Grainger, the co-owner, marrying an employee? For heaven's sake, Grainger started out as a pastry chef himself working on little more than a pie assembly line at Apex Pie! What kind of insanity would it be to imagine we were something special?"

Martha toyed with her piecrust. "I have thought about this for a long time. Now that our daughters and sons aren't children anymore, I fear that he sees them as rivals for his position of authority. Isn't that awful of me to imagine? It's a bit Shakespearean. The Sergeant has been bossing people around for so long that he doesn't know how to accept them graciously and concede that they are capable adults. Our lovely children have scattered and done as they please. They are all slowly being disowned by him."

It was incredibly rude of me and I knew it. But I couldn't help asking, "Why do you stay with him?"

"He's ill. Physically ill. If I left, he wouldn't have anyone to help him through what will likely be the biggest challenge of his life. What kind of heartless person would I be to leave him when he needs me most?"

She was a complicated person. Or maybe she had too many allegiances with her big family and always put herself last?

"By the way, it's not known that the Sergeant is not well. Please keep that under your hat."

"I will." No one needed to know that. "But I'm a little confused. I understand that he's sick and you feel the need to stand by him through his illness, which may actually qualify you for sainthood, but you're okay with telling me you're afraid he killed Grainger?"

"Grainger may be dead, but I'm still his mother. Even if the Sergeant murdered him, the truth, no matter how hard it is to accept, must come out. I owe that to Grainger. And I owe more to Nellie, who has wasted five years of her life in prison for someone else's crime. No matter what the outcome of the Sergeant's illness, the fact that he is sick doesn't diminish the need to right the situation for Nellie. She has a long life ahead of her and deserves to live with joy and freedom."

I thanked Martha for the tea and pie.

She walked to the door with me. "I'm glad you came by, Sophie. I was able to relieve a lot of burdens that have troubled me. I'm counting on you to set everything straight. But I'm sure you understand—we did not meet here today. We have not spoken, and we don't know each other, except through the Hope gala."

I gave her a hug and told her my address. "In case you need anything."

I walked across the silent patio, out the gate, and felt safer once I had exited the alley and was on the sidewalk again. I couldn't help glancing around to be sure the Sergeant wasn't watching. I didn't see him anywhere.

I walked home slowly, trying to make sense of everything Martha had told me. It all boiled down to proving that the Sergeant murdered his own son. The mere thought turned my stomach. But how could I prove that? The only things I could think of were witnesses and that elusive knife. I wished I had asked Martha about the knife.

Witnesses were going to be next to impossible to find. Where had I been on that fateful night five years ago? I didn't have the first clue, except for the fact that I was usually home in bed at five in the morning.

Chapter 20

Dear Sophie,
I have such problems transferring my pie dough to
the pie pan. It always breaks or falls apart!
                    Pie Klutz in Blueberry, Wisconsin

Dear Pie Klutz,
Roll the dough out between two sheets of parch-
ment or wax paper. Gently roll it (with paper) over
your rolling pin, removing the back sheet of paper.
Unroll it in the pie pan and remove the top sheet of
paper.

                                        Sophie

As I neared my house, I could see someone rushing toward my kitchen door. Natasha?

She knocked and peered in the window. Apparently im-
patient, she knocked again. "Sophie!"

"I'm coming," I called, picking up my speed.

She walked out to meet me, looking positively radiant.
"We have to talk," she trilled.

I unlocked the door and greeted Mochie and Daisy.

Natasha ignored them. It was beyond me how she could be blind to their enthusiasm. Daisy waggled from end to end, ready to kiss us, and Mochie head-butted my hand repeatedly.

Natasha couldn't stop smiling. "Sophie, I'm about to pop. I just have to share the news with my best friend."

She squealed like an excited teenager. "The most wonderful thing has happened to me. My dreams are finally coming true. Peter Presley has offered to be my manager. He already set up the pie bake-off with Tommy Earl to be featured on a national network! I'm so excited I can hardly breathe. He's the one who catapulted Patsy Lee to stardom."

I didn't want to burst her bubble by mentioning that Tommy Earl had suspected as much. "You signed a contract with Peter?"

"I did!" She clasped her hands together under her chin. "Can you imagine, he thinks I'm too beautiful! I need to tone it down. He took me clothes shopping this morning. My brand is going to be Upscale Country Gal." She raised her hands and drew them apart in the air as though she was imagining a banner. "Your meemaw's dishes, only better."

I hardly knew what to say. But Peter had made a star out of Patsy Lee, so maybe he could do the same for Natasha. "I'm so happy for you."

I meant it, too. Natasha had been casting about for a long time, trying to find her way to stardom. It was time she caught a break. And if everyone could be believed, Patsy hadn't been much of a cook or a baker, so it didn't matter how Natasha cooked. She had a stubborn streak, though. I hoped Peter was used to dealing with divas.

"I had to share with you. You've always been there for me, Sophie. And now you're not even jealous that I'll be famous and you'll still be stuck in this horrible old

kitchen, plugging away at a boring and unfulfilling job."
She gasped. "Maybe I can hire you to be part of my entourage. Peter is bringing Brock on board. I'm sure we
could find a place for you to do something. Maybe you
could make travel arrangements for us."

That was Natasha. She would probably get worse as her
career took off. "Thank you for the offer. But I'm quite
happy with my *unfulfilling job.*"

"Now don't you worry, Sophie. Even when I'm rich and
famous, I'll still remember you. I'll have Brock send you
fruit baskets at the holidays." She tossed her hair and
placed a hand on the base of her neck. "Peter is just so
sweet. He's not my type, but I could fall for a guy like him.
You know what he said? He told me, 'Now that Patsy Lee
is a star in the sky, there's room for another star on earth.' "
She rubbed under her eye with the back of her finger.

Was she tearing up?

"Isn't that the most lovely sentiment you've ever heard?"

Why did I suspect that Peter was more interested in
money and flattering Natasha so she would become his
next Patsy Lee? "So what does an Upscale Country Gal
wear?" I asked.

"You should see the clothes he bought me. Jeans, of
course. Every country girl wears them. But I wear them
tucked into boots with a long white shirt and a tweed
blazer. It's the ultimate in casual sophistication. That's actually one of the reasons I came over. The bake-off is tomorrow at the Belmont Hotel. Would you come?"

"Absolutely. I wouldn't miss it for the world."

Natasha tilted her head and reached out her arms toward me. "Thank you for being so supportive. Now I'm
off to re-create my nanny's coconut cream pie by adding
avocado."

I was used to Natasha's modern-ingredient combinations. A lot of them didn't appeal to me, but I had decided

I shouldn't be closed-minded about them. I couldn't think of a single pie that would be improved by avocado in it, but I smiled to be encouraging. I closed the door behind her, wondering if Peter had figured out yet that he had a lot of work to do before Natasha would be ready for prime time.

The next morning I took my tea out in the backyard and enjoyed the cool morning air. Daisy roamed my yard frantically, her nose to the grass like she was following tracks. I couldn't see anything, but her dog nose was on the trail of something. Probably a squirrel.

While she had fun, I thought about the Gibbard family. It had taken a lot of courage for Martha to speak so openly. Would I have had the courage to do that? Maybe, if someone had killed my child or my sibling. I wondered if other family members suspected the Sergeant as well but remained silent about it.

After lunch, Nina and I walked over to the Belmont Hotel. A crowd had already assembled to watch the show being taped. There was a buzz in the air, as if something exciting was about to happen.

Television cameras were present to record every minute. It wasn't live, so I guessed some of it would end up on the cutting-room floor. I hoped all would go well.

Natasha was dressed in her new Upscale Country Gal outfit. I was wearing a sleeveless dress and would have wilted in jeans, boots, and a blazer. The stage lights were hot enough to make Tommy Earl sweat. I had no idea how Natasha managed to stay cool.

Wong chatted with Tommy Earl. I knew for whom she would be cheering.

I stopped by to wish him luck.

"Thanks, Sophie. I'm looking forward to this." Tommy Earl rubbed his hands and chuckled evilly.

I eyed Wong. "You're in uniform? Are you expecting trouble?"

Wong yawned. "Everyone's working overtime right now. I'm bushed." She winked at me. "But the hotel is on my beat, so I thought I should make sure everyone was safe."

"Well, thank goodness for that!" I teased.

"Don't worry. As soon as they start baking I'll be back out on the street."

I left the two of them and hurried over to Natasha. "It's hot in here. Maybe you should take off the blazer? I've never seen anyone cook in tweed."

Natasha patted me on the shoulder. "And that, Sophie, is why *I* am here about to go on camera, and you are not."

Okay, fine. Maybe it was a good thing that her impending stardom hadn't changed her. There was a certain comfort in things staying the same.

A man with a wonderfully deep voice was acting as the announcer. He reminded me of a game show host and was busy engaging the crowd that had gathered to watch the show. Next to him a young woman held up cue cards telling the audience when to applaud.

I stood in the wings with Nina and Peter and watched, fascinated by the whole thing and more than a little bit relieved that it wasn't me who was up against Tommy Earl.

Brock walked up to Peter. In a calm voice he said, "The third judge's plane hasn't landed."

Things like that happened to me all the time in my job as an event planner. You had to go with the flow and do the best you could.

Peter looked around and nabbed Nina. "You're our third judge." To Brock, he said, "Introduce her as an experienced pie contest judge."

Nina beamed. "Don't I need some makeup?"

Peter peered at her and called over a makeup artist.

Before I knew it, Nina was in a seat next to Willa and a woman was dabbing concealer on her face.

I hurried over to Brock, eager to ask him some questions. "I'm glad to see you landed on your feet after Patsy Lee's death."

"It was a lucky break. I hardly know Peter because I didn't work for Patsy Lee until after the divorce, but she must have said good things about me. Patsy Lee, for all her faults, was a class act in many ways."

"*Faults?*"

"Aw, come on. Everyone has weaknesses. Peter said he appreciated my discretion. I'm not one to blab on social media."

"A very valuable trait, especially these days when every misstep goes viral in an instant."

"Hey, Sophie, have the cops interviewed you about Patsy Lee?" Brock asked.

"I wouldn't have called it an interview, but Wolf asked me what I saw."

"They're on my back because I brought her the coffee. I get it. I had plenty of time to monkey with her drink. The thing is, I didn't. I can't understand how a drink that I brought to her could have been poisoned. It went from the person at Moos and Brews, into my possession, and straight to Patsy Lee. I know *I* didn't poison it, so when could it have happened?"

"Do you think she might have done it herself? Was she in the habit of taking caffeine for an energy boost?"

"Patsy Lee was definitely a coffeeholic. No question about that. Four cups a day was the norm for her. But I never saw her add a powder or anything to her coffee. I knew how she took it and made sure it was perfect every time, with just the right amount of milk, no sugar."

"Brock, I don't want to pry or ask you to give up confidences, but Patsy Lee allegedly wrote me a check for a lot of money. Do you know what that was about?"

Brock's gaze shot to Peter. He whispered, "I have twin boys back in New York. They're everything to me. When Patsy Lee died, I was in a panic. How would I support them? It wasn't like I anticipated leaving and had another job lined up."

That was very possibly the oddest answer he could have given me. "The money? Are you saying you took the money?"

"No! Oh, please don't think that. I guess the cops have the money. I just can't really go blabbing about what Patsy told me." He raised his eyebrows and tilted his head ever so slightly in Peter's direction.

Okay . . . it had something to do with Peter. "You'll love working with Natasha," I said loud enough for Peter to hear. "And sometime when you're not so busy, I hope you'll show me photos of your boys."

I reached for a hug and whispered my address into his ear. We joined Peter in the wings.

The show began with the introduction of the three judges, Roger, Willa, and Nina. The audience applauded and cheered for each of them.

Peter muttered to me, "This is a big test for Natasha. Think she can bake and engage the audience at the same time?"

How to answer that? "Probably." Maybe not quite in the way Peter had planned, though. I crossed my fingers for her and wondered if she was planning to bake a pie with avocado in it.

Both contestants handled their introductions flawlessly. Natasha came across as the country gal she was supposed to be by telling a story about her mom baking pies at the local diner. That was probably true. Her mom still worked at the diner in our hometown.

And then they were off to collect ingredients to bake their pies.

The announcer interacted with the judges. "How do you think Natasha is doing?"

Willa spoke up. "I'm a little bit confused by the ingredients Natasha has selected."

Peter, standing next to me, whispered, "Flour, sugar, eggs, chocolate. What's she doing? She's supposed to be baking a coconut cream pie."

"Maybe she's making chocolate cream pie instead?"

Peter glared at me. "She can't beat Tommy Earl in the appearance of the pie. It's incredible what that guy can do with pie dough. The only way she can win is fantastic flavor."

We watched as Tommy Earl started his pie dough, deftly cutting in butter.

Natasha, on the other hand, had the mixer going. She appeared to be creaming butter with sugar.

An edge of anger had crept into Peter's tone. "She's baking a cake."

I glanced up at him. His face had turned the color of the luscious strawberries at Tommy Earl's workstation. I couldn't help noticing that while Natasha broke eggs and added them to her batter, Tommy Earl smiled as though he had already won.

The next two hours were pure torture. When the buzzer rang to indicate their time was up, Natasha proudly displayed a stunningly beautiful Boston cream pie, which, as Peter pointed out, wasn't a pie at all. It was clearly a cake, plain and simple.

On the other side, Tommy Earl had baked a strawberry pie with adornments on the top that looked like flowers cascading over the strawberries.

Wong rushed in and whispered, "What did I miss?"

"You made it back just in time to hear the winner announced."

I shuddered at the thought of what was about to happen. Peter no longer stood. He sat on a chair well into the wings, bent over with his elbows on his knees and his head hanging down as if he couldn't bear to see what would transpire.

The announcer seemed at a loss. To his credit he said, "Ladies and gentlemen, we have a unique situation today. Let's see what our contestants have to say."

Natasha smiled and posed for the cameras as if she had done nothing wrong. She looked stunning. The announcer asked, "Natasha, what made you bake a cake instead of a pie?"

Her head pulled back as though she was surprised by his question. "Don't be silly. Everyone knows this is a Boston cream *pie*."

"But there's no crust," he said.

"Where does it say there must be a crust? And, anyway, I used a lot of the same ingredients that Tommy Earl used in his crust, like flour, butter, and salt."

The announcer moved over to Tommy Earl. "How do you feel about this surprising turn of events?"

Tommy Earl said, "It's a *pie* bake-off."

I had to give him credit for remaining composed and not saying anything snarky.

Peter lifted his head, but the look of desperation on his face made me wonder how much money he had already put into making Natasha a star. He got to his feet and walked over to me. In a whisper he said, "When I managed Patsy Lee, I thought I could fix anything. Bad publicity? No problem. Dropping a pie on the set? Time for jokes. But this . . ."

The announcer approached the judges. "Roger, how do you feel about Natasha's pie?"

"I think Tommy wins by default. It's a pie contest. That is clearly not a pie."

"Then why is it called a pie?" asked Nina.

Willa piped up. "There are several stories about the name. The most prominent one is that in the 1800s cake tins were scarce, so bakers baked their cakes in pie tins and called them pies. There's also a theory that the original Boston cream pie was more like a pie than today's version. It's believed to be the creation of a chef at Boston's Parker House Hotel. Curiously, there are also historic references to Washington pie, which was also a cream-filled cake, similar to Boston cream pie and baked in pie tins."

Nina gazed at her. "How do you know all that?"

"I'm something of a culinary historian. I love reading about the history of food."

The announcer moved on to Nina. "And what do you think about this pie-versus-cake issue?"

"I think we should taste both of them," which brought the house down laughing and broke the tension.

Peter grinned. "Your friend Nina has potential."

The tasting commenced. Roger and Willa tasted tiny bits, but Nina cleaned her plate.

Roger was the first to speak. "Natasha, you took a huge chance today. Even if cake had its origin in a pie pan, you did not bake this in a pie pan, and I have to assume that you knew perfectly well that it would not be considered a pie."

Willa was up next. "I find it remarkable that you managed to bake this and fill it with cream in the time allotted, since it had to cool first. So to that, I say well done. Tommy, your strawberry pie is truly a masterpiece. No one else has your touch with pastry. That said, I wish you had chosen a more complex filling. Your pie is delicious, but barring the decoration on top, it could easily have been baked by a beginner."

I suspect I wasn't the only one holding my breath when Nina's turn came up. "I thought they were both wonderful, and I would gladly eat them both again. I understand

Willa's concern about your filling, Tommy, but it sure is beautiful to look at. Natasha, I feel like I taste too much cornstarch in your cream. It's miraculous that it set up for you, but that happened at the sacrifice of the flavor."

The other two judges and Peter gaped. No one had expected a sophisticated response from Nina.

The judges huddled together for a discussion. People in the audience murmured and I heard them defending their favorite baker.

Finally the announcer declared that the judges had come to a decision.

Chapter 21

Dear Natasha,
My father insists that his mom only baked her pies
in foil pans or metal tins and that her pies always
had crisp crusts. Do you think that's true?
Doubtful Daughter in Lemon, Kentucky

Dear Doubtful Daughter,
It stands to reason that metal would convey heat
better. However, the appearance of metal pie tins is
ghastly. If you bake in metal, please pop the pie
into a pretty pan if you want to show it off at the
table.
Natasha

It was Willa who declared, "Both of you made amazing creations today, but the winner is the baker who made a traditional pie, in the current sense of the word as we know pie today, Mr. Tommy Earl Felts."

The announcer wrapped up the show, and Wong ran up to Tommy Earl and plunked a big kiss on him.

I hurried toward Nina. "You were wonderful!"

"Whew! It's stressful to be on camera."

"You were great. You stole the show."

"Thanks. I've been practicing for this my whole life. I eat every day."

Roger reached over and shook Nina's hand. "I thought you might be the comic relief, but you were dead-on about Natasha's cream filling."

Their conversation continued, but I had turned my attention to Natasha. Luckily, a few of her fans had been in the audience. They gushed over her and were telling her how clever she had been to bake something so unexpected.

"Do you think she's going to need a ride home?" asked Nina. "The limo might not be big enough to hold Peter *and* Natasha anymore."

"That's what I'm afraid of. I wonder if her little stunt was a violation of her contract with Peter." I nudged her. "Look over there."

Peter appeared to be in a deep discussion with Tommy Earl.

"Wow," whispered Nina. "That isn't just the coach of the losing team congratulating the other side. What do you bet Peter's in search of a new star?"

Poor Natasha. As her fans left, her expression changed to disappointment.

"C'mon, Nina." I walked over to Natasha and gave her a hug. "You did great. I would never have been so composed under the circumstances."

"It's a pie, Sophie." Natasha's lips pulled tight. "Thanks a lot, Nina," she uttered sarcastically.

"Sorry. Them's the breaks. There are people of the pie and there's the clan of the cake. They know the difference and so do you. You knew what you were doing."

"I should have anticipated that you would side with Tommy Earl. Next time I want judges who don't know me."

"That's a good idea," I said. She would always fare better with people who didn't know her. "But Nina was doing everyone a favor by filling in."

"And I did *not* put too much cornstarch in my cream. How dare you even suggest that? You don't even bake. You know nothing about this."

Uh-oh. Now we knew who would be taking the brunt of Natasha's loss. "That's not fair, Natasha."

She flipped her hair with her right hand and turned her head away from us.

"Do you need a ride home?" I asked.

"Not if she's going to be in the car. I'll take my limo, thank you."

I hoped the limo would be available to her. In any event taking the limo home would probably be painfully awkward.

There was nothing to do except leave. I hoped she wouldn't be as cold toward Tommy Earl.

On the way home Bernie called. On the speakerphone in my car, he told us that he and Mars were tasting new recipes at The Laughing Hound.

"We're on our way," Nina annouced.

"Who won the contest?" asked Bernie.

Nina moaned. "Natasha baked a cake."

We could hear Bernie laughing when he said, "See you soon," and hung up.

Nina asked, "Do you think it's possible that Natasha really didn't understand what she was doing?"

"Natasha's mind is a mystery to me. I suspect she thought she was being clever. Yesterday she was practicing baking a coconut cream pie. The switch wasn't because she didn't have the correct ingredients or she couldn't remember the recipe. She took a chance by pulling a stunt and she lost."

"She's mad at me," Nina grumbled.

"She'll get over it."

"Normally, I wouldn't care. But I know how much this meant to her."

"Are you saying you care about Natasha?" I asked.

"Maybe just a little bit. But don't tell *her.*"

I pulled into my garage and the two of us set out on foot for an early dinner at The Laughing Hound. Nina was still fussing about Natasha's pie catastrophe.

"Nina, you did not force her to bake a cake for a pie bake-off. She made that decision on her own instead of doing what Peter suggested. Now she has to live with the consequences. If she had listened to him, she would have had a chance."

"I know. I just don't like anyone being upset with me. Not even Natasha!"

We were walking into the restaurant when Nina blurted, "With all the craziness of cake versus pie, I almost forgot! The woman who did my makeup used to do Patsy Lee's makeup when she was in town for a show. And guess what—Patsy Lee was seeing someone in Old Town, and it wasn't Peter."

"But we know she went to see Peter the night before she died."

"Exactly. So Peter or this other fellow might have killed her out of jealousy."

I stopped dead in my tracks. "That's the first real lead we've had. The woman didn't know who it was?"

"She said Patsy Lee kept mum about it. According to her, Patsy Lee could keep a secret."

"Unlike you," I teased.

The hostess pointed upward and to her right. "Mars and Bernie are eating on the private terrace."

We thanked her and wound our way through the main dining room to stairs that led to the terrace where Bernie had held the dinner to welcome Patsy Lee.

I opened the door and glanced around. I whispered to

Nina, "I can't believe how much has happened since we were here last."

Mars waved at us. "Is it true that Natasha lost because she baked a cake?"

Nina slid into a seat. "Painfully true."

A waitress took our drink orders and promised to be right back with Chicken Skillet Pie.

Mars passed Bernie a ten-dollar bill.

"Paying for your dinner?" asked Nina.

"Paying my gambling debt. I keep losing to Bernie. He bet me ten bucks that it would be a disaster for Natasha. I thought she'd do well, with Peter coaching her and telling her what to do. I wonder if this is the end of their contract."

"I had the same thought," I said. "I had hoped this would work out for her. From what I gather, Peter took Patsy Lee under his wing and made her into a star. They must have faced some hurdles. Maybe Peter will stick with Natasha for a while in spite of her disastrous error. I did notice him in a discussion with Tommy Earl, though."

Bernie winced. "Natasha isn't exactly the warm and fuzzy type."

"I'm not sure Patsy Lee was, either. I'm beginning to wonder if that was a front. She seemed so sweet and friendly, but she wasn't very well liked by the other pastry chefs in town."

The waitress brought a skillet for Nina and me to share.

It didn't look much like a pie to me. Baked in a cast-iron skillet, thin sheets of light golden phyllo flared in layers around the edge. The middle was covered with browned cheese. "Who baked this? Willa judged the contest today, so I assume it wasn't her."

"It was Honey Armbruster's idea," said Bernie.

Mars shuddered.

"What's wrong with Honey?" I asked.

"She's Mars's latest admirer." Bernie guffawed.

"You don't like her?" asked Nina. "I think she's nice."

In a low tone Mars responded, "She's like a mini-Natasha clone. Pardon me for expressing myself with an overused phrase, but I've been there and done that. Not going back."

I couldn't blame him for feeling that way. "So, will this pie be self-served or will the server scoop it out on the diner's plate?"

Mars shot Bernie a smug look. "Exactly what I asked. You scoop it out yourself and make a mess. If you ask me, it's way too big for one person, so two people have to share."

Nina cut into it with a serving spoon. "Maybe if they cooked it in smaller dishes?"

"It makes a nice presentation," I observed, spooning it onto my plate, "but it falls apart after that. So, Bernie, how well did you know Nellie Stokes?"

"Nellie?" Bernie stopped eating and gazed at me. "Nellie never worked for me, but I would have hired her in a split second. She's a superb pastry chef."

"What about Dooley?" asked Nina.

"I didn't know them well," said Bernie. "I'm told Nellie thought the world of Dooley until Grainger started up with her."

Mars sat back and eyed me. "What's going on?"

"In a nutshell Patsy Lee, Tommy Earl, Nellie, Roger, Willa, and Grainger worked together a long time ago at a pie-making business. Today two of them are dead and one is in prison for life. I feel like there's something odd going on in that group."

"In other words you think one of them murdered Patsy Lee?" asked Bernie.

"It's possible. She wanted to talk with me about something, but she didn't live long enough to tell me what it was. It doesn't seem right to me that she would make a lunch date with me and then kill herself."

"I guess it didn't seem right to Wolf, either," said Bernie, "or he wouldn't have asked us so many questions about Peter renting our little house."

Nina choked and coughed. "Do they think Peter murdered Patsy Lee so he could sponsor a new starlet?"

Bernie's eyes widened. He was clearly horrified by the thought. "I'd hate to think that. But it's common knowledge that Patsy Lee threw Peter out once she was established. If anyone had good reason to resent her, it would be Peter."

"But they spent the night together," I pointed out. "That seems more like a reconciliation if you ask me."

"Apparently, Patsy Lee had a sweetie in Old Town," said Nina. "Do you think that could have been Peter?"

Mars excused himself and returned in a minute with a sheet of paper. On it he wrote, *Peter—ditched by Patsy Lee.*

"Well, we know it wasn't Nellie who murdered Patsy Lee," said Bernie.

We all agreed that she had the best imaginable alibi.

Mars listed all the bakers who had worked at Apex Pie and crossed off Nellie's name, as well as Grainger's. "That doesn't leave many people. Roger, Tommy Earl, and Willa are the only ones remaining."

"It's not Willa," said Bernie. "I know her very well, and she's a gentle soul."

"Did you know she gave up everything to move to New York with Patsy Lee and work for her?" I asked.

"That must have been a while back. She's worked here at The Laughing Hound for years."

Nina waved her fork in the air. "Patsy Lee fired her."

Bernie winced. "Okay, leave Willa on the list, but I guarantee she didn't murder Patsy Lee."

"He's been winning a lot of bets lately," said Mars a bit snarkily. "We're down to Tommy Earl and Roger."

"They're both bitter about Patsy Lee's success," I pointed out.

Mars wrote that notation by their names.

"You're forgetting someone," said Nina. "What about Brock?"

"I need to speak with him," I said. "He was closer to Patsy Lee than anyone. He must have some ideas."

"He goes on the list." Mars wrote down his name and read aloud, *"Peter, Tommy Earl, Roger, Brock, and maybe Willa."*

Mentally, I added Sergeant Gibbard. I didn't know of any reason for him to kill Patsy Lee, but if he murdered his own son, then he was a loose cannon and could do anything.

The four of us indulged in peach cobbler for dessert before walking home.

In the calm of my kitchen I preheated the oven to try baking a s'mores pie. To make it echo the flavors of a s'more, I chopped honey graham crackers, added melted butter, then pressed the slightly moist crumbs into the pie pan and popped it into the oven. In the few minutes it needed to bake, I washed my utensils. I took the crust out of the oven, and set it on the counter to cool a bit before adding miniature marshmallows.

I poured a bag of semisweet chocolate chips into warm cream and watched my spoon ripple through the melting chocolate chips. I added butter and vanilla, then poured the warm liquid over the marshmallows. They floated! I pressed them down with the back of a spoon, to be sure they were all covered in chocolate. I had planned to make a marshmallow topping for the pie, but it would have to cool completely first.

I placed the pie on a rack on my kitchen island to cool

and considered whether any of the people on our list of suspects in Patsy Lee's death might have murdered Grainger. Had any of them had a reason? Or was Mrs. Gibbard correct about her husband slaying their son?

I dressed Daisy in her halter and set out for a thought-cleansing walk. I concentrated on Patsy Lee and Grainger as I strolled.

The two of them ran with the same group of friends for a long time. Had one of those friends wanted them out of the way? But for what reason? Had there been some connection between Patsy Lee and Grainger that I didn't know about?

Evening was descending on Old Town. With the sun nearly gone, the temperature dropped and the humidity abated. It was perfect for a long walk. Diners still filled restaurants, and people walked by us on the sidewalks. Even though we walked in the heart of Old Town, it wasn't abandoned like some downtowns are after the offices close.

Lights shone in the tall windows of the Federal-style buildings. Daisy sniffed her way along the sidewalk, no doubt picking up the scents of other dogs that had passed that way during the day.

We neared Alex's office, and I slowed down. The two of us hadn't left things well. Maybe I should be the one to call and set things right again. A light flicked off in his office window. Maybe he was just leaving for the day. It might be a good time to say hi.

We passed the gold plaque by the door that said, ALEXANDER GERMAN, ATTORNEY AT LAW. A dim light still shone in the plateglass window in front. I knew from experience that it didn't mean he was still there, but I hoped we had caught him in time and peered in the window.

I was deep in thought about not ruining his reputation when a hand slammed the bottom of the window from inside.

Chapter 22

Dear Natasha,
I love the taste of butter piecrusts, but I have such
trouble with them. Do you have any tips? I know
the ingredients should be cold.
                    No Luck in Butterfield, Minnesota

Dear No Luck,
Make your crust using oil. It works fine and isn't as
finicky.

                                        Natasha

Daisy barked and jumped away. I screamed.
    Daisy pulled at her leash, unwilling to get any closer.
But I saw something that chilled my heart. Close to the
bottom of the window was a handprint. At least the fingers were indisputable. The palm had been smeared. As
the fingers ran through it? Even worse, in the pale glow
emanating from the room, the handprint was clearly red.
    I cupped my hands around my eyes and pressed against
the window. "Alex?" I raised my voice. "Alex?"
    I hurried to the door and tried the handle. It swung

open easily. Something was wrong. Alex would never leave the door unlocked.

Cautiously, in case someone else was inside, I scanned the reception room. I didn't see anyone, but in the back of the office, I heard someone moving around. "Hello?" I called. "Alex?"

A door slammed in the back.

Daisy tugged me farther into the room, toward the window where the hand had appeared.

Alex lay on the floor. His beautiful face was a bloody mess. I fumbled for my cell phone and dialed 911. When I was assured that help was on the way, I looked around the room one more time, to be sure no one would attack me. I briefly considered waiting for the police outside, but another glance at Alex and I couldn't let him lie there in agony alone.

I knelt on the floor next to him. "Alex, can you hear me? It's Sophie."

His eyes were swelling. I wasn't sure he could even open them enough to see me.

He grunted. I picked up his bloody hand and clutched it in mine. "An ambulance is on the way. Conserve your strength. You'll be okay, sweetie."

An ambulance siren wailed in the distance as someone opened the front door.

"Sophie?" I recognized Wong's voice.

She flicked on bright lights. "What's going on?" She strode closer and saw Alex. "Whoa! Sophie, don't move. I need to make sure no one else is here, okay?"

"I heard someone in the back and then a door slammed."

I was vaguely aware of Wong checking out Alex's office, the file room, and the restroom.

Speaking into her phone, she returned to us. She clicked it off and jammed it into her pocket. "We have to get out of here. Now!"

"What's going on?"

"I'll help you with Alex. You get his left side and I'll lift on the right."

The two of us dragged him toward the door. I no longer had to ask her why. Flames licked under the door that led to the back of his office. They were coming from the file room.

We had just pulled him onto the sidewalk when the EMTs arrived.

Wong spoke calmly, but was very clear. "Get him out of here. There's a fire inside. Sophie, you and Daisy, too. Get to safety now."

Fire truck sirens wailed. I tugged Daisy across the street and down the block, where the EMTs were checking out Alex in the back of an ambulance.

"Are you the one who found him?"

I nodded. "Alex German. That's his law office."

"Can he speak?"

"I don't know. He didn't say anything to me. But it all happened very fast."

The fire trucks arrived and Wong ran toward us, jumped into the ambulance, and bent over Alex. "Alex!" she shouted. "Who did this to you?"

His chest heaved and his lips parted, but no sound came out.

The EMTs made Wong leave, closed the door, and turned on the siren as they drove away.

"Sophie! Sophie!" Wong tugged at me. "What happened?"

I couldn't tear my eyes away from the flames devouring Alex's office.

"You saved his life," she said.

"We did it together," I murmured, horrified by the thought that he might have died if we had arrived five minutes later.

"What were you doing here?" asked Wong.

"Just walking Daisy." I gazed down at her. She must have been scared but she didn't show any sign of it. When we dragged Alex out of the office she worked alongside us. I reached down and rubbed the spot just above her eyes.

"Alex and I had a little disagreement, and I thought it might be a good time to get past that."

"What did you argue about?"

"It wasn't really an argument. He didn't think I should be snooping around an old murder."

"*Hmpff.* Well, he was probably right about that. Are you okay?"

Part of me wanted to go home and curl up in the safety of my house, but I couldn't rip my eyes away from the flames. "I'll be fine," I choked. My heart beat like crazy and my hands shook. I buried them in the long fur on Daisy's back. I was afraid if I stood up my knees might give out.

"I think you're in shock." Wong peered at me.

"I just need a minute."

"I'm trembling. How about you?"

I was relieved that Wong, a professional who probably saw horrific things every week, has also been shaken. We sat side-by-side with Daisy leaning against our legs.

Eventually the fire department got the fire under control. It wasn't out, but they finally had it under control.

"I think I'd better take Daisy home and get over to the hospital."

"Maybe Nina should drive you."

I blinked at Wong. "You think Alex will die?"

"I don't know, Sophie," she said gently. "I hope not. But you've had a shock."

Daisy and I walked away from the chaos of the fire. All of Old Town seemed to have lights on in their houses. People stood on their front stoops, looking around to see what was happening.

A lone figure hurried along the street away from the fire and turned right exactly where Peter was renting a house from Bernie and Mars.

Daisy and I crossed the street. Staying in the shadows as much as possible, I watched as a slender person rapped on the door of the rented house. Peter opened it, and in the glow of the light by the front door, he wrapped his arms around Willa and kissed her passionately.

I was stunned. Surely, they didn't have anything to do with the attack on Alex? But that embrace, there was something about it—like they had been separated too long or had been through something emotionally wrenching.

We continued on our way home, where Nina waited by the kitchen door.

"Wong called me," she said. "How's Alex?"

Generally, I wasn't the type who cried a lot. I tried very hard to present a stiff upper lip, no matter what happened, but on this occasion I burst into sobs and choked out words. "You should have seen him, Nina. Someone beat him to a pulp. And the flames. There were flames every-where. His hand was covered in blood and he smacked the window."

"You're babbling." Nina unlocked the door for me. "You go upstairs, wash your face, and change clothes. I'll feed Daisy and Mochie, then we'll head to the hospital. All right?"

I drifted up the stairs, my head spinning. It wasn't until I looked in the bathroom mirror that I realized my clothes and face had Alex's blood on them.

Chapter 23

Dear Sophie,
I'm serving pie to friends at teatime. What kind of
beverage is appropriate?
                    Harried Hostess in Pecan Springs, Texas

Dear Harried Hostess,
Serve hot tea or coffee. If it's cold out, you might
consider a warm punch, like a grog. In the summer,
lemonade and iced tea are good choices. But mix it
up! Don't serve lemon pie with lemonade.
                                        Sophie

I slid into the passenger seat of Nina's car.
    She handed me a travel mug.
"What's this?"
"Tea. You're the one who always says it calms a person."
Nina walked around to the driver's side, started the car,
and eased into the empty street. "Feel like telling me what
happened?"
Feeling numb, I recited the events, trying not to ramble.

"No wonder you're like a walking zombie." She glanced in the rearview mirror.

I turned around to see a black plume rising against the night lights of the city. "I hope they can save the building."

"Alex has a lot of criminal clients, doesn't he?"

"Yes. But who would beat up their lawyer? He's on their side!"

"Maybe the outcome of the case wasn't what the client hoped for." Nina swung her car into the hospital parking lot. "He's probably still in the emergency room."

I agreed. We walked around to the emergency entrance and straight into Wolf.

He grabbed me in a quick bear hug. "I'm relieved to see you! Wong is a trouper, and even she was shaken up by this. Are you okay?"

"I'm fine. How's Alex?"

Wolf had a poker face. When we dated, it had driven me crazy because I never had a clue what he was feeling. "I'm heading back there now. I'll let you know after I see him."

Nina and I sat down in the waiting room. It felt like an eternity, but by the clock it had only taken twenty minutes for Wolf to return.

"He wasn't able to speak. They're taking him into surgery now."

"What for?" I asked.

"He took a heavy beating, Sophie. I think they need to operate on more than one thing."

"That sounds ominous!"

"He has some broken bones. His nose, his radius, a couple of ribs . . ."

"Poor Alex. He must have been terrified. I can't even imagine what he went through. He's a nice guy. Why would anyone beat him up like that?"

Wolf gave me a sad look. "Maybe he didn't win a case for his client."

"That's not a reason to beat up the lawyer."

Wolf exhaled. "I wish I could sit around here with you, but I'd better get back to work. I'll be thinking of Alex. Keep me posted, okay?"

Nina nodded.

Time ticked by slowly. Nina sampled the contents of every vending machine in the hospital.

I wasn't convinced that the clock was moving at all, but the small hand switched position occasionally. At two in the morning a nurse told us he had been moved to intensive care.

We took the elevator upstairs and found Alex easily. A nurse was adjusting his IV.

I leaned over him. "Alex? It's Sophie."

"He can't hear you, honey. He's in a coma," said the nurse.

"*A coma!*" I shrieked.

"Now, it's nothing to get upset about. Medically induced comas are very common in cases where there's head injury. They need him to stay still so he can heal."

"He's in a coma, Nina!"

"Soph, she just explained it. I wish my husband were here, they might tell *him* more about Alex's condition. Doctors like talking to other doctors." Nina's husband was a forensic pathologist who was constantly out of town testifying as an expert.

A bald doctor walked into the room. "Which one of you is Mrs. German?"

Nina immediately pointed at me. "She is."

I had opened my mouth to protest when he said, "We'll know more in the next few days. Right now, the important thing is to give him some time to recuperate. We'll deal with the broken arm when he's more stable. You try to get some rest."

The doctor walked toward the door, but turned around and said, "Don't worry about Alex's safety. The police are providing a twenty-four-hour guard. See you tomorrow."

Nina and I stared at each other.

"Wolf and Wong must have asked for the guard," I said.

"And there he is." Nina waved at the uniformed officer who looked in on us. "Come on, Sophie, let's go home."

I waited until we were in the car before I said, "You lied to the doctor."

"Didn't you want to hear what he had to say?"

"He didn't tell us much."

"Yeah, he did. Alex is in bad shape, Sophie."

Every time I closed my eyes, I saw Alex's barely recognizable and puffy face. In spite of that, exhaustion finally kicked in and I dozed off.

The clanking of my door knocker woke me just past nine o'clock in the morning. I scrambled into a bathrobe and headed down the stairs. Daisy and Mochie already waited at the door.

Mars, Bernie, and Wolf stood on the stoop.

"You look terrible," said Mars.

Bernie hugged me.

Wolf handed me a package of Krispy Kreme doughnuts with chocolate glaze.

"Alex died?" I asked.

Wolf chuckled. "Is that what hot-from-the-oven Krispy Kremes mean to you? No, he's not dead, thanks to you."

I followed them into my kitchen and put on the kettle to boil water.

Mars let Daisy out, and Bernie pulled take-out breakfasts from The Laughing Hound out of two giant bags and set them on the island.

Nina, also wearing a bathrobe, brought Daisy back inside. "I knew I was missing breakfast." She spooned ground coffee beans into the French press.

I helped Bernie remove waffles and fried eggs over easy from the take-out packages. He placed each waffle on a plate and topped it with an egg and a white sauce that smelled so divine that my appetite quickly came back. He'd brought sausages and bacon, too. "The waffles are cheddar," he explained.

We gathered around the kitchen table, but I couldn't eat after all. Not until I knew how Alex was doing. "Wolf?"

"You saved his life, Sophie."

"Stop saying that. It was a fluke that I was there."

"Not only did you get there in time to drag Alex out of a burning building, but it appears that you interrupted his assailant in the act of strangling him. There's a ligature mark on his neck."

Everyone stopped eating and drinking, even Nina.

"So that's why they posted a guard at his hospital room," I said. "They're afraid his attacker will return to finish him off."

Chapter 24

Dear Natasha,
I have some leftover apples that I'd like to bake in
a pie. My neighbor acted like I was nuts! Isn't a pie
a good way to use fruit before it spoils?
                    Confused in the Village of Almond, New York

Dear Confused,
You neighbor is correct. Fresh fruit is necessary for
a good pie. Mushy fruit will result in a mushy pie.
                                        Natasha

"Well?" I demanded. "How is Alex?"

"They don't tell me much more than they tell you. My understanding is that he's doing as well as can be expected. Of course, I'm hoping that when they bring him around to consciousness, he can tell us who attacked him."

"So you think he'll live?" I asked.

"He might not be quite as good-looking. I suspect he'll need some plastic surgery."

"Be serious, Wolf."

Mars cut into his waffle and broke the gloomy atmosphere by saying, "Mmm. Best breakfast ever!"

On that recommendation we all had to try the waffles.

"Someone should call Alex's parents," I said.

"Already have," Wolf responded. "They're on their way here. Sophie, I know Alex is a respected attorney who wouldn't blab about his clients, but did he say anything to you that I should know?"

I put down my fork. "I went over to his office on Monday around lunchtime and they were looking for a client who didn't show up for his court date. I have no idea who it was, and there's no reason to think there's a connection. Alex was completely mum about his work, but his assistant would know who the missing client was."

"I'll check with her. I was hoping he might have complained about someone to you. Maybe another lawyer?"

I shook my head. "I'm afraid not. When I asked him about the lawyers who represented Nellie Stokes, he pretty much told me to back off. That I shouldn't be getting involved in a closed case." I gasped. "He warned me that if Nellie wasn't guilty, then there was a killer roaming around who got away with murder and could be dangerous."

"Good point," murmured Mars through a mouthful of food.

I looked straight at Wolf. "You don't think that I somehow triggered the attack on him?"

"Oh, Sophie!" Nina cried. "Of course not. Now you're being silly."

"I agree with Nina." Wolf poured himself more coffee. "That's highly unlikely."

As they chattered, I considered the possibility that I had inadvertently stirred up a hornet's nest. But it didn't seem likely. Even if the Sergeant had returned and seen me speaking with his wife, that wouldn't have anything to do with

Alex. And as far as I knew, none of the Apex Pie crew had any business with Alex. Maybe Wolf was right. I was grasping around for connections that didn't exist. I reached for a Krispy Kreme and bit into the heavenly, pillowy, chocolate-glazed doughnut and felt better immediately.

The nice thing about take-out food is that it's cleaned up in minutes. As soon as everyone left, I fed Daisy and Mochie, then hurried to my office and checked my schedule. Still in my bathrobe, I took care of a few outstanding matters so they wouldn't be overlooked if I took the next couple of days off to worry about Alex.

With those items taken care of, I hurried upstairs for a long, hot shower. Even though Nina had misrepresented my identity to the doctor, I suspected that wouldn't hold up for long. The only person who could really shed light on this was Alex's assistant. But I had a bad feeling she was as closemouthed about his business as he was.

If someone missed a court date, wouldn't there be some kind of public record of that? I hopped out of the shower, dressed in a gray sleeveless sheath that I thought looked professional, donned my cushy sandals, which ruined the effect, and blew my hair dry. I added button-style earrings. Maybe the clerk at the courthouse wouldn't notice my shoes.

I could hope.

I locked up the house and walked over to the courthouse. It was packed. I heard Alex's name mentioned several times as I walked to the clerk's desk.

"Hi," I said. "Sophie Winston. Do you still have a schedule of the hearings that were set for yesterday?"

The clerk retrieved a sheet of paper from her desk and set it on the counter in front of me. "You're not the first to ask." She plunked her fingertip down on *Armbruster* v. *Armbruster.* "That's the one you're looking for."

"Alex was representing Honey Armbruster?" I was stunned.

"Nope. I believe he was representing Mr. Armbruster." She smiled at me. "I hope Alex pulls out of this. He has always been so nice to me. If you talk to him, tell him everybody at the courthouse is rooting for him." She leaned toward me and whispered, "You need anything else, you let me know. Every one of us wants to see the creep who did this to Alex in handcuffs."

"Thank you. I'll pass your message along to Alex."

I was walking away when she called, "Hey, Sophie! I like your shoes."

So much for fooling her, but it was great to know they were all on Alex's side. I hoped the police felt the same way and would hustle to catch the perpetrator.

Alex's office was close to the courthouse. I walked in that direction. The stench from the fire hit me two blocks away from the building.

When I saw it, I could hardly breathe. Not from the lingering odor, but from the shock of the appearance. The large window in Alex's waiting room had shattered. It was nothing but a gaping hole. The interior must have burned hot and fast. Everything looked like charcoal. There wasn't a thing left.

Crime scene tape crossed the door and the window.

I backed up to see how the rest of the building had fared. As far as I could tell from the street, the fire had reached the second floor. I wasn't sure about the extent of the damage to the third floor.

"Good thing Alex can't see this," said a woman's voice.

I glanced over to see Alex's assistant.

"Have you heard anything about his condition?" she asked.

"Not much. As well as can be expected, I'm told."

"I went over to see him this morning, but they were taking him for a scan. I barely got a glimpse of him, but he didn't recognize me or say anything. They told me his parents were on the way."

"He's in a medically induced coma."

She gasped and covered her mouth with long, slender fingers. "It's worse than I heard!"

How could I gain her confidence? How could I coax her into telling me if she knew of any dangerous clients?

"Poor Alex," she said. "Maybe it's a blessing that he can't see this. What a mess. It will take us months to get everything back up and running."

I hugged her just because I was so happy to know that she expected Alex to be back and working, even if it was in the distant future.

She swallowed hard and pulled a card and pen out of her purse. She jotted a number on the back of the card. "This is my cell phone number. Would you call me if you hear anything about Alex's condition?"

I took the card from her. "Yes, of course. I imagine you'll be calling his clients to let them know what happened?"

She nodded. "I'll have to phone the ones with upcoming court dates and appointments." She scratched her forehead. "I hope I can remember them all. I think I can refer them to a couple of his attorney friends who might cover for him."

I decided I might as well come right out and ask her if she knew anything. After all, she would want that person arrested, too. She might even say something to me that she wouldn't tell the cops. "Do you know who did this?"

"I wish I did. The cops asked me the same thing. Honestly, I don't have a clue. No one that I know of was making threats or acting violent. Of course, you know Alex. He might not have mentioned it to me."

"I know what you mean. Protecting the privacy of his

clients was a big deal to him. There's not a doubt in my mind that he expected the same from you. But this isn't the time to stay mum. If there was anyone who could have done this to Alex, I hope you'll tell me or the police. The cops can take it from there. They don't need to know a lot of details about the client's legal issues."

She just stared at me.

"Alex said something to me the other day in another context that probably also applies to you now. There's someone out there who is very angry and not afraid of killing. He meant to murder Alex. He could come after you next. This is the time to speak up and tell Wolf what you know. For your own sake, as well as Alex's."

Color drained from her face, and I felt a little guilty for putting fear in her. But it was true. She needed to be careful and the best way was to inform Wolf.

She gazed around. "It could be anyone."

"Could it be Honey Armbruster's husband?"

I was staring at the building, but I heard her sharp intake of breath.

"Did you ever locate him?"

"Did Alex tell you about it?"

Hmm. How to handle that? Lie and say he did, so she would feel free to keep talking, or be honest? I didn't need to tell her I got it from public information at the courthouse. I sidestepped her question. "I know he didn't show up for his case."

"He finally called Alex. I never did find out why he didn't show, but Alex wasn't too upset about it."

That wasn't helpful. Maybe she didn't know as much about Alex's clients as I had hoped.

"I'd better go. Call me with updates on Alex, okay?"

She walked away in a hurry, looking from one side to the other as though she was nervous.

Maybe it was a good thing I had frightened her. She needed to be careful.

And I needed to pay a visit to Honey Armbruster. Maybe she would blab about her court date with her former husband.

Since Alex was probably still tied up having tests, I decided to pop in at The Laughing Hound. With any luck I might get a chance to talk with Remy.

The restaurant was doing a brisk lunch business. I spied Mars seated at the far end of the bar.

I headed toward him. "Have you taken up residence here?"

Mars put down his sandwich and wiped his mouth. "I would if I could. Have you tried this? It's a grilled cheese BLT. Can you imagine a better combination?" He picked it up. "Here, have a bite."

I bit into it. He was right. The soft, warm cheese mixed with salty bacon, crisp lettuce, and the crowning touch, a slice of juicy tomato, was nothing short of perfection. I hopped up on the chair next to him. "That could be my new favorite."

Remy walked up and wiped the bar in front of me. "Can I get you one?"

"How about an iced tea?"

"The kind with booze in it?" he asked.

"No, thanks. Plain old iced tea."

I watched as he poured it from a pitcher and brought it over.

"Actually, I'm glad you're working today, Remy. Got a minute?"

He glanced down the bar. "For you? Sure!"

"What do you know about the Gibbards and Grainger?"

Chapter 25

Dear Sophie,
I grew up calling the dish in which a pie is baked a
pie plate. But my neighbor always calls it a pie
dish. Which one is right?
                              Pie Lover in Correct, Indiana

Dear Pie Lover,
You are both correct. The shallow ones are called
pie plates. When they are deeper, they are called pie
dishes.
                                                    Sophie

R emy eyed me with undisguised suspicion.
        Mars ate his sandwich, probably blissfully unaware
that Sergeant Gibbard had fired Remy years ago.

"Mrs. Gibbard is nice, but the old man is nuts. I guess
you know that I worked for them once."

I nodded.

"I got the boot when a customer was berating his girlfriend. He was a real jerk. I couldn't stand it anymore, so I
nicely asked him to step outside, then I punched him in the

jaw. His girlfriend was very grateful, but the guy sued the restaurant, so I'm not real popular over there." He grinned. "They settled out of court, but I got the laugh, because the woman dumped him on the spot and started dating me."

Mars chuckled. "Great story."

Not if you were the one who was sued. "Did you work there when Nellie Stokes was the pastry chef?"

"Poor Nellie. I never did think she killed Grainger. She adored him and she had a soft personality. You know what I mean? Some people, you know they're gonna punch you back, like Sergeant Gibbard. But Nellie couldn't bring herself to do that if her life depended on it."

"What I can't figure out is how someone managed to bake a pie with rhubarb leaves in it and talk Grainger into eating it."

"A lot of people speculated on that. They say strawberry-rhubarb pie was Grainger's favorite thing in the world to eat. And some people are easy, you know? Like I could probably get Mars to eat just about anything with bacon in it."

With his mouth full, Mars nodded.

"That suggests to me the killer was someone Grainger knew or was giving a chance at a job," I said. "But it was two in the morning, so the job interview is unlikely, and why stab him?"

"The rumor mill had it that Nellie baked the pie and took it to the restaurant after hours," explained Remy.

"What did you think happened with the knife that was used to stab Grainger?"

"Hey, I'm eating here," Mars protested.

I reached down the bar and slid a bottle of ketchup toward him.

"You're so cruel," Mars muttered.

Remy grinned. "I'm told the cops went in and wiped them out. They took every chef's knife in the place. I remember that because friends who still worked there said the Sergeant was furious about having to pay for all-new knives."

I didn't want to point a finger at anyone and predispose him to agree with me, so I asked, "If Nellie didn't murder Grainger, then who did?"

Remy looked me in the eyes. "Who else? The old man. He's the only one insane enough to have killed Grainger."

"You mean Sergeant Gibbard?" asked Mars.

"That's exactly who I mean." Remy flicked his thumb down the counter. "I better get back to work. Good seeing you, Sophie. I'll put your tea on Mars's check."

"Thanks, Remy!"

"Gee, thanks!" cried Mars in mock dismay. "Think Remy's right?"

"I'm not sure. Thanks for the tea. I'm off to see your new girlfriend."

"Very funny." He took a bite of his sandwich.

"Should I send your best to Honey?" I asked.

Mars coughed.

I winked at him and headed to Honey Armbruster's house.

Pink flowers cascaded down her front steps. It was lovely. She lived in a sizeable Federal-style house, but it was a modern one without a historical plaque on the door. I rang the bell while admiring her pineapple-shaped door knocker, a colonial sign of welcome.

Honey opened the door, looking perfect, as though she had been expecting someone to drop by. How did people do that? A cocker spaniel sat at her feet and didn't bark or jump up. "Sophie, please come in. To what do I owe this lovely visit?"

I stepped into an immaculate entrance hall that was pure Williamsburg in color and décor. "I'm sorry to bother you. You probably heard about Alex German?"

She no longer smiled. "I loathe that guy. But I *am* sorry about what happened to him, even if he's a dreadful human being. Won't you have a seat?"

Her living room was enormous. A stunning Oriental-style rug, with a predominately teal background, anchored the room. Most of the upholstered furniture picked up on a rose tone in the rug, but she had made sure there were teal accents through the room, like the painting of her three children that hung over the fireplace. As I looked, though, I noticed that the paint behind the portrait was faded in spots, as though something else had hung there for a long time.

I had to appeal to her soft side. "Alex can't talk. He's in terrible shape. But I do know that there was a problem with your court date the other day."

"That was all my ex-husband's doing."

Her mouth pulled into a taut line. She sat primly, averting her eyes as though that was all she planned to say on the subject. I hadn't expected that. Was it true that she was chasing Mars? Maybe if I let his name slip . . . "Mars thought you might be able to help me with some details about that."

Her chin rose a little bit. "Of course. You understand, I'm sure, that with the children getting older, they have greater needs. Sports, camps, and the like. They shouldn't be denied those things simply because their father left me for a woman with five children. It's clear that he owes his first allegiance to his own children, not to someone else's. Right?"

She didn't wait for an answer and kept on talking. "I'm sorry. I've been holding this in. I can't go blathering about it to *anyone*. I have a reputation in this community. Mars left you, so I'm sure you understand what I mean. You have to hold your head high and keep going. I *need* more child support, but my ex-husband has been yanking me around, pulling stunts like avoiding his court dates. And now he wants the house! *This house!* Alex was there in court. When my ex-husband didn't show, Alex managed to get yet another continuance for him. Meanwhile I need money now! And my jerk of an ex-husband has stopped making the mortgage payments. Doesn't he have any love for his children? How can he pull this house out from under them?" She drew a deep breath and gazed at me in horror. "That's all strictly confidential between us. Please don't tell Mars."

"I'm sorry, Honey. You're not alone, and no one would think any less of you if they knew. Everyone goes through trying times in life. You'll get past this, too. And I won't breathe a word. I feared his absence might have something to do with the attack on Alex."

Honey blinked at me. "Oh! That's why you're here. Silly me. Well, if one of us had a reason to attack Alex, it would be me, not my ex. Alex has done a bang-up job for him. He would have rescued Alex instead of beating him up."

I knew she was trying to make a point when she said it would have been her who had a reason to attack Alex. Still, I couldn't help wondering. "School will be starting soon. Do you and the kids have any fun plans for the remainder of the summer?"

"No vacation at the shore for us this year. We spend most afternoons at the pool. The cheap one. But it's clean and they have fun. Yesterday my youngest learned to dive."

What time did the pool close? "That sounds like fun. Movie night afterward?"

"How did you know? Thank heaven I can still afford to buy hot dogs and make popcorn. They've been running the Star Wars series every night this week. My kids are mesmerized by it."

I thanked her for talking to me. "Before I go, do you know the Gibbards?"

Honey snickered. "Really? You don't know? I'm the eldest of the grand clan. They adopted me and then Harry about a year later. There was a time when our mom thought she couldn't have children. But surprise! When I was about three, she became pregnant after all. The doctors told her that happens sometimes. But postdivorce I'm keeping my husband's name, Armbruster, because that's the name of my children."

"I had no idea." My head reeled. "I'm so sorry about Grainger."

"Thank you. It was one of those tough times you mentioned. Just horrible. It changed our lives."

"Do you think Nellie murdered him?"

Fear flickered in her eyes. But Honey was nothing if not stoic. "She was convicted."

That she was, but I was surprised by the manner in which she sidestepped the question. I thanked her again and promised not to breathe a word of her personal problems. But I walked away from her home, wondering if she knew more than she was letting on.

I strolled home, thinking that I knew nothing more than I had in the morning. Honey's husband probably hadn't been involved in the attack on Alex.

As I passed Bernie's mansion, I heard voices.

"Sophie!"

That didn't sound like Bernie or Mars. I paused and spied Brock jogging down the stairs from their porch.

"I was looking for you. The guys saw me and invited me in."

"You're probably sick of pie, but I have one in the fridge."

Mars overheard me. "Are we invited, too?"

I looked at Brock. "Can you speak freely in front of them?"

"Sure."

I raised my hand and signaled for them to come over. Brock settled comfortably in my kitchen and made friends with Daisy and Mochie.

"Hot tea or iced?" I asked.

"Do you have that iced sweet tea they serve around here?"

"I do." I poured the dark amber liquid over ice cubes and set the kettle on the stove for my hot tea.

Bernie and Mars barreled in and it felt like a party.

I pulled the incomplete s'mores pie from the fridge. A slice was missing! I hadn't tried it or served it. But I had a sneaking suspicion I knew who might have sampled it. I had never even gotten around to putting the marshmallow topping on it. Instead of whipping up a marshmallow topping, I quickly added marshmallows to the top and took a minute to brown them under the broiler.

When everyone sat on the banquette with the s'mores pie and tea in front of them, I waited for Brock to speak.

Chapter 26

Dear Sophie,
How much larger than the pie pan should the
dough be for the crust?
                    Precise Baker in Inchelium, Washington

Dear Precise Baker,
A one-inch overhang is recommended. Fold it under
and crimp into a pleasing rim.

                                        Sophie

"When Patsy Lee had a little too much to drink, she would ramble about some of the things she had done to get to the top. Most of them were stupid pranks," said Brock.

"Like what?" I prompted.

He swallowed a bite of pie. "At a competition that Tommy Earl would probably have won, Peter snuck into the pantry and stole an ingredient that Tommy Earl needed. He had to bake without it, which gave Patsy Lee a huge advantage."

"I hope she felt guilty about it," I muttered.

"I think it weighed on her conscience. According to her, Peter didn't have that problem. He walked by the oven and turned it down once when she was in competition with Roger. When Roger pulled his pie from the oven, it was still raw. They played tricks on everyone. Patsy Lee was at a big conference where they were doing demonstrations and Peter kicked loose the power to Nellie's oven."

Mars stopped eating. "I'm in politics, and I thought people threw dirty punches in my business. That's insane. It doesn't matter, anyway."

"It does to them! And it makes for drama when something goes wrong for a chef on TV," said Brock.

"Did you do things like that for Patsy Lee?" asked Bernie.

"No! Never. I think it's slimy. By the time I came along, she turned down competitions. She did demonstrations and judged contests, things like that. And she had her own show, of course, which wasn't live in case anything went haywire and we had to reshoot."

"So basically you're saying that Peter used unethical tactics to assist her rise to stardom," said Mars.

"Yeah. When she came in on Saturday morning, she said to keep an eye out for Peter because she was through with him. Apparently, they had a big blowup about something when she went to see him on Friday night. I didn't know what to make of it. She was angry, yet sort of sad at the same time."

"That's what you couldn't say in front of Peter." Now I understood why he had come by. "Yet you took a job with him," I observed.

"I don't have the luxury of not working. I figured I'd hang in with him for a few days to collect a paycheck, then head back to New York. I've got nothing to lose, and it bought me a few days to cast around for another job."

"Did you tell Wolf?" I asked.

"Not the details. But I let him know that Patsy Lee and

Peter had an argument. The rest of the stuff is petty and in the past. But the fact that Peter and Patsy Lee fought about something hours before she died, well, I figured that was important. Peter clearly has no integrity. And his principles of decency are severely impaired."

Brock wiped his brow and sat back. "I held Patsy Lee in high esteem and it always bothered me that she managed to get ahead through slimeball tactics. But now she's gone and it doesn't matter anymore. And I think she was a decent person deep down. She had a hard life before she met Peter. Her dad drank, and when she was a kid, she never knew what to expect when she came home from school. Sometimes he didn't show up for days, and other times she tiptoed around afraid of triggering a rage. She was the kid who went without dinner most nights and couldn't wait to get to school in the morning for breakfast."

It was hard for me to imagine that Patsy Lee had grown up living in terror. "I had no idea."

"Do you think Peter killed her?" Bernie asked.

Brock's jaw hardened and his fingers coiled into balls. "It was my fault. I was supposed to watch out for her, but I missed it. Somebody got by me. I'll never forgive myself for that."

I placed my hand over his fist. "It wasn't your fault. Hey, I heard a rumor that Patsy Lee had a sweetheart in Old Town whom she used to visit. Do you know who that was?"

"For years I was paid to keep her secrets." He shrugged. "I guess it doesn't matter anymore. It was Roger."

Mars almost spewed tea. Fortunately, he caught himself in time. "Roger Mackenzie? Are you kidding me?"

"I know," said Brock. "Who'd have thought it? He's like the exact opposite of big, blustery Peter. Maybe that's what she saw in him. I always felt like she was embarrassed about her relationship with Roger. Maybe that's why she kept it a secret."

Bernie finally spoke up. "So Patsy Lee had a romantic relationship with Roger, but spent Friday night with Peter. Either one of them could have been sufficiently angry to have killed her."

"Roger is very envious of Patsy Lee's success," I said. "What did he say to me? Something about her finally stepping on the wrong person." All three of them looked at me. "I'll tell Wolf. One other thing, Brock. Do you know anything about a check that Patsy Lee wrote out to me?"

"All I know is what the cops told me."

"She wanted to have a private lunch with me that day. Do you know what that was about?"

"She was very happy about it. I'm trying to remember her exact words. It was something like she couldn't change the past, but she could change a future."

I was totally bewildered. Could it have involved Nellie and Grainger's death? Did she plan to come clean? Did she intend to offer money to Nellie's family? Or to pay for legal costs that might help Nellie get out of prison?

"Do you have the check?" asked Mars.

"No. I knew nothing about it until Wolf told me. She had my address, too, so maybe she mailed it? I'm completely clueless."

Bernie gazed at Brock. "You're sure you don't know what this is about?"

"Only that she seemed to feel good about it."

"Why would she need you?" asked Mars. "If she was setting up a baking scholarship or some kind of fund to help people, then why would she make out a check to you?"

"Maybe she wants to sponsor a convention or begin an annual charity event. I guess I won't know until the check arrives. Though I have to wonder why she would have mailed it when she was going to see me that day, anyway. It doesn't make any sense. Did she ever mention Grainger or Nellie to you?"

Brock shook his head. "Those names don't ring any bells for me."

Brock stretched his legs. "Thanks for the pie, Sophie. It was delish. I'll be in town for a few more days. If you need anything from me, I'm staying at the Belmont."

I saw him to the door. "Thank you, Brock. I guess you won't be working for Natasha."

His eyes opened wide. "Man! I thought Peter was going to blow a gasket. Gotta give him credit, though. He just walked away from her like she didn't exist. He didn't yell at her or say she was fired, nothing like that. He was just *done*. Poor Natasha was the one who was all fired up. I had to walk her to the taxi stand at the hotel to get her to leave!"

"Thanks for handling it. I'm sure she'll be appreciative, too, once she has had a chance to chill out."

He walked away, and I closed the door.

When I returned to the kitchen, Mars and Bernie asked about Alex.

"I'm headed that way now to check on him. I don't know if they'll let me see him."

Mars stacked the dishes in the sink. "We'll take you."

On the trip to the hospital, I told them about Alex's missing client and how that had bombed as a lead.

"It could be anyone," said Bernie. "His assistant is in the best position to guess who might be suspects."

"If she has a hunch, she sure wasn't sharing it with me."

Mars had been uncharacteristically silent on the drive. "What would a person tell his attorney that would make him want to permanently silence the lawyer and set fire to his files?"

Chapter 27

Dear Sophie,
I read that one shouldn't freeze pie dough. I'm completely flummoxed. I thought it was a good thing to freeze it. Doesn't freezing the dough make it more flaky?

Pie Pro in Pie Town, New Mexico

Dear Pie Pro,
You are correct. The old saying goes "make it cold, bake it hot." Some recipes even recommend freezing the pie for fifteen minutes before baking it.

Sophie

It was a good question. Mars had put his finger on the precise thing we needed to know in order to uncover the monster that had attacked Alex.

"Could be anything. Everyone has secrets," said Bernie.

I twisted in my seat to look at him. "What's *your* deep, dark secret?"

He grinned at me. "I'll never tell."

"Does a lawyer know?"

"Why are you questioning me? I didn't set fire to Alex's office!"

I glanced at Mars, who was laughing. Personally, I thought Bernie was getting a little testy and wondered if he did have some kind of secret. He probably beat someone up. Maybe that was why he had that kink in his nose.

"Okay," I said, "so it might be a previous scrape with the law that would ruin a reputation?"

"Or anything personal. Lawyers have a lot of details about their divorce clients. Maybe someone told him too much," Mars suggested. "Something that can now be used against the client?"

Mars parked the car. We found Alex's room without difficulty.

Wong had pulled guard duty. She gave me a hug. "I'm so sorry, Sophie."

We walked inside. Alex was barely recognizable. If they had swapped him for another person, we wouldn't have known. His face was practically swaddled with gauze.

I picked up his hand and leaned toward him. "Alex? Can you hear me? It's Sophie."

He didn't move. There wasn't even a twitch in his fingers.

"I guess he's still in the medically induced coma," I murmured.

Mars and Bernie tried to talk with him, too.

It was worse than depressing. I couldn't believe this had happened to Alex. He was such an upstanding guy. He always played by the rules. What could have happened? I forced myself to shove those thoughts aside until later. I needed to be cheerful for him now. Who knew if he could understand anything that was being said?

Bernie was teasing him about missing out on the s'mores pie that I had baked. I promised to bake one just for him when he was released from the hospital.

A nurse bustled in to check his IV. "We have a ten-minute limit for nonfamily visitors. Are any of you family?"

Mars and Bernie looked at me.

"Does girlfriend count?"

"No, ma'am, it does not. But I'm sure he appreciates your visit."

I knew she was only doing her job. I wished I could sit with him, but realized that he probably needed peace and quiet. We said goodbye to Alex and walked into the hallway.

"Have you seen his parents?" I asked Wong.

"We're expecting them anytime."

Bernie, Mars, and I left. The two of them gabbed, but I was thinking if I couldn't be with Alex, maybe I could figure out who had done this to him. But how?

I asked Mars to drop me off at Alex's house.

Bernie and Mars perked up immediately. "Do you have a key?" asked Mars.

I admitted that I did.

"We're coming with you," said Bernie. "As guards."

They were being silly, but to be completely honest, I didn't mind the company.

Alex had bought a historical home built in 1800. Smaller than my house, it had only two floors, unless one counted the ancient basement. It shared walls with neighboring houses on both sides. Built of red brick, it featured black shutters and a black front door, which seemed suitably masculine. It bordered the sidewalk and had only enough front yard for a few azalea plants under the front windows.

Mars parked half a block away from the house.

I pulled out my key and unlocked the front door. Without Alex, the building was eerily silent. I left Mars and Bernie in the living room, which always reminded me of an elegant home library, filled with books and cushy brown leather furniture. I bounded up the stairs to the room he used as a home office.

Apologizing to Alex, who might be offended by my behavior, I pawed through the orderly drawers of his desk. The top one on the right contained what I had hoped for—a password booklet.

I turned on the laptop, flipped through the password book, and found the key word on the inside top cover. I typed it in and the computer screen opened up for me.

Mars walked in. "What are you doing?"

"That idiot who attacked him might have burned his paper files and melted his computers at the office, but if I know Alex, he has a backup somewhere."

"Sophie, I think this is called *hacking*. Maybe this isn't such a great idea." Bernie scooted a stool up next to me and peered at the computer.

Mars picked up the password book. "Try a file called *Office*."

I clicked on the Spotlight Search on his Mac and typed in *Office*.

"There are a lot of matches."

Bernie pointed at a file. "Try that one."

I clicked on it and when it opened, it revealed Alex's calendar for the month of August. "Those look like appointments," I said.

"And they include Armbruster," Mars noted.

I stopped what I was doing. "I'd like to snoop, but you're right, Bernie. It seems wrong to violate his privacy, especially since he was so careful about guarding his clients' secrets. I'm just going to check his appointments for the day he was attacked."

Mars leaned over my shoulder. "Agreed. That seems reasonable to me."

I clicked on the date. "I'd like to find a client list to take to Wolf."

"Wolf might arrest you," said Bernie.

I scowled at him.

"I'm serious, Sophie. If there's something on his desk, that's one thing, but I don't think we should hack into his computer files."

I understood his point. And deep down I knew he was right, but I didn't want to agree with him. "One of his clients tried to kill him."

"Bummer," Mars murmured, studying the screen. "Not a single entry on the calendar for yesterday afternoon."

I didn't want to give up. There had to be useful information in his files, but I reluctantly logged out and turned off the computer.

Chapter 28

Dear Sophie,
I watched a pie show on TV the other day and the
baker froze the flour! Isn't that overkill?
                    Keeping It Simple in Icedale, Pennsylvania

Dear Keeping It Simple,
Some bakers do refrigerate or freeze their flour.
And their bowls and utensils, too!
                                        Sophie

Daisy and I returned to the scene of the crime that evening, a little bit earlier than the time it had happened. We began behind Alex's office, where the burned-out windows were a grim reminder of the horrible event. I didn't let Daisy go close, for fear of broken glass on the ground. Smoke had curled up the redbrick walls, leaving them black with soot.

A lone fireman studied the back of the building.

"Hi," I said. "It's quite a mess."

The fireman looked over at me. "Don't come any closer, please. Are you the girlfriend or the assistant?"

"The girlfriend. How did you know?"

"You're not old enough to be Alex's mom, so that leaves the girlfriend, the assistant, or the perpetrator. No one else would be interested in coming back here."

He ran a sturdy hand through short blond hair that was graying. "It was brave of you to enter the building and rescue Alex."

"It wasn't burning then. The perpetrator had just started the fire in the back room and left. I heard the door close."

He looked at the door. "This one?"

"I assume so. I don't think there are any other doors back here. It was his only way out without passing by me. So how do you figure out who set the fire?"

"Mostly by interviewing people like you. No one came to talk with you yet?"

"No. But I've been out a lot. If I knew who did it, I wouldn't be here right now. I'd be hounding the police."

He picked his way over to me and held out his hand to shake. "Harry Gibbard."

"You have to be kidding. You Gibbards are everywhere. Sophie Winston."

"And who is this?"

"Daisy." She lifted her paw as though she expected him to shake it, which he did.

"Very nice manners, Daisy."

"I was just talking to Honey this morning," I said.

He grinned. "My partner in crime."

"Oh?"

"In a manner of speaking. As the first two kids we were often in mischief together. Plus we were the only ones who were adopted. Don't get me wrong, the Gibbards treated us all alike, but Honey and I had a special bond because of it. We related in a way that the other kids didn't really understand."

"I'm sorry about Grainger's death."

Harry nodded. "Thanks. I don't know if my mom will ever get over losing him. Any of us kids. We're her life."

"I heard he was a good guy."

"Grainger? Yeah, I guess so. The two of us got into it over a girl when we were young. We got along after that, but I think we both saw the flip side of each other's personalities."

"Who got the girl?"

"Grainger did. He was tenacious. Exactly like our dad, he was stubborn and strong-willed. Heaven help us all when those two butted heads. And then the girl went off and married someone else, so we both lost in the end and the whole argument was for naught."

"Harry, do you think someone else might have murdered Grainger?" I asked.

He appeared to be surprised by my question. "They nailed Nellie. The lesson of that story is, if you're going to murder your fiancé, you shouldn't bake him a pie using rhubarb from your ex-husband's garden." He patted Daisy's head. "Could I buy you two an ice cream?"

"Sure. We'd like that, wouldn't we, Daisy?"

The three of us rounded the corner to a restaurant that sold ice cream to passersby through a window.

Harry handed me a Hound Dog Delight cone for Daisy and a pecan praline cone for me. Harry went for triple chocolate with chips in it.

We strolled over to a bench that faced the marred building. I noted with some irony that the brass sign on the wall with Alex's name was still there, only it was black now.

"Would you mind telling me exactly what happened?" asked Harry.

I filled him in on all the details. "I never saw the guy. I was concentrating on Alex, and then Wong arrived and

204 *Krista Davis*

spotted the flames. It was all we could do to drag Alex out of the building."

"You're sure Alex never mentioned a client who might have been a headache? Or maybe he lost a case and felt terrible about it?"

"You don't know Alex, do you? The most closemouthed man you're ever likely to meet. He took a lot of pride in being a lawyer and keeping his clients' secrets safe."

"You were walking Daisy around here before you saw the hand in the window?"

"Right. That's why I came back today. I was hoping some people might walk by who would have seen something. You know, someone who goes this way every night."

"It was a good thought. But I suspect you might know more than you realize."

"I wish I did, Harry."

Before Daisy and I left, I gave him my phone number. "Thanks for the ice cream. If there's any way I can help, I hope you'll give me a call."

Harry tucked the slip of paper into a breast pocket.

Daisy and I walked away, but when I looked back, Harry was still sitting on the bench, staring at Alex's building. I was glad to know that someone else was thinking about who the perpetrator might be.

On the way home I considered what Harry had said. But no matter how I wracked my brain, I knew that Alex hadn't talked about his clients. He hadn't mentioned them by name, nor had he told me about their legal issues.

It wasn't until I stuck the key in my door that I realized Alex might have let on about something after all, and I had been too obtuse to see it.

Chapter 29

Dear Sophie,
I struggle with pie dough every time I make it. Is
there anything I can do when it isn't working?
                    Hopeless in Cold Fork, California

Dear Hopeless,
If the pie dough is too stiff, you can try adding a
few drops of ice water. If it's too soft, try refriger-
ating it for a half hour or more.

                                        Sophie

Alex hadn't disguised his dismay at my poking around
in the case of the Grainger murder. He had come right
out and said I could damage his reputation. At the time I
thought he was worried because I was looking into a case
that had been closed. But now I wondered if it could possibly have been the case of Grainger's murder specifically
that he wanted me to stay away from. Did he know something about it?

I closed the door behind us and leaned against it. "Oh,
my gosh!" I yelped. Alex had warned me that if Nellie was

innocent, it meant the real killer was still on the loose and might stop at nothing to hide his guilt. I had even told his assistant as much, without understanding Alex's complete meaning.

My knees quaking, I locked the front door, then dashed into the kitchen, where I sat down in one of the chairs by the fireplace.

What had I done? It *was* my fault that Alex was in the hospital. It was my fault that someone had tried to kill Alex and destroy his files so the truth wouldn't come out. It was all my fault.

A whimpering sound brought me out of my train of thought. Daisy was dragging her leash behind her. "Poor Daisy. I'm sorry that I forgot to take off your halter."

Mochie jumped up on the chair and pawed me. "I forgot about you, too." I listened to his contented purr while I stroked him.

But that didn't prevent my thoughts from wandering back to Alex. He had tried to make me back off. He had tried to warn me. And now it was Alex who was paying the price for my nosiness. I would never be able to forgive myself.

I sat in my kitchen for a long time, feeling miserable and guilty. I kept coming to the same conclusion. I couldn't go back in time and do things differently. Nor could I heal Alex, but I could find the person who did this to him. And in doing so, I might just find the person who murdered Grainger.

I phoned Bernie, Mars, and Nina, who agreed to come over. Before they arrived, I reviewed the transcript of the trial that Aly had left with us. I was scanning fast, but there was simply no mention of Alex's name at all. I hadn't imagined that or overlooked it.

I stacked the papers, put on the kettle, and pulled the s'mores pie out of the fridge. In the dining room I opened the liquor cabinet and found marshmallow vodka and chocolate liqueur. If I knew Nina, she would want a drink, and a s'mores cocktail sounded just right.

Bernie, Mars, and Nina arrived simultaneously.

I pointed Nina to the liqueurs and made tea for Bernie and me.

"So what's up?" asked Mars as we settled at the table in my kitchen.

I cut the pie while I told them that the attack on Alex was probably my fault. "He tried to warn me, but at the time, I thought he was stating the obvious. I didn't realize that he was warning me because he knew something."

Mars sipped his s'mores cocktail. "Sophie, you're over-reacting. You just admitted that Alex wasn't involved in Grainger's case at all."

"Do you really think it was just a coincidence that some-one attacked Alex only days after Patsy Lee's death and at the time when we started poking around in Grainger's murder?" I handed everyone a piece of pie.

"Yeah. I think exactly that. Not everything is about you or because of you, Sophie." Mars dug a fork into his pie.

"What about you two?" I asked Nina and Bernie.

"First it's important to note that this pie is fun," said Nina. "I do agree that it's entirely possible that the attack on Alex had nothing to do with the people of the pie. He has a lot of clients and there's no telling who was angry with him. In fact, the field of suspects is even bigger than his client list because, as in Honey Armbruster's situation, the person who was angry with him might have been the person on the other side of the case. It could have been anyone."

Bernie had been eating quietly and sipping his tea. "Per-haps the wisest course of action here is to examine Patsy Lee's murder and Grainger's murder because they appear to involve the same group of people. If Sophie is correct about the attack on Alex, then narrowing down the suspects in the two killings might lead us to the person who attacked Alex."

I couldn't help flashing Bernie a smile. He was so logical.

Mars nodded and pulled his list out of his pocket. "Okay then, let's review what we know for sure. Tommy Earl?"

"He's too nice a guy," said Nina.

I sipped my tea. "You have to include him. He told me Grainger stole a TV-show idea from him. I would say he might have been a little bit bitter about Patsy Lee's success, but he wasn't furious with her like Roger."

Mars made a note and said, "Roger?"

"He claims Patsy Lee stole his recipes and his meemaw story," I said.

"Seriously?" asked Mars. "Come on, Sophie. Who would murder over something like that?"

"Don't forget that he was Patsy Lee's secret beau. He might have blown a gasket when he found out that she spent the night with Peter."

Mars nodded reluctantly.

"Roger told me that all they have is their reputations, and once that's gone, they're finished," I said.

"That's true in a lot of professions," said Mars.

"Especially in the restaurant world." Bernie set his fork down. "I've steered clear of hiring Tommy Earl because of his reputation for drinking. I can't deal with someone who is unreliable or drunk on the job."

"That came as a surprise to me," I said. "I have hired Tommy Earl to bake pies for several events. I've never had a problem. He always comes through on time with perfect pies."

"Makes a person wonder where that rumor started," said Nina. "I've never known him to drink. But there's something about Roger that gives me the willies. Does anyone else feel that way?"

"He spooked me a little bit when he was so angry with Patsy Lee, even after her death," I said. "Of course, everyone gets angry, and if Patsy Lee stepped on him the way he claimed, then maybe that festered into a rage."

"What about Willa?" asked Mars.

Bernie wasted no time speaking up. "I can vouch for Willa. She's a great employee, an excellent pastry chef, and a genuinely nice person."

Nina glanced at him. "She and Patsy Lee were best friends until Patsy Lee fired her. I'd have been mad, too. Can you imagine packing up and moving, leaving your home and your life, to work for a friend and then being kicked out the door a few months later?"

"That would be a rotten thing to do to anyone, not to mention a good friend." Bernie grimaced. "But I don't see Willa murdering a friend over something like that. Besides, she's back up on her feet. What reason would she have to murder Patsy Lee now?"

I gasped. "What with Alex's condition, I forgot all about it. Last night when I walked back from Alex's office, I saw Peter and Willa kissing in a passionate manner at your rental house."

"Willa is in love with Peter?" Nina's eyes grew large. "That changes everything. If she knew that Patsy Lee spent the night with Peter, she might have been wildly jealous."

Bernie groaned. "Not Willa. How could she get involved with a guy like Peter, who is completely devoid of ethics?"

"Peter rises to the top of the suspect list," said Mars.

"Patsy Lee gave him the heave-ho and from what I gather he lost just about everything," said Nina.

"Any chance Alex represented Patsy Lee?" asked Bernie.

"This is what we get for being honest and not hacking into his files," I grumbled.

"Did Peter have a motive to knock off Grainger?" asked Nina.

"Could he have been involved in the TV show that Grainger allegedly stole from Tommy Earl?" I asked.

"Willa might have helped him," suggested Nina. "Maybe he beat up Alex while she set the fire?"

"That's wild speculation." Bernie clearly wasn't pleased. "What we do know is that they appear to be in a relationship. That doesn't mean they teamed up to kill anyone. And sorry, Sophie, but the TV show idea is also mere speculation."

"I have my doubts about Peter because I'm not sure he can bake," mused Nina. "Might Willa have baked a poisonous pie for Peter, even back then?"

"Or Patsy Lee for that matter," Bernie added.

"What if Patsy Lee threatened to expose Peter's slimy tactics, and that's why he killed her?" I sipped my tea and added, "And somehow Alex knew about it."

"We have to add two more names to the list," Mars said. "Honey Armbruster and Remy Tarwick."

"What is this obsession with my employees?" Bernie shook his head. "Remy was fired from Star-Spangled Pies. I'll come right out and admit it. But it was because he defended a female customer whose boyfriend wouldn't let her eat. Weird, huh? Apparently, he was obsessed with her weight. He was belittling her and allowing her only two forkfuls of food to eat. Remy was waiting on their table and finally intervened, which resulted in a brawl on the sidewalk. Obviously, one can't have that kind of behavior. I have been very clear with him about that. But I understand why he tried to help that woman."

"That doesn't mean Remy didn't go back and get into a fight with Grainger," said Mars.

"Think he went home and baked a poisonous rhubarb pie first?" asked Bernie.

"Good point. Though I hear anyone can bake a pie if they try. Still, I agree with you, highly unlikely. That leaves Honey, who we know for sure can bake a great pie," said Nina.

"Maybe she was chasing Grainger?" suggested Mars.

"I don't think so," I said wryly. "They're siblings."

"Are you sure?" asked Mars.

"Confirmed this afternoon by her brother. Honey loathes Alex, but we all know she was obsessed with Patsy Lee, so while she certainly could bake a great pie, I would have to say she's low on the list of suspects. I guess we need to include her, just in case."

"So what now?" asked Nina. "How do we confirm that it's Peter?"

"Hmm, what would you do now if you were Peter?" I asked. "I'd get out of town while the gettin' was good, but then, I wouldn't have murdered anyone, either."

"I'll talk to Willa when she comes in tomorrow morning," Bernie volunteered.

"Discreetly!" Nina reminded him.

"Of course. Is there any other way?"

"I have Brock on this list," said Mars. "Can I scratch him off?"

"As far as I know, his only connection is to Patsy Lee. I don't think he was around here five years ago when Grainger was murdered," I said.

Mars crossed his name off the list. "Willa is our best bet for information, Bernie."

"I'm on it."

I cleaned up the kitchen after they left, feeling just a tiny bit better. Maybe we were finally on the right track.

But I was wide-awake and the last thing I wanted to do was toss in bed.

Mochie and Daisy were napping, so I grabbed my laptop, hopped in my car, and drove to the hospital.

A police officer, whom I recognized, sat outside Alex's room. He waved me in.

Alex lay still as death. The monitor on a screen to his right showed his heartbeat. It looked even to me, but what did I know?

I lay my bag on a bedside table that was loaded with flower arrangements. I poked through the blooms to find the cards from his colleagues and friends, which I read aloud to him. "You're very much beloved, Alex." I read them out loud a second time in case somewhere, deep down in his brain, he could comprehend what I was saying.

I sat down and took his hand into mine. "I'm so sorry, Alex. Can you hear me? Squeeze my hand if you know I'm here."

Nothing happened.

"Alex, I'm so worried that I inadvertently caused this. You tried to warn me, but I didn't listen and now you're the one paying for it. Honey, you have to come around and tell us who it was. Was it a client? Was it another attorney?"

It was useless and I knew it. He couldn't hear what I was saying.

Nevertheless, I opened my laptop and jabbered about my upcoming schedule. "I landed the Convention of Neuroimmunology. And a couple of weeks after that, I have the World Conference of Corporate Brokers. There's not much coming up that involves lawyers."

After a bit I just held his hand and watched him, wondering what was going on in his brain.

A nurse came in, smiled at me, and checked his IV. She left without a word. Maybe being there by myself in the middle of the night was the key to not getting kicked out.

Every fifteen minutes or so, I talked with him again. I tried to mention the names of his friends and told him about Natasha's stunt with the Boston cream pie.

At one in the morning, I finally went home, hoping against hope that he had known I was there.

Mochie, Daisy, and I went up to bed, and I fell dead asleep.

At five in the morning Daisy nudged me and whimpered.

"Not now, Daisy." I opened one eye to look at her.

Daisy's ears perked up. I heard it, too. The tiniest tapping sound. "Where's that coming from?" I whispered.

Chapter 30

Dear Natasha,
My bottom crusts always come out soggy. What
am I doing wrong?

Swimmer in Big Water, Utah

Dear Swimmer,
You can try dusting the bottom pastry with a little
bit of flour, blind baking it, pricking the dough, bak-
ing in a dark-bottomed pie plate, or sprinkling nuts
or a small amount of bread crumbs in the bottom.

Natasha

Daisy padded down the stairs and headed straight to the sunroom door. I followed her in the predawn darkness and could see someone standing outside, tapping lightly on my door. I flicked on the outdoor light, squinting at the brightness.

"Natasha?"

The second I unlocked the door, she bolted inside. "Turn that light off. He'll see me!"

I hit the switch and walked her to the living room, where we were less likely to be seen by someone outside. I turned on a small light on a side table.

"Natasha, it's the middle of the night. What are you talking about?"

"This is all your fault."

She was right, of course. Alex's condition might well be my fault, but she didn't have to rub it in. "I agree."

"At least you realize it. You ruined everything! If it weren't for you, everything would be different."

"Okay, okay. I already feel terrible about it," I said.

"You do?" she asked, surprise in her voice.

"Of course. I didn't want this to happen. I'm horrified."

"Sophie!" she cooed. "I've never seen you like this. Thank you. But what do I do now? And by the way, it's not the middle of the night. I waited until morning. I haven't slept since the bake-off."

She looked completely fine to me. Her makeup had been applied perfectly. Not a hair strayed. She wore a white dress cinched at the waist with a wide belt made of a tan fiber. I wished I looked that good when I didn't sleep. "The bake-off? Is that what you're talking about?"

"Of course. What did you think?"

I was half asleep. Otherwise I would have realized that she wasn't worried about Alex.

"You should wear more makeup, Sophie. I'm a mess underneath it. It took concealer, base, and powder to hide the dark rings under my eyes."

I squinted at her. Maybe that was the truth. There were very faint blue crescents just under her lower eyelashes.

"I'm glad you recognize that you single-handedly ruined my chances to be a star," she blathered.

"Actually, I was talking about something else."

"Sophie! I hate to admit that I read your advice column, but I do. You told that woman not to bake a pie but to bake a cake. You said she couldn't compete with her pie expert mother-in-law. That's why I baked the Boston cream pie! It was your idea."

I kept my tone level. "That woman wasn't in a contest. You should have done what Peter told you to do, Natasha."

"I certainly will never follow *your* advice again. Remember how Peter Presley told me there was room on earth for another star?"

I was tired. "Yes, very touching."

"He picked me out of the crowd at the pie festival. Oh, Sophie," she wailed. "He saw me and made room for another star on earth."

It took a minute for her meaning to compute. "You think Peter murdered Patsy Lee so he could make you a star?"

"Now you've got the picture!"

"Why would you think that?"

"It all fits, Sophie. Peter is broke. When Patsy Lee divorced him, she hired a different manager. Peter made her successful and then she kicked him to the gutter with her expensive high-heeled shoes. He needed a replacement for her. He knew how to *make* a star, but Patsy Lee had to be gone first. Don't you see? Now he has to get rid of me."

"You embarrassed him, Natasha." It wasn't the time for a lecture on how she ruined her chances all on her own, so I bit my tongue about that. "But I don't think he'll murder you." I wondered if I should share what Bernie, Mars, Nina, and I had discussed about Peter. Maybe not. Natasha was already agitated.

"You're so naïve! Listen to me, Sophie. He's going to kill me next."

I yawned, which surely gave her the wrong impression, but it *was* early in the morning, and I hadn't gotten much sleep.

"Sophie!" she screeched.

"Fine. Why would he want to kill you?"

Natasha reached into her pocket and pulled out a clear plastic vial with a white powder in it.

Chapter 31

Dear Sophie,
My mother-in-law insists that pie dough cannot be made in a food processor. I think food processors would be perfect for pie dough. Who's right?
            Crossing My Fingers in Bacons, Delaware

Dear Crossing My Fingers,
You definitely can make pie dough in a food processor. Just remember to pulse, not let it run!
                                            Sophie

I drew in a sharp breath and was suddenly wide-awake. "Where did you find that?"

"In the limo."

"Put it down on the coffee table. I'll be right back." I rushed to the kitchen. I couldn't find a paper bag, so I grabbed a birthday gift bag covered with a colorful fireworks print, grabbed my phone, and dashed back.

I stared at the little vial for a moment. How could I get it into the bag without touching it or smearing fingerprints? I gazed around and spotted long matches for lighting the fire in the fireplace. I snagged one and used it to roll the vial into the bag.

Relieved that it was secure, I said, "You may have found the very thing the police need." I skipped mentioning that she could have spared Alex if she had brought it to Wolf's attention right away. "Of course, I'm sure other people rode in that limo. But if it has Peter's fingerprints on it, and if it contains caffeine powder, this might just be the key to putting Peter away."

"So you do agree with me?"

"I still don't think you would have been his next victim, but he may have murdered Patsy Lee, and this little vial is the key to establishing that."

I picked up the phone and called Wolf's number.

"It's a little early to be calling people, Sophie," cautioned Natasha.

I stared at her in wonder about how her brain worked. "It's not too early to wake me, though?"

"It was an emergency, and I waited until a quarter of five before I came over here."

Wolf's phone rolled over to voice mail. He was probably asleep. "Wolf, this is Sophie. Please come to my house as soon as you possibly can. I think we may have the key to Patsy's death."

Natasha smiled at me. "Aren't you going to offer me a cup of coffee?"

I chuckled all the way to the kitchen.

Natasha must have felt safer because she didn't complain when I turned on the kitchen lights. Dawn was breaking in the sky and that probably helped, too. If someone happened to be hanging around outside, it would be much harder to hide.

I turned on the kettle and ground coffee beans while Natasha paced the kitchen.

She looked over my shoulder when I spooned fresh grounds into the French press. "Did you add charcoal?"

"I'm so sorry, but I happen to be out," I said sarcastically.

"I suppose we'll have to make do. I would run over to my place to get some, but I think I'll hang around here until I know that Wolf has Peter in custody."

"What did Peter say to you after the show?"

"Not a word! Everyone who tried my Boston cream pie raved about it. But Peter snubbed me!"

"I'm sorry your dreams of stardom didn't work out."

"It's just as well, I suppose." Natasha stretched as she poked around the kitchen. "I wouldn't have wanted to work for a killer, anyway. I shudder to think what might have happened if I had gone off with him to New York and other cities, all the while thinking he was a great guy. He could have murdered me and left my body somewhere!"

"Would you prefer an omelet or French toast with strawberries for breakfast?"

Natasha paused in front of the bay window. "French toast. What's taking Wolf so long? Oh, good! Mars is on his way over here. Did you call him?"

I hadn't. I opened the kitchen door to let him in. "Good morning."

"You'll never believe this. The police arrested Willa this morning."

Chapter 32

Dear Sophie,
I used to watch my meemaw make pies in her country kitchen. She did it so fast! She barely even rolled out the dough. How did she do that?
Meemaw's Girl in Lick Skillet, Virginia

Dear Meemaw's Girl,
Your meemaw was doing it correctly. The less you handle the dough, the better it will be. Don't keep rolling it. Use a few firm moves to roll it out. If you overwork the dough, it will become tough.

Sophie

"Willa?" I cried. "Are you sure?"

"Bernie is over at the police station, trying to bail her out." He stopped petting Daisy and looked at me in an oversized T-shirt and Natasha in her lovely dress. "What's going on here?"

"I'm running upstairs to shower and change clothes. Natasha, you tell him what you found. Neither of you touch the vial."

Daisy stayed with the two of them while I ran up the stairs, took a very quick shower, and slid into a periwinkle blue dress and white sandals.

When I walked downstairs, Mars was holding the birthday bag and looking inside it.

"Can you believe it?" I asked.

Mars looked over at me. "What I can't believe is that Peter didn't get rid of the caffeine powder. Why would anyone run the risk of being caught with it? I'd have flushed the powder down the toilet, washed the container to remove any remnants and fingerprints, and ditched that thing in a Dumpster behind a busy restaurant. Or the river. They'd never find it in the river."

"Mars," said Natasha. "You're scaring me. How long have you had these kinds of thoughts?"

Mars winked at me. "Since I moved in with you."

For a moment Natasha appeared stunned. "I hate it when you tease me."

"So why did they arrest Willa?" I poured coffee into Blue Denmark breakfast cups for each of us and brought them to the table with sugar and cream.

"I have no idea," said Mars. "Willa called Bernie, but he didn't wait for details. He hightailed it over there."

"How interesting that she didn't call Peter . . . ," I mused as I fed Mochie and Daisy.

"I told you," said Natasha. "Peter's broke. He couldn't bail her out. Besides, Willa doesn't have what it takes to be a star. She's kind of frumpy. She doesn't have style like Patsy Lee and me."

I beat some eggs with cinnamon and the tiniest pinch of nutmeg, and heated the flat top griddle on my stove. While we talked, I quickly washed and sliced plump red strawberries, and sprinkled sugar over them so they would release their delicious juices into a sweet sauce.

Happily, I had challah on hand, my favorite bread for making French toast. I cut it into thick slices and dipped them in the eggs long enough for them to soak up the eggs and the spices. The griddle sizzled when I placed the bread on it.

I noted that Mars had taken a seat at my banquette as far away from Natasha as possible.

"Do you miss my cooking?" asked Natasha.

Mars was a remarkably confident person, but at that moment it was obvious that he didn't know what to say. "Sure," he blurted.

That was kind of him. When they were living together, he had dropped by my house more than once hoping for a meal.

We ate our French toast with the fresh strawberries and a splash of maple syrup, except for Natasha, who declined the French toast and picked at the strawberries.

Meanwhile we speculated about the arrest of Willa.

"At the pie festival," I said, "Willa returned to the tables of professional pies asking if she left her coffee there. I didn't think much of it at the time. But if she's the one who poisoned Patsy Lee, that would have been a good ruse for claiming someone took her coffee."

"That's wicked!" exclaimed Natasha. "But then, why did Peter have the poison?"

Mars flicked a glance at me. "Maybe they were in cahoots."

Our speculation ended half an hour later when Bernie arrived with a distraught Willa. Tears stained her face. She wore jeans with a short-sleeved T-shirt and sneakers. But she looked like she'd been through a terrible experience.

Willa scooted into the banquette and said, "Bernie thought you wouldn't mind if we came here. Would you like me to leave?"

"Of course not." I worried about Wolf dropping by, though. I poured coffee for both of them and put more bread on the griddle.

"What happened?" asked Mars.

"That cop, the one they call Wolf, came to my condo late last night. He read me my rights and took me down to the police station."

Just hearing her talk about it gave me shivers.

"At the food festival I lost my cup of coffee." Willa gasped and pointed at me. "Sophie! You're my witness. I told you I was looking for it."

Bernie turned hopeful eyes to me.

"That's absolutely true."

"When you say *cup*, do you mean one of those imprinted paper cups like they have at Moos and Brews?" asked Mars.

"Exactly. I never did find it. I figured someone picked it up by mistake or threw it out. There were so many people there! Wolf said they tested Patsy Lee's coffee cup for poison and then they checked for fingerprints." Willa's voice broke. "They claim my fingerprints are on the cup."

Chapter 33

Dear Sophie,
Can I freeze pie dough?
                        Busy Mom in Kid Valley, Washington

Dear Busy Mom,
Pie dough freezes very well. Wrap it tightly in wax
paper and store in a freezer bag.

                                                Sophie

Natasha looked over at me, her eyes wide.

Oh, boy. We had a merger of clues here. I delivered the French toast to Willa and Bernie, who reached over to Willa and patted her on the shoulder.

"We'll get to the bottom of this," he assured her. "Won't we, Sophie?"

"Absolutely." But at that moment I saw Wolf's car pull up outside. I froze. Willa had just been interrogated by him. He was the last person she wanted to see.

I didn't have many choices, and I had to act fast.

"Natasha, could you help me with that bush outside?" I asked.

"What bush?"

"I'll help you," offered Mars.

Ohhh! This was not going as I had hoped. I grabbed the HAPPY BIRTHDAY bag and tried not to rush to the door. Forcing myself to walk calmly, I headed to the foyer, flung the front door open, and stepped outside, with Mars right behind me.

"Wolf!" I whispered.

Mars and I met him at the sidewalk, and I handed him the bag.

"It's not my birthday," said Wolf.

"It was all I could find. It contains a vial of white powder that Natasha found in Peter's limo."

Wolf peered in the bag. "From what *I* heard, Peter dumped her at the pie bake-off. How come she's only telling us about this now?"

"You'd have to ask her. Where is she? Mars, could you ask her to come out here, please?"

He trotted toward the house.

"Wolf," I said in a low voice. "I know you found Willa's fingerprints—"

"How could you possibly know that already?"

"As it happens, Willa is sitting at my kitchen table."

"Oh. That explains a few things."

"What you need to know is that I saw Willa and Peter in a romantic embrace and kiss right after the attack on Alex. I'm worried that they might have been in this together."

"Yet you invited her to breakfast?"

"Bernie showed up with her! What was I supposed to do?"

A grin spread across his lips. "Only you, Sophie. This could only happen to you."

"Have you heard anything about Alex's condition?"

"Nothing I would want to tell you."

"No!"

"I don't think he's any worse. But they're keeping him in the medically induced coma for now. He needs to stay still."

"Do you think it was Peter or Willa?" I asked.

Wolf blinked in surprise. "Why would you think one of them attacked Alex?"

The thing was that I didn't really have a good reason to think it might be Peter or Willa who had wreaked havoc on Alex and his office. My theory that I had inadvertently instigated the attack on Alex evaporated if Peter and Willa murdered Patsy Lee. "Have you checked his client list?" I asked. "Don't you think it's one of his clients, or a person on the other side of a lawsuit?"

"We've been trying to reach his assistant but so far we haven't had any luck. Do you know of a way to get his client list?" asked Wolf.

"Maybe."

Wolf gazed at me questioningly. "Show me."

I hurried into my house for my purse while Mars escorted Natasha outside.

On my return Natasha was explaining how she had found the vial of white powder.

Wolf thanked her and said he might need to contact her with further questions.

Natasha beamed as though she had just won a pie competition.

"Will you watch Daisy?" I asked Mars. "I'm going to show Wolf something."

Mars frowned at me, and I knew he wanted to come with us.

"I'll be back soon," I assured him.

Wolf shot me an awkward look. "Where are we going?"

"To Alex's house."

For a long moment he was silent. "I, um . . . We shouldn't be seen . . ."

I smiled. His wife was sensitive about the fact that Wolf and I had dated. "No problem. You drive over, and I'll meet you there. Nina can probably come with us." I gave him Alex's address and walked to Nina's house.

She was fully dressed and on her way out when I arrived at her door.

"Where are you off to?" I asked.

"Your house. What's going on over there?"

I told her the whole story about Natasha, Peter, and Willa as we walked to Alex's place.

Wolf was waiting for us when we got there. He handed Nina a bag of croissants and a cup of coffee. "Heard *you* didn't get breakfast at Sophie's this morning, either."

I laughed at them, stole a croissant from the bag, and unlocked Alex's front door.

The three of us trooped up the stairs to the home office. I pulled the password book out of the drawer where I'd left it and switched on the computer. In no time I opened the *Office* file, entered a second password, and found a complete list of Alex's clients.

"It worries me that I think you've done this before," grumbled Wolf.

I kept quiet and neither admitted nor denied that I had poked around previously in Alex's private files.

"So you think I'm right?" I asked. "It was probably an irate client?"

"Someone sure wanted him out of the way."

I printed off Alex's calendar for the year, too.

Wolf examined the pages as they churned out of the computer. "Interesting information here."

"Have you talked to Alex's assistant?" asked Nina.

"Can't find her," said Wolf.

Nina and I gasped at the same time.

"She went missing?" asked Nina in between bites of croissant.

Wolf shook his head, but kept his eyes on Alex's schedule. "No one has reported her missing. But we haven't been able to reach her."

"She's scared." I turned off the computer. "Alex told me if Nellie didn't murder Grainger, then there was a killer on the loose who would do anything to hide the truth. I told his assistant the same sort of thing. She needs to be careful. Whoever did this to Alex was the worst kind of human being imaginable. He would think nothing of hurting her, too."

"Wish you hadn't told her that." Wolf grunted. "She probably has a better idea than anyone but Alex of who might want him dead."

I shuddered at the thought. "Are his folks here yet? Have you talked to them?"

"I have spoken to them. They're in touch with his doctor. They were out in Idaho in their recreational vehicle when Alex was attacked. They thought the fastest way back would be to fly, so they booked the next flight out, which was the following day. But when they arrived, the airport had closed due to an encroaching forest fire. Their only choice was to drive south, significantly out of their way to avoid the fire, so they've been delayed in getting here."

"They must be sick with worry," I said. "I'll go over there and sit with him for a while today if the nurses let me."

"I'm going to take the vial straight back to forensics. Never thought I'd say this, but thanks to Natasha, we may be able to wrap up the investigation of Patsy Lee's murder."

While I locked the door, Wolf drove away.

"It was thoughtful of him to bring me breakfast," said Nina.

"Thanks for coming over here with me. He's still sensitive about being seen alone with me."

"He always will be," said Nina. "You're such a dangerous and wicked woman."

We couldn't help giggling a little bit.

"So"—I said as we walked home—"if Willa and Peter murdered Patsy Lee, then who murdered Grainger?"

The words were barely out of my mouth when someone shouted my name.

"Sophie!"

"Don't look now, but it's Peter," Nina whispered. "Think we can pretend we didn't hear him?"

Of course, I had to look. He waved us over to a restaurant where he was seated at an outdoor table.

"What do we do?" asked Nina.

I squinted at a guy in a baseball cap eating breakfast not too far away from Peter. "Play it cool. There's a cop watching him. Pretend you know nothing, maybe we can learn something. Do *not* mention that vial!"

"I can do that. Hi, Peter!" she called in a melodious voice.

"Won't you ladies join me?" he asked.

"We had an early breakfast," I said. "But thank you for the invitation."

"Well then, how about keeping me company while I eat?"

I was pretty sure that I stopped breathing for a moment. But we were outdoors and there was a cop only a few tables away. What was Peter going to do? Stab us with a butter knife? "That would be nice. Thanks."

Nina and I skirted the little fence around the tables and joined him.

"I'll be leaving Old Town fairly soon." Peter picked up a slice of bacon and noshed on it. "Sure you don't want some? Nothing is better than good bacon."

We declined.

"I'm sorry things didn't work out with Natasha," I said, enjoying the soft breeze.

His beefy face turned the color of the meat in his bacon. "She sure taught me a lesson. You know, when I met Patsy Lee, she had a warmth that everybody wanted to be around, including me. I should have known something was off when I didn't see that in Natasha. Turned out the network liked the show, anyway, but I believe I'll steer clear of pigheaded people like her."

He took a big bite of ham. "I feel like a heel eating in front of you ladies. You sure you don't want anything to eat?"

"We've had breakfast," Nina said in a hurry. She held up the bag she'd been carrying.

"Well, I tell ya, I'm gonna miss Patsy Lee somethin' fierce."

"But you divorced her," Nina blurted.

"That was Patsy Lee's doin'. She got to thinkin' I was just a country fellow who couldn't hold my own with the city slickers. We didn't end well, did we? But we had a great time on the road there. Nobody else has ever made me laugh as hard or feel as loved. Don't suppose anyone ever will. For a while there Patsy Lee and I had something special. Not everybody gets to experience that." Peter gulped coffee and swiped his mouth with a napkin.

He spoke about her so lovingly, it was hard to imagine that he had poisoned her.

"Rumor has it that you two had a fight the night before she died." Nina said it sweet as honey, like she was totally innocent and making conversation, but I nearly panicked. What did she think she was doing?

"Is that why the cops are on me like fleas on a dog?" He looked past us and raised his coffee cup as though he was toasting someone.

Nina and I turned around. The plainclothes cop wiggled his fingers at us and continued eating his breakfast.

"I have come to recognize," said Peter, "that memories are a lot like photographs. You ditch the lousy ones, get rid of everything that is out of focus, and in the end you keep the ones that were the way you wanted them to be. Patsy Lee and I had a little discussion that night about how she made it to the top, but it wasn't worth remembering."

I played dumb. "I don't understand. What do you mean?"

Peter wiped his mouth again and sat back in his chair. "You got to psych out your competition. Make 'em worry about somethin' else so their minds aren't focused on baking. Haven't you seen shows where a really great chef gets the boot because he forgot to use an ingredient? Or something slowed him down and he didn't get the food on the plates on time?" Peter laughed. "Makes for excitement on the show."

I tried to sound clueless in the hope that he would tell us more. "Those aren't just glitches?"

"Not all the time."

"It seems kind of underhanded," said Nina.

"Patsy Lee didn't think so when she was a nobody, but seeing her old pals made her feel guilty. Especially about Nellie."

Nina and I shared a look. Was he about to confess? Why didn't I have a recorder with me? Did my phone have one? There wasn't any time to find out now.

Chapter 34

Dear Natasha,
Why does my pie dough crack? It's so frustrating.
Can I patch it or do I have to start over?
Breaking Up in Coffee, California

Dear Breaking Up,
You need to add liquid to your dough. Not much,
though—only drops. You can patch it by moisten-
ing your fingers and sprinkling with a teeny bit of
flour.

Natasha

"Now hold on there. Don't go jumping to conclusions." Peter's eyebrows dipped in dismay. "I may have pulled a few stunts. Everybody does. I'm not proud of everything I did to get Patsy Lee to the top. Did you think all those stars get there by being sweet and lettin' people walk all over them? You got to be tough. You got to use everything you have to move up in this world. But, ladies, I have never murdered anyone."

"That's a relief," I said, not believing him. "But then why would Patsy Lee feel bad about Nellie?"

Peter pulled out his wallet and handed the waitress his credit card. "I don't believe I'll use that tactic again. It seemed clever at the time, but it went too far."

I couldn't help myself. I pushed him a little by asking, "Did it involve Grainger?"

"Naw. Honey, it doesn't matter now, anyway. Everybody has moved on. It's time I did."

"I heard Grainger was planning a TV show about his restaurant. Were you involved with that?" I asked. "It sounds like something right up your alley."

"A clever deduction, Miss Sophie. I was shocked when Grainger was killed. Whoever murdered him axed the show, too. Would have been a huge success with that loony old man shouting at everybody. Huge. Has Tommy Earl told you the good news?"

"No," we chimed.

The waitress returned with a charge slip for him to sign. I noticed that he added a very generous tip.

"The next time you hear Tommy Earl's name, he'll be on his way to fame and fortune."

"You're taking him on as a client?" I asked.

"But what about his bakery?" whined Nina.

"The bakery will continue, sugar pie, don't you worry about that. I signed him as a client right after the bake-off." Peter rose to his feet. "It's been delightful meetin' you, ladies." He eyed me for a moment. "Sophie, darlin', you have a little bit of Patsy Lee's charm. If you ever decide to make the move to superstar cook, you give me a call." He handed me his card and left the table.

"Do it!" Nina screeched.

"Nina," I whispered, "the man is a murderer and a cheat."

"Too bad. I could have been your sidekick. We could have bought side-by-side beach mansions."

I elbowed her and pointed discreetly. The cop had left and was casually ambling along behind Peter.

"Wolf obviously put a tail on him. It's just a matter of time before they arrest him."

We left the table and headed home.

"Do you think Peter murdered Grainger?" I asked. "Grainger's brother told me he had a hot temper. Maybe two hotheaded bullies faced off alone in the middle of the night."

"What about the poisonous rhubarb pie?" asked Nina.

"You could bake one."

"Excuse me? I believe you saw my mangled dough in Tommy Earl's class."

"It's easy enough to buy piecrust and nab rhubarb leaves from someone's garden," I said.

"Patsy Lee might have done the baking," Nina suggested. "Maybe that's what they argued about. The guilt finally got to her. If she baked it, he might feel like he never killed anyone, even though he did."

I stopped walking. "Patsy Lee could have baked the pie and taken it to Grainger as a peace offering."

Nina nodded. "They sat outside and Grainger ate it, but Peter was in the alley, listening. When Grainger didn't die, Peter stabbed him."

"I'd call that murder," I said.

"Me too. But that could be exactly how it went down."

"Do you think they stole the rhubarb from Nellie's ex-husband's garden?" I asked. "It does seem odd that he happened to be growing rhubarb."

"I'm game to check out their garden," said Nina. "My husband is out of town until Saturday. I don't have anything pressing to do."

We walked along our street. My house seemed fairly peaceful. I wasn't sure if Bernie and Willa were still there.

We continued to Dooley's house.

"He's probably at work," said Nina. "Maybe we should just peek in the garden."

"Let's at least knock on the door first." We walked up to the door and Aly opened it before we could bang the dragonfly-shaped door knocker.

"Is Mom out of prison?" asked Aly, her eyes wide with excitement.

"I'm sorry, honey. We're still working on it," I said.

Dooley appeared behind her. "Won't you come in?"

"Actually, we were hoping we could see your garden," I said.

Aly rolled her eyes like a bored child. "You just made my dad the happiest person in the world."

Dooley chuckled. "I love to show off my garden, but not many people are interested in it. I'm glad we were home. Somebody has an appointment with the dentist today."

Aly groaned. "We could skip it and spend time in the garden."

He led us through the house to the kitchen, which over-looked a back porch and an expansive garden. We stepped outside.

"It's gorgeous!" I exclaimed. "I've never seen a garden quite like this."

Nina frowned. "Is it a vegetable garden or a flower garden?"

"It's an insect garden," chirped Aly.

Bees flew peacefully between flowers that bloomed around a pond. Trees offered shade in a back corner, but the other corner was bare dirt.

"Are you working on that spot in the back?" I asked.

"The dirt? No that's intentional," said Dooley.

"For burrowers," explained Aly.

I understood the look she'd given us. This was a very unusual garden and she must have heard her dad tell peo-ple about it many times. To Aly it was all old hat.

"My favorite part is the butterfly diner." She took me by the hand and led me around tall grasses on the right side of the pond to pink and purple butterfly bushes, orange butterfly weed, bright yellow coreopsis, lavender wild geranium, and small golden sunflowers.

"Those plants are native to our area," Dooley explained.

"The hibiscus is my favorite." Aly pointed at vivid pink flowers with ruby centers.

Nearby a row of tomato plants offered hefty red, orange, and yellow fruit.

I spied Swiss chard and cabbage. "Do you still grow rhubarb?" I asked.

Dooley and Aly exchanged a look.

"It's behind the tomatoes, near the dock weeds. I wish Dad wouldn't plant rhubarb," said Aly. "It got Mom into trouble."

"I plant them for the rhubarb curculio beetle," said Dooley. "They're such fascinating creatures. They have little snouts, kind of like miniature anteaters."

He bent to examine a stalk and pulled a miniature magnifying glass out of his pocket. "There's one! Do you see it? About half an inch long."

He aimed his magnifier at it, and I bent to examine the beetle. "Oh, cool! It does have a snout."

I made room for Nina, but when I looked at her, I realized there was no way she was going to examine a snouted bug or any other bug for that matter.

She wrinkled her nose. "Is something burning?"

"Tommy Earl built one of those fire pits in his yard. It's quite impressive. He was entertaining a lady friend the night before last. The breeze picks up the scent for days."

"Wong!" said Nina. "I bet he had a date with Wong."

It was a good guess, but my thoughts ran darker. The night before last someone had set fire to Alex's office.

Chapter 35

Dear Sophie,
Isn't there an easy way to crimp a pie edge? I wear
my nails long and they get in the way!
             Manicured Lady in Snapfinger, Georgia

Dear Manicured Lady,
The simplest edge by far is achieved by crimping
the edge with the tines of a fork!
                                       Sophie

It would be easy enough to confirm Tommy Earl's date
with Wong. There was something else that I wanted to
ask Dooley about, but not in front of Aly.

"Aly, do you think your dad would let you pick a couple of nice tomatoes for us to take home?"

"Sure. Would you like some ears of corn, too? We've
been eating it every night."

"That would be lovely. Thank you."

Aly grabbed a basket from the kitchen and retreated
into the garden to collect a harvest.

"Dooley," I said, "I really need to know who you were

seeing when you received the blackmail letter. It could be key to getting Nellie out of prison."

"But I wasn't seeing anyone."

"Then why would someone send you a blackmail letter? The person who did that must have had reason to think you were involved with someone else."

"I have thought about that for years. It ruined my marriage. I was sick over it. But truly, I wasn't having an affair."

"What about a woman at work?" suggested Nina. "Maybe someone was friendly with you and someone else jumped to incorrect conclusions?"

"You think it could be someone in my office? There *are* a few ladies in my department."

"Do you have the letter?" I asked.

"Yeah. I'll get it for you."

Aly carried the basket full of goodies up to the porch.

"They're wonderful. Thank you so much, Aly!" I said.

Aly led the way into the kitchen, where Dooley handed me a clear plastic food storage bag with a letter in it.

"Dooley, did you ever make any payments?

"Many nights I have lain awake wishing I had made payments. I guess it wouldn't have changed anything. But perhaps it would have. Nellie wouldn't have left me and might not be in prison now." He seemed sad when he added, "In the dark of night when it's quiet, one thinks these things."

Aly reached for her dad's hand.

I was tearing up. "Thank you for the veggies. We'll be in touch."

Nina took the basket and we left. On the short walk back, she examined the contents. "How are you going to use these?"

"I guess you'll have to come to dinner and find out."

"You're on." Nina handed me the basket, and I turned to my house.

I opened the kitchen door to find Mars with Daisy and Mochie. "What happened to Bernie, Willa, and Natasha?"

"Bernie took Willa to see a lawyer. Natasha went to meet someone for lunch." He peered in the basket. "I love fresh corn!"

I put away the vegetables and took strawberries out of the refrigerator. I poured them into a large colander to wash them.

"Are you baking a pie?"

"Yes, want to help me?"

He sighed. "Sure. What do I do?"

I handed him the colander of strawberries. "Take off the stems and cut them into quarters."

He groaned. "This better be a great pie."

I pulled cornstarch, sugar, and graham crackers out of the pantry and preheated the oven. "Where were you two nights ago?"

"I did not beat up Alex."

After spinning the graham crackers in the food processor with melted butter, I pressed them into a pie pan and slid it in the oven. "I know you didn't. I'm just thinking."

"That's always trouble."

"Very funny. Did you know that Wong is dating Tommy Earl?"

"Really? You know, I can imagine them together."

"Apparently, he has a fire pit in his backyard."

"I see where you're going with this. Fire pits are still all the rage. Bernie has one. You have a fireplace in your backyard. That doesn't mean one of you set fire to Alex's office."

I scooped out two cups of cut-up strawberries and mashed them in the pot. "Bernie seems very close to Willa, doesn't he?"

"I don't think it's anything romantic. He believes in her, just like I believe in you. Friends have to stick together in moments like this."

I poured the cornstarch and sugar over the mashed strawberries and smashed them all together before adding water. "You don't think Willa was in cahoots with Peter? He seems almost like a Svengali. I don't see the attraction, personally. But Patsy Lee and Natasha were crazy for him. Then again, Natasha was also crazy for you," I teased.

"That's me—a Svengali. It's the same in politics. Men with big ambitions seem to attract women."

"Has anyone ever tried to blackmail you?" I asked.

"You're making my head spin. Are we talking about Bernie, Willa, Natasha, Tommy Earl, or Peter?"

I took the mashed strawberries off the stove. I picked up the bowl of strawberries, placed a layer on the bottom of the pie pan, and ladled the mashed berries over them. I finished assembling the strawberry pie and placed it in the refrigerator to set up.

Pulling on a pair of gloves, I sat down at the table with Mars and took the letter out of the plastic sleeve.

The envelope was unremarkable. It was the simple white letter size that I used to send payments to people. There was no return address. It was postmarked Washington, DC.

I slid the letter out and read aloud to Mars.

I know you cheated on your spouse. You really should be more careful if you're going to sneak around. For a mere $2,000 paid in bitcoin, you can buy my silence on this subject.

Don't think that telling your spouse about your infidelity will rid you of the problem. The humiliation and anger will result in you being alone.

*To avoid this and make me go away, you need
only pay me by bitcoin. Precise instructions are
enclosed.*

Still watching you.

"You have to be kidding me!" Mars reached for the letter, but I snatched it away.

"You have to wear gloves. There could be fingerprints on this."

"What kind of jerk would send a letter like that?"

"What would you have done if you received it while we were married?"

"That's easy. I would have trashed it. I might have shared it with you first, just for a laugh."

"It wouldn't have worried you, even if you weren't having an affair?"

"I don't think so. It's clearly some kind of scam. But I see what you mean. Some people might have flipped out about it."

I handed him gloves to put on. "Nellie left Dooley because of this letter."

"Dooley? That skinny guy you were worried about?"

"That's the one. It ruined his marriage."

"Was he having an affair?"

"He says he wasn't."

"You know, this is really very anonymous. I mean in terms of the recipient. Look at it carefully. It doesn't mention his name or Nellie's. Not even on the envelope. It's like someone stuck this in his mailbox."

"In a way that almost makes it scarier. Someone knew where he lived."

"You're missing my point. You could put these in every mailbox on any street. Chances are good that you'd hit a couple of guilty people."

"*Eww.* That's just sick."

"It's totally twisted. Think about it. It doesn't matter whether the husband or wife finds it. If they're having an affair, they panic. If they're not having an affair, they assume it was meant for their spouse and they flip out."

"Which is exactly what happened to Dooley and Nellie."

"But no one else on this street received one, right?" asked Mars.

"It was years ago. But we lived here then. I suspect we would have heard something about it." I started laughing. "Unless we received one and you never told me."

"This pie better be really good if I have to take that kind of abuse."

"I don't think anyone else got a letter. It would be sufficiently upsetting to throw a person off in a competition, wouldn't it?" I asked.

"It's just enough to put a seed of doubt in your head. You think it was one of Peter's stunts to give Patsy Lee a leg up?"

"That's exactly what I think. What's more, I suspect that's what Patsy Lee and Peter argued about that night. Maybe he intended to do it to someone else, and Patsy Lee wouldn't stand for it."

At that moment the phone rang. It was Wolf. "Just wanted to let you know that the fingerprints on the vial are a match for Peter's. We're picking him up for questioning now and sending the vial to the lab to be analyzed."

"So it's over."

"I wouldn't go quite that far yet, but it looks like we might be wrapping it up soon."

"Thanks for letting me know, Wolf." I hung up the phone. "They have Willa's fingerprints on the coffee cup and Peter's fingerprints on the vial Natasha found in the limo."

"I'd say that's pretty conclusive."

Feeling a little melancholy about not making more progress for Nellie and Aly, I slid into the banquette opposite Mars. "I really thought the person who killed Patsy Lee had also murdered Grainger and tried to kill Alex."

"That would have been a neat little package. I don't think that happens with murder. Those three incidents are probably all unrelated."

"Alex had nothing to do with Nellie's trial, yet I feel like he tried to warn me against looking into that case."

Mars shrugged. "That's sound advice."

"Why? Why is that sound advice? Nellie may be doing time for someone else's crime."

"If that's true, then a killer is on the loose and you wouldn't want to aggravate him."

"Thank you. That's what Alex said. I thought I had somehow angered one of Alex's clients, and that led to the attack on him."

"That would mean—"

"That Alex knows who really killed Grainger. And worse, he let Nellie rot in prison for five years," I said, finishing his sentence.

Mars folded his arms across his chest. "Attorney-client privilege."

"How could that even happen?" I asked. "It seems impossible that he would know."

"Maybe he'll spill the beans when he wakes up."

I glanced at my watch. "His parents have been detained. I went to see him last night. He was totally unresponsive."

"When's the pie being served?"

"That's what's important to you? Tonight for dessert."

"Am I invited?"

"Of course. Would I ask you to cut the strawberries and then not give you any pie?"

"I'll bring Bernie."

"Great. We can eat outside with a fire in the fireplace."

Mars took off with Daisy, and I spent a couple of hours

working, but Nellie and Alex were never far from my mind. After a short nap I headed to the grocery store, but changed my mind and stopped by the hospital first.

When I walked along the corridor in the hospital, I noticed immediately that the guard was gone. My heart beat faster and I sped up to a jog.

I swung open the door to Alex's room and could feel the blood draining from my face. It was empty. The bed was made, waiting for the next patient. The flowers were gone, and there wasn't the first shred of evidence that Alex had ever been there.

Chapter 36

Dear Natasha,
Why do I have to cut slits in the top of my pie?
                              Curious in Piddleville, Georgia

Dear Curious,
The filling steams in fruit pies. By venting the top
crust, you're allowing the steam to exit the pie.
                                                    Natasha

I backed away from the door and gazed around. Did I have the wrong room? The wrong floor? Everything seemed to be correct. I retreated to the nurses' station and asked for Alex.

The nurse barely looked at me. "He's been moved to a different floor. Take the elevator down one level."

That had to be good news! I waited impatiently for the elevator and nearly leaped out of it on the floor below.

I didn't need anyone to tell me where his room was. I spotted Wong sitting outside his door. I hurried toward her.

"Alex is better?"

Her eyes were sad. "Not that I can tell. But I hear his

parents might arrive today." As I started to go inside, she said, "Sophie, don't expect much."

I peered in the room, expecting the worst. Some of the bandages on his face had been removed, revealing swelling and bruises.

"Can you hear me, Alex?" I took his hand. "Squeeze my finger if you can."

Nothing happened. He wasn't any different at all.

I sat with him for a few minutes, telling him about the fingerprints on the vial and the coffee cup.

Pretending he could hear me, I said, "Hey, I hear your parents will be here today."

Clutching his hand in mine, I tried to position his fingers so that he could squeeze mine and tried again. "Squeeze my fingers, Alex. Try really hard to let me know you hear what I'm saying."

Nothing happened.

I kissed his forehead gently. "You get some rest, and I'll stop by later on today. Okay?"

I left the room, and asked Wong, "What have you heard? Is he off the meds that induced a coma?"

Wong swallowed hard. "Yes. Now it's up to him. The nurses tell me that it can take days, even weeks, for them to come around."

"How awful. Maybe the voices of his parents will reach him. How come you look so gloomy?"

"Tommy Earl and I were just getting to know each other and now he's leaving for New York."

"I'm sorry, Wong. Peter told me he has big plans for Tommy Earl." What was I saying? When Peter was arrested, it would put a quick end to Tommy Earl's plans for stardom. Suddenly I was at a total loss. What could I say? I waited for her to speak.

"Just my luck, huh?"

"I'm so sorry." I said goodbye and got out of there fast before I felt compelled to tell her that Tommy Earl probably wasn't going anywhere. It seemed to me that Peter left a trail of disappointed people in his wake.

On the way home I stopped at the grocery store. I picked up eggs, steaks, Panko, jumbo shrimp, lemons, and six gorgeous apples, which made me want to bake another pie. I drove home, parked the car in the garage, and toted my groceries into the kitchen.

How soon would Alex be able to eat pie? I took some buttery pie dough out of the freezer to let it thaw while I put things away and preheated the oven. Then I set to work peeling apples and slicing them as thin as I could. In a microwave-safe container, I heated sugar and heavy cream for caramel sauce. I tossed the apples with heavenly scented apple pie spice and lemon juice, and then added the caramel sauce to them and tossed them again. After rolling out the dough and transferring it to the pie pan, I poured the sliced apples on top of it. I poked at them just a bit to get rid of any obvious air holes and sprinkled just a pinch of coarse salt over them. I cut strips of the remaining dough and crisscrossed them on the top. A quick egg wash on the exposed dough, a sprinkle of coarse sugar and salt, and it was ready to go into the oven. I had just closed the oven door when I saw Wolf's car pull up outside my house, followed by a squad car.

Nina bolted out of her front door and ran across the street.

Wolf and a uniformed officer walked up to my front door.

I hurried to the foyer and flung open the door. "What happened? Did you arrest Peter?"

Wolf looked me in the eyes and swallowed hard.

"Is it Alex? What happened?"

"Ma'am, are you Sophia Winston?" asked the uniformed officer.

"It's Sophie, not *Sophia*," I corrected him. "And Wolf knows who I am."

"I'm sorry, Sophie," said Wolf. "I'm so sorry."

"Is Alex dead?"

"Ma'am," said the uniformed officer, "I'd like you to accompany me to the police station."

I gazed at Wolf, who looked miserable. "Just go with him, Sophie."

"I don't understand. Am I under arrest or something?"

"We need to ask you some questions, ma'am. It would be helpful if you came with me willingly."

It had been years since I was carted off to the police station, but that nightmare came flooding back to me. I felt weak in the knees, even though I knew I hadn't done anything wrong. "I have a pie in the oven."

Those words were possibly the most ridiculous thing I could have said under the circumstances, but I had to turn off the oven before I left the house.

"I'll take care of it," said Nina. "And I'll call Mars and Bernie. They'll know what to do."

I hoped so. Wolf probably knew exactly what to do, but I had the sinking feeling he couldn't help me, or he wouldn't be standing there apologizing to me.

"Thank you, Nina." It came out as a whisper, although that wasn't what I had intended. I walked to the squad car.

The uniformed officer opened the back door and I slid inside like a criminal.

Chapter 37

Dear Sophie,
I love meringue pies, but they always weep! How do I prevent that?
            Crying in My Pie in Shoo Fly, Illinois

Dear Crying in My Pie,
Be sure the filling is hot when you add the meringue so it cooks a bit from underneath. Storing in an airtight container will help, too. And beware rainy weather. Meringue behaves better on dry days.
                                    Sophie

The officer didn't say a word all the way to the police station. He opened the door and escorted me inside. Another officer took over and showed me to an interrogation room.

And there I sat for what seemed an eternity. Finally a plainclothes cop entered and identified himself as Sergeant Mikulski.

"I guess you know why you're here?" he asked.

I knew I wasn't supposed to answer questions without an attorney present. But *my attorney* was in a hospital bed, in a coma. I figured it couldn't hurt to answer that particular question. "I don't have a clue."

He gazed at me intensely, like a buzzard looking for dinner.

"Now, Ms. Winston, we have never met before, but they tell me you're fairly sharp. I'd think you might have some idea why we brought you in."

I did not like this guy. "Where's Wolf?"

"Wolf is busy working."

I looked up at the mirror on the wall and suspected I knew exactly where he was. Wolf was too close to me to be in the room, but I would have bet my shoes that he was on the other side of the mirror watching and listening. "What is it that you want from me, Sergeant Mikulski?"

"You seem agitated."

"Do you bring in many people who aren't agitated about being here?"

Mikulski sat back and stared at me. "Most of them have committed a crime."

I looked him straight in the eyes. "I have not." Unless it was computer hacking! Had Wolf turned me in?

"Then why are you upset?"

"Why don't you cut to the chase, Sergeant? Tell me what you want to know."

"Things will go easier on you if you cooperate, Ms. Winston."

"I appreciate that. But you'll have to tell me why I'm here."

"I hear you have a nice house."

Was he kidding? Was that some misguided attempt to chat or was it some kind of threat? I kept quiet. If he didn't tell me what he wanted to know, I wasn't going to give him any information. I guessed he wanted me to break down and confess something, but I had nothing to confess. I stared at him.

"Do you mow your own lawn?"

What?! What kind of nonsense was that?

He folded his arms across his chest. *Uh-oh.* He was irritated with me. Well, too bad.

"Sergeant," I said gently, trying very hard to speak softly and not show how aggravated I felt, "I'm sure you didn't bring me in just to ask who mows my grass."

He sat forward and eyed me. It was like a chess match in a nightmare.

"A lot of people around town are calling you a hero for saving Alex German."

A glimmer of a lightbulb went on in my head. This was about Alex? I chose my words carefully. "I'm not a hero. It was just lucky timing."

"Was it?"

I tilted my head. Surely, they didn't think *I* set the fire?

"Why were you there, Ms. Winston?"

My brain went into overdrive—lawn, lawn mower, gasoline, fire. Why would they think I set the fire? It made no sense to me.

"Did you surprise him by going through the back entrance?"

Aha! It was a trick question. Neither *no* nor *yes* would be a good answer. I continued to stare at him, doing my best not to look scared about where he was going with this.

"Did you have an argument? Is that why you attacked Alex?"

At last he had gotten to the point of the interrogation. I frowned. Had someone told them we argued? Suddenly I was feeling the heat.

"I would like to call an attorney."

He sighed, and I knew why. Merely uttering those words forced him to bring the questioning to a complete halt.

He left the room. I could imagine him out in the hallway talking with Wolf about me and how I refused to answer his questions. What a nightmare. I hoped Nina, Mars, or Bernie had phoned an attorney. There was nothing I could do but wait.

Fortunately, I didn't have to wait long. Benton Evans walked in, cool as a cucumber.

He carried a black leather briefcase and wore a navy blue suit. I knew him well from the social circuit. He was a big supporter of the library and the animal shelter. Well into his sixties, Benton carried himself with the confidence of a man comfortable with himself and his life. He spoke with a Southern drawl. "Sorry to take so long, Sophie. I was in court."

He sat down with me. "What do you say I buy you a cup of coffee and we have a chat?"

I grinned. "You're on."

Benton escorted me out of the interrogation room. It was wrong of me and I knew it, but I smiled broadly at Sergeant Mikulski.

When I had passed him, I heard him ask Wolf, "Did you really date her?"

Benton grinned and I giggled.

Benton opened the passenger door of a gleaming red MGB convertible for me. It was vintage, if not an antique. I hoped that creep Mikulski noticed that I was getting a lift home in a most enviable car.

Benton drove us to King Street, parked, and escorted me into a café, where he led me directly to a table in a back corner.

When we had lattes in front of us, Benton said, "Darlin', there's a rumor around town that you and Alex had an argument at Market Square."

"That's why they arrested me?"

"Y'all do a little bit of yellin', did you?"

"No. Not at all. I was asking him about Grainger Gibbard's murder and Alex didn't think I should be looking into a closed case."

"No screaming?"

"I'm afraid not. I would guess most people didn't even know we were having a little disagreement. In fact, I'm somewhat surprised that there would even be a rumor of that sort."

He nodded. "Then you argued about it again in his office?"

"No. Never. I didn't even see him again until the night of the fire. Who would spread that kind of malicious rumor? And why would they bring me in for interrogation over something so flimsy?"

"Well, darlin', it seems they found your fingerprints on the gas can at the scene."

Chapter 38

Dear Sophie,
What's your favorite way to decorate a pie?
                              Unoriginal in Surprise, Indiana

Dear Unoriginal,
Use small cookie cutters to cut leaves out of your dough and place them on the edge of the pie all the way around. It makes a lovely presentation.
                                                    Sophie

I spewed latte on the table.

"I'm so sorry!" I dabbed at it with a napkin and fetched more paper napkins to clean it up. Benton was always so unflappable and there I was spitting latte. How vulgar of me. "I'm sorry, that took me totally by surprise."

"I can see that."

"Sergeant Mikulski asked me if I mow my own lawn. I guess he was trying to get me to say I had a gas can."

"Do you?"

I shrugged. "Don't you? Everybody has one for their mowers and weed-whackers and such."

"Did you tell him that?"

"No. I clammed up because I didn't understand what was going on. I didn't want to say the wrong thing."

"Very shrewd of you. Have you seen this gas can lately?"

"No. I'll look for it when I go home, but I guess we both know it won't be there."

Benton settled back in his chair, so I told him exactly what had happened, from the discussion about the Grainger Gibbard murder to finding Alex beat up in his office. "I even had Daisy with me. Who would take a dog with them to beat someone up? And what's my motive? I had no reason to attack Alex or burn down his office. *No, no, no.* That had to be someone who had something to hide—something that Alex knew and that was in his files."

Benton's eyebrows lifted. "Why would that person want to frame you?"

I pointed at him. "That's the real question. It had to be someone who knew about my relationship with Alex."

"Which is just about everyone in town," said Benton.

"Maybe I know the secret," I mused.

"What secret?"

"Whatever it is that Alex knows and that person wants to hide. I've thought all along it must be one of Alex's clients. Why else would he burn the office? He was trying to get rid of files. What do you think?" I asked. "You know your clients' secrets. What would be so bad that they would want to kill you to prevent you from talking?"

Benton took a deep breath. "Some people don't want anyone to know what's in their wills, or who the beneficiaries are. Other folks are fussy about their business transactions and don't want the details to be public."

"Bernie says everyone has a secret."

Benton smiled. "I suppose he's right in a way. Most of

our secrets are important to us, but not to many other people."

"What do you mean?"

"Let's say you are charged with assault on Alex and setting his office on fire."

"Heaven forbid."

"But you have an alibi. Because right up until the very moment when you saw his hand in the window, you were with Wolf."

I gasped. "That would be an excellent alibi. But that didn't happen."

"This is just an example. You and Wolf might not want to admit that because he's married. So the two of you would have a secret that not many other people would care about, but it would matter a lot to Wolf and his wife."

I couldn't help thinking about Dooley and the letter accusing him of having an affair. Someone was banking on exactly what Benton was talking about. A secret that wouldn't matter to most people, but would create havoc for Dooley and Nellie. And it just might throw Nellie off her stride if she was baking in a competition. *Peter.* That was what Peter did to Nellie that Patsy Lee regretted.

"Sophie? Are you okay?" asked Benton.

I nodded my head. My mind was spinning. What if Mars was right? Maybe the murders weren't connected at all. It was looking like Peter and Willa murdered Patsy Lee. What if Sergeant Gibbard killed Grainger, just like Martha thought? "Is there any way possible that Alex would know one of his clients was a murderer, but someone else was convicted?"

Benton appeared surprised. In a scholarly tone he said, "What an interesting proposition. In that case Alex would have to keep his client's secret. And what a secret that would be!"

"It would also be an overwhelming motive."

"Just so I'm clear, we're not talking about you, are we?" asked Benton.

I leaned toward him. "No. But I think Alex knows who killed Grainger Gibbard."

Benton squinted at me. "That's quite an assertion."

"That's the person who stole my gas can, assaulted Alex, and set his office on fire."

"If that's the case, then all we have to do is ask Alex."

"They've had him in a medically induced coma. Think you can keep me out of the slammer long enough for him to recover?" I asked.

"That's a tall order. But I'll do my best."

Benton offered to drive me home, but as fun as it was to ride in his convertible, I declined. I felt like walking. It wasn't far and I needed some time to think things through.

What I didn't understand was why the perpetrator would have fingered *me*. Why try to frame me? To get me out of the way? Because I was an easy target? Or did I know something that worried him?

I turned at the corner and walked along the alley behind my house. It would have been easy for someone to open the gate to the alley. I pulled up the latch and let myself in. My garage was connected to the house by an open outdoor porch with a roof over the top of it. I opened the door to the garage and looked for my gas can. It came as no surprise to me that it was gone.

When I finally walked into my kitchen, a cheer went up. Daisy pranced in circles, and Mochie stood on the table and reached a paw out to me. It was as if even the animals knew I had been in trouble.

"Are you okay?" asked Nina. She peered in my face like she was checking to see if someone had punched me.

Bernie let out a huge sigh. "We're glad you're home."

"What took so long?" asked Mars.

I sat down on one of the fireside chairs. Mochie jumped into my lap, and I patted Daisy at the same time. "In a nutshell, whoever started the fire at Alex's office stole the gas can from my garage. It has my fingerprints on it."

Nina handed me a mug of hot tea. "Just the way you like it."

"Thanks, Nina." I gazed around at my friends. "Did any of you hear a rumor that Alex and I had an argument?"

"The mailman asked me about it," said Nina.

"I heard it at the restaurant," Bernie admitted.

"Mars?" I asked.

"I got it from Remy."

"Interesting. Everyone in town was talking about something that was a private conversation at Market Square while we ate lunch. It wasn't heated. There was no yelling or anything like that. How did that morph into an argument that everyone heard about?"

"It sounds like the kind of thing Peter did to Patsy Lee's competitors," said Nina. "It's easy to start a rumor."

"What do you bet that's how Tommy Earl got a reputation for drinking on the job?" I said.

"And Roger being inappropriate with women," Bernie suggested. "He's always been a gentleman in my experiences with him."

"So Peter may be behind this. I'm glad they nabbed him before he could hurt anyone else. Hey, which one of you sent Benton to the police station?"

Mars raised his hand. "I told you that if you were imprisoned like Nellie, I would move heaven and earth to get you out."

"Thanks, Mars. I owe you."

"Are you still up for dinner tonight, Sophie?" asked Nina. "I could order takeout."

"And let that gorgeous fresh corn go to waste?" Mars looked horrified.

"I can throw everything on the grill," said Bernie. "And Sophie made two desserts before she got grilled."

Everyone moaned at his terrible pun. Oddly enough, that silly remark made me feel much better. It had been an awful day.

It was six thirty when we gathered for dinner out on my covered deck. Bernie had brought Willa along. She chatted about her interrogation by Wolf while Bernie manned the grill. Mars stoked the fire in the fireplace, and Nina whipped up strawberry bourbon lemonade. I felt totally pampered as I sipped my drink through a straw and listened to Willa.

"Honestly, how anyone could think for a second that I could harm someone, much less Patsy Lee, is simply beyond me. And how do you defend yourself against fingerprints on a coffee cup? It's not like you have an alibi and can claim you weren't there. I was there. I bought a cup of coffee from Moos and Brews, just like hundreds of other people did that day."

And that was when it hit me.

Chapter 39

Dear Natasha,
I hate pie. I hate making the dough, and I loathe trying to create an acceptable edge. But I like the fillings! Any suggestions?
    Fillings for Me in Horsetooth Heights, Colorado

Dear Fillings for Me,
Bake cobblers.

                            Natasha

"There are too many fingerprints!" I announced.
    They looked at me like I had lost my mind.
    "Don't you see? What do they call it? A modus operandi? It was the same person. He thought the best way to frame other people was through their fingerprints. He knew the police would check for them. It's so basic. And it worked for him. I bet you anything that the person who murdered Patsy Lee is the same person who attacked Alex."
    "Peter?" asked Bernie.
    "I don't think he would have been so precise. Whoever

did this made sure his or her fingerprints weren't there. It was someone else."

I sipped on my drink and tuned them out while they speculated. Nellie had been framed, too, by the missing rhubarb from Dooley's garden. One person had murdered two people and almost killed Alex.

Sergeant Gibbard had been on my mind as a possibility, but I now mentally crossed him off. If I was right, and one person had committed all three acts, then Sergeant Gibbard was in the clear. He had no reason that I knew of to want to murder Patsy Lee. In fact, I didn't think he had even attended the pie festival.

It always seemed to come back to the Apex Pie group. Now that I was a person of interest in Alex's attack, I didn't think Wolf would tell me if any of the Apex Pie gang were clients of Alex's.

I gasped and they all looked at me. "Do you think they'll let me in to visit Alex, now that I'm a suspect in the attack on him?"

Nina reached over and patted my arm. "Sophie, if I were you, I wouldn't go anywhere near the hospital. They're likely to arrest you."

I looked at the others, hoping for a different response, but I could see it in their faces. "Wow. Can one of you go by to check on him once in a while? I guess I won't be seeing Wolf, either."

Bernie gave me a stern look. "They might send him to see if he can weasel information out of you. I'd be very careful if Wolf shows up."

He was right. Wolf was a friend, but he was conscientious about his job. If they sent him to ask questions, he would probably do it.

"You really need to date men who aren't so principled," said Nina.

"Ahem," said Mars. "Who sent her a knight in a red convertible to save her today?"

Amid the laughter Bernie said, "Are you kidding? You're one of the most virtuous people I know. How you got involved in politics is beyond me."

"*Au contraire.* I have a rebellious nature," Mars insisted.

"A rebel without a clue," said Bernie. "Help me with these steaks."

We gathered around the table, on which Nina and I had spread a festive French tablecloth. I poured wine into the blue blown-glass goblets, and we sat down to eat.

I had just sliced some pieces of my steak for Daisy when Wolf strode into the backyard. I couldn't believe it. Even though I knew deep in my heart that he was probably doing the right thing, I thought he cared about me enough to be on my side.

"Don't tell him anything," whispered Bernie.

"He might be wearing a wire," said Mars.

I pasted on a fake smile. "Would you care for some dinner?"

"Thanks, but I really can't. Could I have a word with you privately, Sophie?"

Feeling everyone's eyes on me, I stood up and walked over to him. "I have no more gas cans. Nor do I have any secrets. My friends can hear what you have to say."

He gazed at them briefly. "We'd like you to turn over your computer, phone, and iPad. Basically, whatever electronics of that sort that you have."

"Do you have a search warrant?" I asked.

"Sophie, come on. Please don't make this difficult," said Wolf.

"No," I said firmly. "I'm not turning over a thing. I did nothing wrong, and if you want to get a search warrant, you'll have to go through my lawyer."

I was quivering inside, but I did my best to hide it.

Wolf's voice softened. "This isn't up to me. They will get a search warrant. You can do it the easy way or the hard way."

"Wolf! I can't believe you would do this to me. You know perfectly well that I had nothing to do with the attack on Alex or the fire. Can't you see? There's a thread between that event and Patsy's murder, and probably even Grainger's death. Someone is framing me."

"Oh, Sophie."

I was glad he sounded miserable.

"Now if you don't mind, I believe I'll get back to my dinner. Or would you like to take that, too?"

"I'll try to be here when they come with the search warrant."

I turned and walked toward the table, quaking.

"Sophie?" Wolf called.

I didn't want to turn around, but I did.

"Don't be sassy with them. That won't go over well."

When I sat down at the table, Mars was on his phone. I was too nervous to eat, something that rarely happened to me. I listened unabashedly to his end of a conversation about search warrants.

Mars hung up. "That was Benton. He says they'll probably get what they want. We need to look at it to make sure it's specific and not open-ended. They can't take just anything."

That didn't make me feel better at all!

"They're not supposed to come after ten at night, unless they think you might destroy evidence."

I snorted. "Then that's when they'll come. Just to annoy me, I'm sure. Why do they have to be so rude?"

"Mars and I will stay over tonight, okay?" said Bernie. "So you won't be alone."

"Thanks. I appreciate that."

Nina made an effort to change the subject, but during dessert Willa whispered to me that we had to figure out what was going on. We couldn't continue this way.

At exactly nine fifty-five that evening, squad cars pulled up outside.

"They're here," murmured Mars.

Bernie, Mars, Daisy, and I gathered in the foyer.

Chapter 40

Dear Sophie,
I have a recipe for pie that uses butter in the crust.
I'd rather use shortening. Can I swap them or will
it throw the recipe off?
                    Living Dangerously in Crisp, Illinois

Dear Living Dangerously,
Butter contains more water. Swap one cup of but-
ter for one cup of shortening plus two tablespoons
of water.

                                        Sophie

I opened the front door before anyone could knock. That ought to show some degree of cooperation. A uniformed officer announced that he had arrived with a search warrant, which I assumed was the paper he held in his hand.

I reached my hand out for it.

He waved other uniformed officers into my house.

"Everything you're looking for is right here in the foyer."

The officer gazed at the phone, iPad, and laptop on the console. "That's all you have?"

"Yes."

Mars snatched the search warrant from his hand and read it.

"Thank you for assembling these things, but we still have to search."

I'd had a feeling that was the case. The truth was that there just wasn't anything else. I had sent off old cell phones to an organization that recycled them for use by abused women. And I traded in my old iPad and computer when it was time for new ones. There just wasn't anything else that fit into that category.

I could hear the officers tromping around upstairs, no doubt opening doors and drawers.

"Is there a basement?" asked the officer who seemed to be the leader of the pack.

"Yes. The door is just off the kitchen."

They wouldn't find anything down there but my laundry and Christmas decorations.

Wolf walked up to the door. I was plenty mad at him, even though I knew he probably didn't have much, if any, control over this. He couldn't just tell them that I was a decent person and hadn't harmed Alex. But I couldn't help feeling betrayed, anyway. I knew that was petty of me, but it was how I felt. I walked away from him and into the kitchen.

A uniformed officer came up from the basement and passed by me without a word. Why did they have to be so unfriendly? Is that how they would want their mothers to be treated?

I could hear murmuring in the foyer. The front door closed with a click and I heard the clank of the lock.

Mars and Bernie came into my kitchen.

"Are you okay?" asked Mars.

"Yes. They didn't stay as long as I expected."

Bernie winked at me. "I think most people have a lot more computer stuff."

"I wonder when I'll get it back? Do I have to buy something new to get into my own files and work?"

Neither of them had an answer for me. I had a bad feeling that I might never see the removed items again. The one thing I knew for sure was that they wouldn't find anything incriminating. I hadn't even texted Alex in the last week.

After a restless night I rose early, showered, and dressed in a sleeveless white shirt and a navy skirt. I bothered to put on makeup and curl my hair in the hope that it would help restore me to my usual self. I didn't like being out of sorts.

The smell of bacon wafted up to me and I had a hunch Bernie was up. Neither Daisy nor Mochie was in my bedroom. I padded down the stairs.

Bernie, Mars, and Natasha were seated around my kitchen table.

Natasha rose and held out her arms to me. "I had no idea you tried to kill Alex! Oh, Sophie! What have you done?"

"What did you tell her?" I asked Bernie and Mars.

"It's all over town," said Natasha. "Everyone has heard about the huge fight you had with Alex."

"That's total garbage. I did no such thing." Determined to be my usual self again, I smiled at her and asked, "Did you make breakfast, Bernie?"

I sat down and he brought me a plate of banana pancakes and bacon.

"This smells so good. I'm hungry!"

Mars sat down next to me with his coffee mug. "Bernie and I have been talking. This situation has gotten entirely out of hand." He looked upward. "That fly is going to drive me nuts. I've been chasing it with a dish towel all morning."

"It probably came inside last night when we brought the dishes in," I said.

Bernie sat down opposite me. "We're not going to let this person frame you like he did Nellie. Mars and I are taking the day off to check some things out. We'll go over and visit Alex. It's probably wishful thinking, but the best-possible scenario is that he finally wakes up and can tell us who attacked him."

Mars frowned at me. "Think you can stay out of trouble for one day?"

"I appreciate your help. I never anticipated that this could happen. It's crazy! Most of all, though, I appreciate your belief in me and my innocence." Which was more than I could say about Wolf.

I hugged them all like crazy before they went on their way. The second they were gone, I phoned Harry Gibbard and asked if he could meet me. He readily agreed.

I suited up Daisy in her halter and set out to meet with Harry. The way I saw it, we were down to three people. The killer had to be Tommy Earl, Roger, or Willa.

They were all intriguing options. Tommy Earl was getting ready to head out of town. He also happened to live where he had easy access to Dooley's rhubarb.

Roger had been unbelievably bitter about Patsy Lee's success, yet he had a secret affair with her for years.

And while Bernie thought highly of Willa, I couldn't exclude her. If she was the killer, she had a lot of guts to tell me she had lost her coffee cup at the pie festival. And even more guts to steal my gas can and then enjoy dinner at my house!

Harry met me on the sidewalk in front of Moos & Brews.

"I presume you know my fingerprints were on the gas

can and that I have been questioned. Will you get into trouble if you're seen with me?"

Harry grinned. "Who cares? Talking to you is part of my job."

That set off red warning flags in my head. Just like Wolf, he might repeat what I said. "I guess I can't swear you to secrecy."

"You could, actually. But it wouldn't do you any good."

I bought us both coffees and we walked toward Alex's office and sat on the bench.

"For the record, while Alex and I had a disagreement, it wasn't a big deal, and I certainly did not murder him."

"Good to know."

"My gas can was stolen."

"Why would someone want to frame you?" he asked.

"I've been pondering that very question. All I can imagine is that Alex's attacker thinks I know something and he wants to get rid of me. This is an easy way to do it. After all, it worked for him with Nellie."

"So how can I help?"

"Tell me about Grainger. Specifically, tell me about his relationships with Willa, Roger, and Tommy Earl."

"I hate to let you down, but you're asking me about details of my brother's life from more than five years ago. I have no idea. Didn't anyone see you when you were out walking Daisy? Someone who could refute the claim that you argued with Alex in his office that night?"

"I've got nothing. It was getting dark. I must have passed dozens of people while we walked. But I didn't go into his office until I saw his bloody hand in the window. Right now, I would love to unravel that rumor and follow the thread back to the idiot who started it."

"You'd probably find you were looking at the person who attacked Alex."

I tried to recall whether I stopped somewhere, spoke to

a neighbor, waved at a friend. And then it dawned on me—I had three suspects. All I had to do was figure out where they were that evening!

I leaned over and kissed Harry on the cheek.

"Now *that* will get me into trouble," he said.

"No, it won't. Because I don't plan to be a suspect for much longer. Thanks for helping me."

I walked away and heard him mutter, "I have no idea what I did that was helpful."

I reached for my cell phone and remembered that I didn't have it. So annoying! I would have to locate Wong. She had a sweet tooth. If she was on patrol, I might find her on King Street, more specifically, in the neighborhood of Big Daddy's Bakery.

Two minutes later I spotted her one block away from Big Daddy's. I hurried toward her.

Wong saw me coming and held up her palms like she meant to stop me. "I can't talk to you, Sophie."

"Funny how all my police friends abandoned me the second I was accused of something I didn't do."

"Sophie," she groaned, "we're still friends."

Didn't sound like it to me. "I only wanted to ask you how things are going with Tommy Earl. Does he plan to come back on weekends? After all, he has a house here."

Wong relaxed her stance. "He's not putting it on the market yet. Peter has a issues. Tommy Earl is keeping an open mind for now. He's eager to see what Peter can do for him, but Tommy Earl isn't holding his breath. Look how fast Peter dumped Natasha."

"Tommy Earl has more sense than to pull that kind of stunt." I tried to sound casual. "Has he cooked dinner for you yet?"

"Sophie, he's such a fantastic cook. I knew he could bake, but he put together a lasagna from scratch that was the best thing I've ever eaten."

"Sounds yummy. Was that the night you sat around his fire pit?"

"It was."

"And that was when? Three nights ago?"

Wong yawned. "Sorry, these double shifts are beginning to get to me. It was the night of the fire in Alex's office. I was late because of it, but Tommy Earl was very nice about it."

"I'm sure he understood when you called to tell him you wouldn't be there on time."

"Everyone was very kind."

"Everyone?"

"He invited another couple. They all had to hang around waiting for me. I was so embarrassed."

And there it was—Tommy Earl's alibi. A cop and another couple could vouch for him. While I suspected that he could have put together the lasagna in advance and slipped out to set Alex's office on fire, I didn't think that had happened. He would have come home bloody and possibly reeking of smoke. Nope, as far as I was concerned, Tommy Earl was in the clear.

"I hope you two can work something out."

"Me too, Sophie."

I walked away, thinking *one down, two to go,* and headed for the Belmont Hotel. It was just past noon when I arrived.

The morning PiePalooza classes were ending and the halls teemed with eager bakers. I found the registration desk and nosed around for a schedule of events.

Roger had done a good job of organizing. I picked up a yellow booklet that contained all the activities and flipped back to three days earlier. In the late afternoon there had been a cocktail get-together before a dinner at The Laughing Hound.

"Sophie!" Roger greeted me warmly. "What are you doing here?"

"I wanted to see how the PiePalooza was going."

"It has been marvelous. There's talk of doing a dozen of these across the United States! Honey, I think I may have found my calling."

"I am genuinely happy for you, Roger. That's terrific. I see you had dinner at The Laughing Hound. How was it?"

"The food was marvelous. Bernie arranged for us to dine on the private terrace and he helped me choose a menu that was just to die for. It was wonderful, until the fire, of course. That put a damper on the festivities, since we were outdoors and could see the smoke in the air."

I gave him a hug. "Stay in touch and let me know how you're doing with the PiePalooza events."

He hurried off, and I mentally crossed Roger's name off my list of three people. Unless I missed my guess, it was Willa who had killed Patsy Lee and Grainger, and tried to get rid of Alex.

Chapter 41

Dear Sophie,
What exactly is lard? It's in my great-grandmother's
pie recipes.
           Modern Woman in Burning Fork, Kentucky

Dear Modern Woman,
Basically it's pig fat.

                                              Sophie

Normally, I would phone Wolf and let him know. Would he believe me this time? Would he even take my call?

I walked through the streets of Old Town, amazed by the calm and the friendly people who passed by me with a warm greeting. They had probably already forgotten about the fire three days ago. But I hadn't.

I had, however, gotten very used to having a cell phone and being able to call anyone from anywhere. There was nothing I could do but walk home and make my phone calls from there.

I walked slowly, wishing I had some kind of physical evidence of Willa's guilt. The only thing the cops had, as far as I knew, was the coffee cup with her fingerprints on it. I suspected she had done that on purpose. She must have switched her cup with the caffeine overdose in it for Patsy's cup. Since she wasn't serving pie, it would have looked odd if she had worn gloves. But she shrewdly made sure she told me, and possibly others, that she was looking for her coffee. If more people testified that she had lost her coffee, it would surely put doubt into the minds of the jurors.

As I walked home, I neared the house Peter was renting from Mars and Bernie. Peter stood on the stoop with Wolf, who held out his hand. Peter shook it. They were both smiling. Wolf walked away and Peter closed the door.

"Wolf!" I called, jogging toward him.

The smile on his face vanished when he saw me. "I was going to phone you."

I put my hands in my pockets and flapped them. "Whoops! No phone!"

"On your landline."

"As you can see, I'm not home."

He took a deep breath like I was annoying him. "The white powder in Peter's vial was not caffeine."

"He's in the clear. I figured that. What was it?"

"Seems he has a common little problem when he travels." A grin crept back on Wolf's face. "It was a laxative."

I hated to be so juvenile, but I chuckled with him, which cracked the ice between us a bit. "I was going to call you, too. It was Willa. She poisoned Patsy Lee, she murdered Grainger, and she attacked Alex."

"I know about Patsy Lee, but I don't have any reason to believe she did those other things."

"She relies on fingerprints and framing people. I don't know what her motive was for murdering Grainger, but I'm certain she baked the pie and brought it to him. It had to be someone he knew and trusted. She stole the rhubarb from Nellie's ex-husband's garden to make her appear guilty."

"Do you have any proof of that?" asked Wolf.

With great reluctance I said, "No. The key was the attack on Alex. She took my gas can, knowing my fingerprints would be on it. I bet if you ask around, she won't have an alibi for that time of day."

"Sophie, I'm sorry you're in this mess. I'm even sorry that they took your computer and phone, but I don't want you to get your hopes up. What you're telling me is only speculation."

I knew that. "Look in Alex's files. I'll bet anything there's a file on her that contains some kind of secret."

Wolf nodded. "I'll check it out. In the meantime you stay out of it."

Yeah, sure, like that would happen. "See you later, Wolf." I started to walk away.

"Sophie! Promise me!"

I turned around. "If the police were interrogating you about something you didn't do, and they had confiscated your computer, iPad, and phone, would you stop trying to prove your innocence?"

"No."

It was the tiniest whisper, but I heard it. I walked home, hoping he would follow up and check Alex's files.

Nina was waiting at my kitchen door, holding a pie box. "Look what I found! Must be a gift from Tommy Earl."

The logo on the top of the box indicated that it was from his bakery.

"Have you had lunch?" she asked.

"No, but I have lots of leftovers."

"Would that include a slice of Tommy Earl's pie? Wonder what kind it is?"

I unlocked the door. Mochie mewed at me, which I took as a complaint because he had been home alone.

Nina gasped. "You didn't wash the dishes this morning."

"I had some things to take care of."

She untied the string on the box. "And what did you find out?"

"It's Willa. She did it all, but I have no proof."

"Except for her fingerprints on the coffee cup."

"Exactly."

Nina opened the box. "Lemon meringue," she cooed. "I might just eat this for lunch."

"I'm just going to check my landline messages. I'll be right back." I walked to my little home office. Sure enough, the message light was blinking. I pulled out a notepad. The first two messages were complaints about not being able to reach me at my mobile number. Clearly, I would have to buy another phone. I had no idea when I might get mine back.

While I noted the callers' names, my thoughts drifted to the pie from Tommy Earl. I dropped the pen and ran to my kitchen shouting, "Nina! Nina! Don't eat that!"

She had cut a slice of the pie. It was gorgeous. The lemon gleamed under a cloud of lightly browned meringue.

Nina had a fork in her hand and was about to take a bite of the pie. I raced at her and grabbed the fork. "No!"

"What's wrong?" she asked.

"Why would Tommy Earl leave a pie at my door?"

She shrugged. "To thank you for something?"

"There's nothing to thank me for."

As the two of us looked at the gorgeous pie, a fly landed on the slice Nina had cut. It feasted on the sweet lemon portion.

She was about to flick it away, but I stopped her.

Seconds later the fly fell off the pie. It lay on its back. Its legs twitched briefly. And then it was dead.

"Don't touch anything. And don't let Mochie touch or sniff the pie." I dashed to the kitchen phone and dialed Wolf's number. It rolled over to voice mail. I said I thought someone had left a poisonous pie for me and that I was at home, waiting for a cop to collect it.

"That could have been me." Nina's voice quavered. "Why would Tommy Earl send you a poisoned pie?"

I wrapped an arm around her shoulders. "I don't think it was from Tommy Earl. Willa probably baked it and slid it into a box that had his fingerprints on it. That's how she operates."

I looked around for Mochie. Cats didn't generally like sweets, but I didn't want him trying it. He lounged in the bay window. "We'll leave everything exactly like it is for Wolf to see."

Nina nodded. "If you're right, this sort of thing has worked well for her in the past."

"I told Wolf my theory. He says it's all speculation, which is true. It's amazing that Willa has managed to get away with so much. I just wish we had tangible proof."

"The pie might provide that."

"Unlikely. She probably wore food-prep gloves to keep her fingerprints off it. There has to be some way to snag her."

"What if you were dead?"

"What?!" I yelped.

"Pretend dead. You know, let her think the pie killed you?"

"And how would that help?"

"I don't know. I'm in shock. We need to set a trap of some kind."

"We might really end up dead if we do that."

"I knew there was something wrong when she wasn't excited about seeing Patsy Lee," said Nina.

"Let's walk this through from her perspective," I suggested. "She couldn't poison a pie at The Laughing Hound because everyone knew who baked it."

"So she bought a coffee at Moos and Brews," said Nina, "dumped the caffeine into it, and swapped her coffee for Patsy Lee's coffee. That would be easy to do."

"Except it had her fingerprints on it, so she walked around asking if she left her coffee, to build the notion that someone took her coffee."

"And it worked perfectly, except for the fingerprints," Nina observed.

"Then, because Alex knew something, she stole my gas can and paid Alex a visit."

"She must have left the gas can outside, in back of the office, so he didn't see it," Nina noted.

"Probably. She went in to talk with him. She must have surprised him by hitting him with something. I can't imagine how she could have overpowered him otherwise."

"She grabbed a cord of some kind and meant to strangle him, but he smacked the window, and you came in so she had to flee."

"And she set the fire, hoping it would obliterate the files," I said. "If we assume we're somewhat correct about the scenario, the only other tangible evidence would be whatever she used to hit him."

"Didn't Mars say he would have gotten rid of evidence in a big Dumpster behind a restaurant?" asked Nina.

"I wonder how often it gets emptied." I jumped up and phoned Bernie on his cell phone. "Bernie's not answering. Why doesn't anyone ever answer their calls?"

"Call the restaurant."

I hung up, dialed the restaurant, and asked for Remy.

When he came to the phone, I asked if he knew how often they emptied the Dumpster.

He seemed perplexed when he said, "Once a week. It's scheduled for tomorrow."

I thanked him and hung up. "Daisy isn't here, so I'll put Mochie upstairs in my bedroom and close the door. Can you write a note saying *Do not eat or touch*? Just in case Mars lets himself in."

Nina shouted up the stairs that she was going home to change clothes.

I took a minute to do the same thing. Old jeans, grubby sneakers, and a T-shirt ought to do the job. I left Mochie napping on my bed, and on the way out the door, I grabbed two pairs of gardening gloves.

Nina met me at the sidewalk. We walked to The Laughing Hound, but turned down the alley to the Dumpster. A few people were dining on the doggy deck in the back.

Nina and I were not very tall. We turned over some five-gallon buckets and stepped on them to see inside the Dumpster.

"Ugh. That stinks," moaned Nina.

"Three days ago. It would be in the middle somewhere."

"What do you think we're looking for?" asked Nina.

"A bat would have been too big and obvious. It had to be something she could fit into a purse, or something that was already in Alex's office."

"A wine bottle."

"That would have broken and been left at the scene," I said. "I bet you're right."

"Thank goodness." Nina flicked her hand in front of her nose. "I hate to tell you this, but there's no way I would have jumped into that stinking pit. Not even to save you from prison."

"Maybe the firemen know if there was a wine bottle," I suggested.

"We're not too far from the firehouse."

"Good point. Think they would tell us?" I asked.

"Can't hurt to ask. Maybe we'll get lucky."

We walked a few blocks to the fire station. A handsome young man greeted us.

Nina smiled at him. "We could use some information about that terrible fire in Alex German's office the other day. Do you think you could help us?"

Did she wink at him?

"I can get someone who would know more about it."

He disappeared into the back.

"I think you scared him," I muttered.

"I keep forgetting I'm not as young and cute as I used to be."

"We're probably his mother's age."

Harry Gibbard walked out to talk with us.

Chapter 42

Dear Sophie,
I love entertaining my friends and family. And I'm
always sending leftover pie home with them. But I
never see my containers again! Is there a nice way
to tell them I want the containers back?
                    No Storage in Suckerville, Maine

Dear No Storage,
Use disposable cake pans. They come in various
sizes and work equally well for packing cakes,
meats, casseroles, and pies. Buy the kind with a
cover made to fit it, or cover it with aluminum foil.
                                              Sophie

"Sophie! I didn't think I would see you again today."

I introduced him to Nina. "We were discussing how Alex might have been attacked and we thought someone probably caught him off guard and hit him with something like a wine bottle."

"And now you want to know if they found wine bottle remnants in the blaze."

"Exactly."

"Good thought, but the only glass appears to be from the shattered front window."

I must have looked very disappointed because he added, "You're probably right in theory, though. Alex isn't a small guy. Overpowering him would have required the advantage of surprise."

"The Lady Justice," I muttered.

"I beg your pardon?" said Harry.

"There was a bronze Lady Justice in his reception room. If someone had swung that down on his head, he would have been in big trouble."

"Depending on the alloys, bronze can melt in high heat. I'll check for it."

"Thanks, Harry. I appreciate your help."

Nina and I walked away. "Is he married?" she asked.

"I have no idea."

"How have I never met him?" she wondered.

"Nina! Concentrate." We walked by Bernie's house and I stopped dead. "We're all wrong. She's trying to frame me. If she used something to slam Alex, she would have hidden it at my place!"

We picked up our speed and hurried past my kitchen door to the backyard.

"She stole the gas can from the garage. That's probably where she would have left any other evidence."

We opened the door and peered inside. I pressed the garage door opener for extra light. We searched the garage for a few minutes.

"Found it!" Nina shouted.

The Lady Justice lay on her side under a shop table. The scales were missing, and I suspected the dark red spots were dried blood. "If the cops had looked in here, I would be in jail right now." My heart beat like crazy. How was I going to explain this?

"Maybe they did look in here and thought it belonged to you. They might not have known it was used in an attempted murder."

"That's even scarier. What now?" My voice came out in a squeak. "If I report it, they'll think I used it against Alex."

"Are your fingerprints on it?"

"I wouldn't think so. But she probably wiped her fingerprints off of it."

"Good point," said Nina. "Normally, I would ask my good friend Sophie what to do in a situation like this."

"I need to call Benton. Maybe he'll know."

"Sophie?" called a man's voice.

I gasped. "That's Wolf!" I hit the button to close the garage door, and whispered to Nina, "Lock the door behind us."

"Hi, Wolf." I hoped I didn't appear as nervous and queasy as I felt. "Thanks for coming."

I walked hastily to the kitchen and unlocked the door. "There it is."

"Looks like an ordinary lemon meringue pie to me."

Nina stepped inside the kitchen. "Sophie saved me. I was about to take a bite when that little fly"—she pointed at it—"took a bite instead and keeled over dead."

Wolf frowned. "It's from Tommy Earl's shop?"

"That's what the box says." I felt stupid for stating the obvious and hastened to add, "But I don't think that's where the pie came from."

Wolf rubbed his chin. "I'm trying to figure out the best way to collect this. Maybe I'd better call in a crime scene processor."

That was all I needed! More cops snooping around. No way! "Why don't you close the box and slide it into a paper bag? I'm pretty sure I have a paper grocery bag." I hurried to my pantry and pulled out a disposable cake pan. I liked to use them to send leftovers home with friends. "Then you could place the little plate and the fork in here. Just remember that I'm holding it, so my fingerprints are on this part of it."

Wolf flashed me a look. "Thanks. That's actually a good idea." He gazed around. "Where's Mochie? Is he okay?"

"I left him upstairs in the bedroom so he wouldn't touch the pie."

Wolf nodded. "Good thinking." I handed him the cake pan and waited for him to pack everything.

"I would like to point out," said Nina, "that *my* fingerprints are on the box and the plate and the fork. I found the box on Sophie's doorstep, opened it, and cut a slice."

"But Sophie stopped you from eating it?" Wolf did not look happy.

"Oh, come on!" I was irritated. "Cut me a break here. Now you think I'm baking poisonous pies and leaving them on my own stoop? Are you kidding me?"

Wolf was completely calm in spite of my outburst. "I know Nina didn't bake it."

"I might be offended, if it weren't a relief to hear that," Nina chuckled.

Wolf smiled, but I was in no mood for levity. Not with Lady Justice in my garage and Wolf imagining that I was baking poisonous pies. At that moment all I really wanted was for him to leave.

He dutifully pulled out gloves and packed the pie. "Nina, could you help me carry this out to the car, please?"

"Sure." She picked up the cake pan and followed him out the door.

I watched them from the window. They exchanged a few words. I trotted upstairs and opened the bedroom door. Mochie stretched and yawned, then curled up again.

Back downstairs I carefully folded the tablecloth so no crumbs, if there were any, would land on the floor. I whipped a fresh tablecloth onto the table and took the soiled one to my basement, where I put it straight into the washing machine and let it run on hot.

When I returned, Nina was in the kitchen.

"What did he want?" I asked.

"He's just worried about you. He thought you looked nervous."

I sighed. "I'm not a good actress. How did you respond?"

"I told him you had every right to be upset because you're being framed. And then he said the weirdest thing."

"What did he say?" I held my breath.

"That Willa was working at The Laughing Hound when Alex was attacked. Remy saw her and it was confirmed by the restaurant computer records."

Chapter 43

Dear Natasha,
I managed to burn the beautiful lattice on my apple
pie. How do I avoid that? It definitely wasn't done
when the crust started burning.
                    Frustrated in Burning Bush, Georgia

Dear Frustrated,
Keep an eye on your pie. As soon as the crust is
golden, place aluminum foil over it to prevent it
from burning.

                                        Natasha

I sank into a fireside chair, barely able to breathe. "That can't be. Something's not right. They can't all have alibis."

Mars, Daisy, and Bernie burst into the kitchen and stopped short. Daisy trotted toward me and placed her head in my lap.

"What happened here?" asked Mars as he closed the door.

Nina put on the kettle and made tea while she told them

everything that had happened from the pie to Lady Justice and the fact that Willa had an alibi.

Bernie's forehead crinkled. "I have never thought it was Willa. But now I have to wonder if Remy was covering for her."

I felt as though he had handed me a ray of hope. "Why?"

"That was the day you came by to try the chicken pie made with phyllo, right?" asked Bernie.

"Yes."

"Willa had the day off. She was a judge at the bake-off between Tommy Earl and Natasha. Either he misunderstood the date when Wolf asked him about it, or he's covering for Willa."

"Or they're cheating you," said Mars.

As I felt better, Bernie grew paler. He pulled out his phone and tapped it a few times.

"What are you doing?" I asked.

"I'm checking to see if Remy was clocked in for that day."

"If you can do that on an app, what's to stop him from clocking in when he's actually at a party across town?" asked Mars.

"Only I can do it from a remote location. They have to clock in on the register in the restaurant. Remy isn't clocked in for that day."

I wanted to dance a jig. Maybe I had been correct about Willa after all.

Bernie poked his fingertip at his phone. A furrow developed between his eyebrows.

"Something wrong?" asked Mars.

"Someone changed Remy's status for the day in question. Now the program shows him as working." Bernie rose from his seat. "Excuse me, please, but I have to go."

"Hold it, Inspector Clouseau." Mars held a palm toward Bernie. "I understand that this involves The Laughing

Hound and that it's important. But we have to think this through, because Sophie comes first."

Bernie sat down again, but he didn't look happy. "You're right. What if I call Wolf and he's there, or they put a wire on me when I talk to Remy?"

We were all in agreement with that plan. While Bernie phoned Wolf, I shared the story about the contents of the vial Natasha had found in Peter's limo.

"Wolf's going to meet me at the restaurant," said Bernie.

"I wish we could be there!" Nina beamed with excitement.

"You go ahead," I said. "I'll stay here with Daisy and Mochie."

"Are you worried about them?" asked Mars.

"Not really. But we know that Willa set a fire. I wouldn't feel right leaving them alone in my house."

Bernie shook his head. "I feel so guilty. I trusted Willa. I brought her into your home, thinking she had been wronged. I don't want to leave you here by yourself until they have her in custody. We'll take Daisy and Mochie with us."

With harnesses and leashes on both Mochie and Daisy, we walked over to The Laughing Hound. Mochie didn't walk quite as fast as Daisy, so he was carried for a good bit of the way. We went in through the back entrance, where Wolf discreetly waited for us.

Bernie led the way upstairs to a meeting room, where I had had some business lunches with small groups. When we were seated, Bernie explained the situation to Wolf, who shot me an apologetic look.

With the door to the meeting room open just enough for us to hear what was going on in his office, Bernie called in Remy.

While we waited for Remy, I realized I was clenching my teeth. After all, my future depended to some degree on what Remy might say.

We heard him enter and sit down. "Hi, boss. What's up?"

"We have a little problem. I was checking the time schedule about an hour ago and, right before my eyes, your status three days ago changed."

"Must be a glitch in the system," Remy said. But I could hear his discomfort.

"You want to tell me why you changed it?" asked Bernie.

"Look, that cop called Wolf came in this afternoon asking if Willa worked that day. I told him she did, that I had seen her here. Then I pretended to look into the system and told him she had been clocked in."

"Why would you do that?"

There was a long silence. "I just felt like I should have her back. A cop asking about somebody's work schedule is always bad news."

Another long silence. I could imagine Bernie letting him squirm.

"I'm going to be fired, aren't I?" asked Remy. "Okay. I owed her. There was a guy in the bar who was a real jerk. He was being rude to the female patrons, so I tossed a drink in his face, took him outside, and punched him. There you have it. Willa knew about it, but she was a good egg and didn't mention it to you. I'll stop by in a couple of days for my last paycheck."

A chair scraped along the ground.

"Remy, wait. Did you tell Willa that Wolf was here asking questions about her?"

"Yeah. I called her as soon as he left."

"Where is she now?" asked Bernie.

"What did she do?"

"Do you know Alex German?"

"Sure. The whole town is talking about what happened to him," said Remy. "It's been the number one topic at the bar."

"The cops want to talk to her about that."

Remy snorted. "No way, man. This is Willa we're talking about."

"You gave her an alibi. Do you think you could get her to come over here now?"

"Oh no, I'm not getting involved," Remy protested.

Wolf stood up and walked to the open door of Bernie's office. Mars, Nina, and I snuck to the door of the meeting room to peek. Wolf did a pretty decent job of filling the doorway by standing with his feet apart as if ready to block Remy's escape. "Too late, Remy. You got yourself involved when you lied to me."

"Aw, man."

For half an hour I was hopeful they would find Willa and bring her in for questioning. But she had stopped answering her phone.

I knew I was still in deep trouble unless they could find her and get her to confess.

There was nothing to do but go home. Bernie brought barbecued ribs, coleslaw, and baked potatoes from the restaurant. The poisoned pie had dampened our appetites for pies, but when we remembered the ice-cream pie, we were back in the game for pie.

Fortunately, my home was still standing and not aflame. I fed Mochie and Daisy, who ate ravenously and then snoozed after their unexpected excursion to The Laughing Hound.

Bernie, Mars, Nina, and I gathered around the kitchen table with our take-out dinner. No one, not even Nina, was interested in alcohol. We were exhausted and needed to keep our wits about us.

"I'm so ashamed," I said. "I've been so self-consumed today that I didn't ask about Alex. How's he doing?"

"Better." Mars picked up a rib. "His parents are here and they're hoping he'll respond to them. They say he's healing really well."

"That's great news! Let's hope this nonsense is over by

then so I can visit him again." I sat back in my chair and thought about how lucky I was to have wonderful friends who stood by me, no matter what.

"Where do you suppose Willa went?" Nina helped herself to more coleslaw.

I gazed out the bay window. "Maybe she's at Bernie and Mars's rental house, hiding out with Peter."

"Peter checked out today." Mars salted his potato. "He and Tommy Earl are on their way to New York City."

"Then it would be a perfect hiding place," I said.

Bernie and Mars exchanged a look.

"Maybe we should go over there and check it out after we eat." Mars took a bite of potato heaped with so much sour cream I was tempted to ask if there was any potato underneath it.

"Maybe you should call Wolf and ask if he can have a beat cop check it out periodically," I suggested.

"Does anyone else feel like we're the ones in hiding?" asked Nina, licking barbecue sauce off her finger. "Like we can't go out in the dark because Willa could be lurking somewhere?"

Bernie pulled out his phone and concentrated on it for a moment. "I've texted Wolf about the house."

I rose and started packing leftovers in containers. When I opened the refrigerator to stash them away, a chill ran through me. "Nina," I said quietly, "did you eat some of yesterday's leftovers?"

"Are you counting?" she teased.

"I'm being serious. This isn't how I left the fridge."

Mars laughed. "You've lost your mind, Sophie."

"You don't understand. There were so many pies in here that I had to wedge the leftovers in. They're not how I left them." I took out the leftover steak and peered inside the aluminum foil. "There's definitely some steak missing."

"She's here," hissed Nina.

Chapter 44

Dear Sophie,
What's the one mistake you think beginning bakers
make when baking pies?
  Beginning Baker in Thief River Falls, Minnesota

Dear Beginning Baker,
Not having everything ready before they start. Pie
baking needs to move swiftly. No wasting time run-
ning around the kitchen in search of the rolling pin!
  Sophie

"You're being ridiculous, Sophie." Mars peered in the refrigerator. "Your fridge always looks like that."

"Shh," I cautioned.

We all listened, but the only sound was Daisy's gentle snoring.

"I'm calling Wolf," I said.

"You'll get him here faster with a text," said Bernie.

"How do you know that?" asked Nina. "I always call him when I need something."

"That's why you get his attention faster with a text.

Everyone thinks he's their pal and calls him when they need something. He has time to glance at a text, but he can't always answer a call."

Gritting my teeth a little, I reminded Bernie, "I don't have a device that can text."

He flushed the color of the barbecue sauce. "I'm so sorry. I completely forgot about that." He handed me his phone. "Help yourself."

I texted as fast as I could—**Wolf, we think Willa could be inside Sophie's house.** "Okay. Let's hope he takes Bernie seriously and comes right away."

"No one go to the bathroom. We'll be fine if we stick together," said Bernie, yanking open my knife drawer and pulling out a chef's knife.

"Gee, thanks. Now the bathroom is all I can think of," Nina complained.

"Should we turn off the lights?" I whispered.

"No!" Nina shouted.

"So we just hang out in the kitchen, waiting for Willa to show up like a deranged ax murderer?" I asked in a low voice.

"I am *not* an ax murderer," the voice came from the foyer.

Willa emerged from the darkness. I should have been afraid. But when I saw Willa, I felt sorry for her. She was pale as a ghost and had dyed her hair blond, which made me wonder if she had planned to leave Old Town and go into hiding.

"A knife, Bernie?" she asked. "You can put it down. It won't do you much good against Sophie's Taser. Besides, I thought we were friends." She sniffed the air. "Ribs. I recognize the smell of the sauce."

Mars brushed by me, holding the ice-cream pie, and whispered, "Engage her."

I had no idea what he planned to do, but I was game.

Maybe we just needed to run out the clock until Wolf came to arrest her.

"What happened, Willa?" I asked, inching toward the wine rack. "What brought you to this?"

"Betrayal," she spat. "Patsy Lee and I were so close, like you and Nina. Back then, Patsy Lee didn't have the first clue what to do in a kitchen. It didn't make sense to me that she would be the one who would become a star. But she was my friend in those days. I was happy for her when she married Peter and things started looking up for her. I couldn't believe it when she fired me. I had made the mistake of believing she would always be there for me, like I was for her." Willa snorted. "I had nowhere to go. It was like she had thrown me to the wolves. I came back to Old Town, where I had connections, to see if I could get a job. Grainger was in the process of getting his restaurant going. He hired me and even let me stay in an apartment over the restaurant until I got back on my feet."

"But you killed him," said Nina.

"You would have, too. I was so supportive of him. Who do you think picked the colors, and made up the logo, and had the menus printed? That restaurant was as much mine as it was his. I worked my tail off for him. We spent a lot of time together, and I thought I had finally found the right man. But when the restaurant was up and going, and he stole the idea of a TV show from Tommy Earl, Grainger dumped me and brought in Nellie, who was younger and way prettier than me."

"I'm sorry," I whispered.

"It wouldn't have been so bad if I had lost one thing. But I lost Grainger, I lost the apartment because he wanted me out, and I lost my job! Suddenly all our friends were asking me about his engagement to Nellie, and wasn't it great that they were going to have a TV show? How would you have felt?"

She wiped tears from under her eyes with the hand that wasn't holding the Taser. "It was like Patsy Lee all over again," she murmured. "I was good enough when they needed me, but when success was on their doorstep, I became yesterday's garbage."

Trying to be subtle, I gazed around. Mars had managed to slip out of the kitchen. He must have gone through the small family room and through the sunroom. He should appear in the foyer anytime now.

"So you cut rhubarb from Nellie's ex-husband's garden?" asked Nina.

"Seemed like a good idea at the time. But the rhubarb leaves didn't work as fast as I expected. I had to stab Grainger, too. I lived in fear that they would find the knife."

"It's in the Potomac River?" Bernie guessed.

"I was so sure that they would figure out that I had killed him. I was terrified, like I am now because there are four of you. I'm not sure how I'm going to do this."

"That was when you went to Alex?" I asked.

She stepped toward me. "I needed someone on my side. He promised, Sophie. He promised he wasn't allowed to say a word unless he thought I would kill someone else. I assured him there was just no way I would ever do that. For a long time I feared every knock on the door. And then they convicted Nellie. For a while I was fairly content. Patsy Lee dumped Peter, and when he came back to town, he looked me up. For years Peter and I had a relationship, but then Patsy Lee came back to town for the pie festival."

Willa's eyes and expression changed right before me. The sad woman morphed into an angry one. "The night of her welcome dinner at The Laughing Hound, I seriously considered taking a knife and killing her on the terrace. But I had gotten away with murder once. All I had to do was be calm and figure out a way to kill Patsy Lee. Did you know that Patsy Lee spent that night with Peter?"

Willa started breathing faster. Her nostrils flared like a bull's. I tried to inch away from her again.

"But I ran into a problem with fingerprints on the coffee cups. It was easy enough to pour the caffeine powder into my coffee and then swap her cup with mine, but after I did that, I realized my fingerprints were all over it. As a precaution I told people my cup was gone, so they'd think the killer swiped it. I hovered in her vicinity, hoping I could snatch the cup when everyone was watching Patsy Lee die, but Wolf and Wong were there immediately. I never got the chance."

I finally spotted Mars in the foyer. My old floors creaked, but he had managed to sneak around her. I needed to keep Willa focused on herself. "But why did you go after Alex? Didn't you think you might need him again?"

She leaned toward me, her eyes wide with fury. "He promised he wouldn't say anything unless he thought I was going to kill someone else. He knew about Grainger. It wouldn't be long before he suspected me of killing Patsy Lee. And then I saw you talking to him on Market Square and I had to get rid of him before he spilled the truth."

She was so agitated that I didn't dare broach the fact that his files were electronically stored in a cloud backup system and she hadn't gotten rid of them. "So you started the rumors about Alex and me having an argument?"

At that moment a wooden floorboard creaked under Mars's foot.

Willa whirled toward him, hitting the button on the Taser exactly as Mars smashed the ice-cream pie in her face. I leaned over and opened a drawer to grab my French rolling pin. Using both hands, I whacked her over the head as hard as I could. She wobbled for a few seconds and then fell to the floor.

The commotion woke Daisy, who jumped up and barked

nonstop until she discovered the ice cream on Willa's face and started licking it.

Bernie opened the kitchen door for Wolf, who raced inside.

I jumped over Willa and knelt next to Mars. "Are you okay?"

"I wish I had never given you that Taser."

I figured he would be fine.

For the next couple of hours EMTs and cops swarmed through my kitchen. An ambulance whisked Willa to the emergency room. The EMTs checked out Mars, who had taken a nasty hit from the stun gun, but they thought he would be fine. Wolf took statements from everyone.

Bernie proudly presented his iPhone to Wolf. He got the whole thing on tape.

"So you *can* record with a phone!" I exclaimed. "You have to show me how."

At long last, everyone went home, and I went up to bed with Daisy and Mochie. I closed my eyes without worrying about landing in prison.

Bright and early the next morning Nina came over, her coffee mug in hand. We stood in front of my house with Daisy.

"Did you tell Wolf about Lady Justice in your garage?" she asked.

"Absolutely. I didn't want them thinking I was hiding something. The cops took it with them last night."

Natasha crossed the street to us. "What happened over here last night? It was so noisy!"

I didn't have it in me to tell her the whole story at that moment. "They arrested Willa for murdering Patsy Lee and Grainger, and for attacking Alex."

"Thank goodness! That should finally end the rumor that you set fire to Alex's office."

"Hopefully. Where have you been?" I inquired.

"Roger is putting together a tour with cooking celebrities who will give classes and demonstrations, and he has asked me to join him!"

Nina shot me a horrified look.

"I'm pleased for you, Natasha. It sounds like something you would enjoy."

"Roger will live to regret that," muttered Nina.

A little boy approached us, his parents beaming behind him. "Are you Sophie Winston?" he asked.

"Yes."

He didn't look happy about it, but he handed me an envelope. Gazing at me expectantly, he crossed his arms over his chest.

My name and address had been scrawled on the envelope.

Nina asked, "Aren't you the kid who won the junior pie contest?"

"Yeah. I found that envelope on the ground when everyone was being rushed out."

"Thank you very much," I said.

"No tip?" he asked.

Nina said, "I liked the way you piped your meringue. Did you do that with an icing bag?"

"Is that how we did it, Mom?" he asked.

"Yes, sweetheart. Don't you remember squeezing the bag?"

I peered inside the envelope and found the check that Wolf insisted Patsy Lee had written out to me. It was for $100,000! I excused myself, dashed into the house, dug in my purse, and pulled out a twenty-dollar bill.

I returned to the boy and handed it to him. "Thank you for bringing that envelope to me."

"That's all? I shoulda just thrown it away."

"Now, sweetheart," said his mom, "not everyone can be as generous as we are."

I balked, determined not to give the little devil another cent.

"Did you really bake that pie all by yourself?" asked Nina.

A rosy flush hit his mother's cheeks. "How dare you!"

"My mom baked it, but I got the trophy," bragged the kid.

Nina glared at his mother.

"Excuse us. We have to go." The mother ushered her child away as fast as she could.

"I guess we know who will be banned from next year's festival," said Natasha. "The nerve of that woman."

When Nina and Natasha went home, I made a second mug of hot tea and sat down to read the letter from Patsy Lee.

> *Dear Sophie,*
>
> *Since we just met for lunch, you'll think it odd that I took the time to write this. But it's an emotional subject for me, and I'm worried that I won't make sense or that I'll skip the important part and you won't understand. If I can't quite bring myself to explain it all to you, I'll give you this instead.*
>
> *I was only seventeen and on my own when I gave birth to a baby girl. I had nowhere to go and was struggling to support myself, so it was clear to me that I couldn't take care of a child. A nurse told me about a couple that couldn't have children of their own and were looking to adopt. They were everything I would have liked in my own parents. A private adoption was arranged.*
>
> *I have thought of that child every single day of my life. Honey Armbruster is everything I ever*

would have wanted in a daughter. Who would have expected her to be a huge fan of mine? I wish I had the guts to tell her the truth. Maybe I can find the strength someday. In the interim, though, Honey has encountered some hard times of her own, and I would like to assist her anonymously. Please arrange for this money to be awarded to her as an up-and-coming baker.

Thank you,

Patsy Lee Presley

I hadn't expected that. There was a certain lovely irony to it, though. I retreated to my office and made a couple of calls.

Chapter 45

Dear Natasha,
I served the most beautiful cream pie to my mother-in-law, but the knife tore the filling. By the time it was on her plate, it looked like it had been massacred. What did I do wrong?
                    So Embarrassed in Rescue, Missouri

Dear So Embarrassed,
The next time you cut a cream pie, run the knife under hot water first. It will glide through without tearing the pie.
                                        Natasha

Three miracles occurred on the last day of August. At eight in the morning, on a day when the sky was a vivid blue and the only clouds were like big fluffy lambs, Nellie Stokes walked out of the detention center a free woman.

The second she was out the door, Aly ran into her arms. Nellie swung her up, and even though Aly's feet were off the ground, it looked to me like a dance of celebration.

Tears rolled down my cheeks just to see the two of them together. They had a lot of lost time to make up.

Dooley embraced them both in his awkward praying mantis–appearing way. For Aly's sake I hoped everything would work out for their family, and that they would stick together.

Still holding Aly's hand, Nellie walked toward Nina and me. "I'll never be able to thank you enough. You gave me my life back when no one else cared."

At noon I met with Honey Armbruster, Benton Evans, and the interim CEO of Patsy Lee, Inc. Everyone except Honey knew what it was about.

I handed Honey the check and the letter. "This is from your mother."

Honey burst into tears. "Why didn't she tell me? She was too proud. . . . I might have done the same."

The interim CEO had been watching Honey carefully. "Patsy Lee left a considerable estate and, of course, a thriving business. We would like you to come on board and be our new representative. Basically, you would take over for Patsy Lee."

Honey looked at each one of us. "I can't believe this is happening. I'm on the verge of foreclosure and suddenly I have money and a business?"

I gave Honey a big hug and left them to work out the details.

At two o'clock in the afternoon Alex arrived at his home. Seated in a wheelchair, he rolled through his front door and into his living room, his mom hovering nervously behind him. I had cooked all his favorite dishes and set up a buffet. His assistant was there, along with most of the fire department, and a host of Alex's friends and clients.

The bruising on his face had almost vanished, and the

broken bones were on the mend. He was under strict orders from his doctors to take it easy, which he promptly violated by insisting he could walk. And he did—to the cheers of everyone around him.

While Alex was on the mend, I had a lot of time to think about what had transpired. I felt enormous guilt for Willa's attack on Alex. Even though my friends assured me that she had attacked him because he had told her he would turn her in if he thought she would kill someone else, I still believed my nosing around had influenced her.

I was torn, though, about Alex's behavior. I knew he was an attorney and that he had responsibilities to his clients—even to the guilty ones.

When I walked by his office days later and spied him inside, I thought perhaps the time had come for me to face what I was dreading.

I strode into the office. The walls had been painted and movers were bringing in new furniture. "It looks great!"

"I'm treating myself to an antique desk. What do you think?"

The partner's desk was massive and masculine, with inlaid woods and a rope carving all around the top. "You deserve it."

"I hear you saved my life."

"Are you kidding? I almost got you killed. And I couldn't have dragged you out without Wong's help."

He winced. "I was worried about you. After all, I knew to watch for Willa, but you were out there floundering around without a clue."

"I still don't understand why you never said anything to anyone."

"Because she was my client. She came to me because she was afraid she would be charged with Grainger's murder. I owed her complete confidentiality. No one was more surprised than I was when the cops never brought charges against Willa."

"But what about Nellie?"

Alex rubbed a scar on the side of his face. "To be honest, when you said you were looking into Grainger's murder, part of me was relieved. I couldn't tell you anything, but I knew I would be glad if you managed to spring Nellie."

"But what if I hadn't? How could you live with yourself knowing that a woman was spending her life incarcerated for a crime she didn't commit?"

"It was something I had to come to terms with. I didn't like it, but my allegiance had to be to my client. For that matter, if I had exposed her, I could have lost my license to practice law."

I looked into his eyes. I wanted to understand. I wanted to go back in time, before Patsy Lee was killed and before Aly came to me for help, before I knew the truth. I understood how much Alex loved practicing law. It was what he was meant to do. But I would never have been able to live with myself knowing that an innocent woman was spending her life behind bars. He would have allowed Aly to grow up without her mom. He would have let Nellie waste her whole life in prison. All to protect a killer.

I would have taken the heat and allowed myself to suffer, even if it meant losing my job. In this equation, as far as I was concerned, there was only one decent thing to have done—I would have made sure Nellie was released.

"I'm sorry, Alex. I didn't see this coming. You're a decent and honorable person in most ways, but you called this one wrong. And it was a huge thing. Not some little quirk that I can live with. I can't be with someone who would let an innocent person languish in prison for something she didn't do. You alone had it in your power to right that wrong. But you chose to protect yourself and your murderous client. Goodbye, Alex."

* * *

On a Saturday evening, almost three weeks later, life in Old Town had settled down. I was gearing up for the US Pet Expo, where manufacturers of items for pets would be showing their products. Mars was busy with November elections, and Nina was fostering a Jack Russell terrier. We all made the time to get together in my backyard for an end-of-summer barbecue.

Bernie, Nina, and Mars showed up first. Nina brought strawberry bourbon lemonade, which we were all eager to try. I was pouring it into tall summery goblets when Nellie arrived with six pies! I had no idea how we could eat them all.

Nellie was radiant. Aly wore a dress that matched her mom's. Dooley looked as awkward as ever, but he couldn't stop smiling.

Natasha had eyes only for Mars again, causing Bernie to snicker. She ambled over to me. "I'm just sick. Did you see Tommy Lee on TV last night? That could have been me if I hadn't taken your advice and baked a cake."

They say to pick your fights. Natasha would always blame someone else when things didn't work out for her. I offered her a glass of lemonade. "Maybe it worked out for the best, Natasha. If you had gone with Peter, you wouldn't be able to participate in the pie seminars that Roger is putting on. That might be even better for you."

"Do you really think so?"

"They say things happen for a reason."

Natasha gazed at Mars. "Sometimes we have to give luck a big push."

Uh oh. Trouble ahead. And that was when Brock walked into the backyard with Honey.

Honey and Natasha exchanged a glance and the only two women wearing high heels in the grass picked their way over to Mars like chickens doing a fancy dance.

Brock pecked me on the cheek. "I hope you don't mind that I came along with Honey."

"Are you kidding? If I had known you would be in town I would have invited you. How's life back in New York?"

"You won't believe this, but Patsy Lee's gift to Honey turned out to be a blessing for me, too. Patsy Lee, Inc. hired me. I'm working with Honey now. She's so much like Patsy Lee that you wouldn't even believe it."

"How are your twins?"

"Lively! But I'm loving every minute of being a dad. Hey, I thought you might want to know that I ran into Peter. Over drinks, he told me that the big fight between him and Patsy Lee was because he had wrecked Nellie's marriage by sending a letter accusing one of them of having an affair."

"I suspected he was behind that."

"Nellie was big competition for Patsy Lee. Of course, Peter regrets it now. He'll be happy to hear they're back together." Brock shook his head. "How low can you go?"

Mars intercepted him, probably in an effort to get away from Natasha and Honey.

I had just joined Bernie at the grill when Wong and Roger arrived through the back gate.

"Is Tommy Earl going to be here?" I asked Wong.

She frowned. "Of course not. His life is in New York now. Peter is keeping him busy. I wasn't very impressed by Peter, but the man knows how to promote!"

"I'm sorry things didn't work out. Any other beaus on the horizon?"

Wong wrapped an arm around me. "We single ladies will have to pal around together."

"Sounds good to me!" I thought about Alex often and heard through the grapevine that he was doing well. Maybe one day I would stop by to see him. But I wasn't ready for that yet.

"Did you ever find out who Patsy Lee was running from on Friday night?" asked Wong.

Roger's face went pale. "I fear that might have been me."

Wong's eyes widened. "Surely not. You're such a gentleman."

"I'll miss Patsy Lee. She was a spitfire. Would you believe that we had a long romance over the years? We kept it completely secret."

Wong looked surprised.

I didn't want to spoil Roger's fun so I didn't tell him I knew about it.

"Oh, yes! She rolled into town on Thursday and the two of us had a quiet little rendezvous. On Friday, I hoped we would get together again but she had plans to meet with Peter that she didn't tell me about. Patsy Lee knew I wouldn't like *that*. I planned to tail her to find out what she was up to. It was actually funny. She was dodging me, trying to lose me! Life was never boring with Patsy Lee!"

When we all sat down to eat at my outdoor tables, the mood was jovial, the barbecue smelled heavenly, and the strawberry bourbon lemonade was the perfect touch.

Bernie clicked a knife against his glass. "I realize that our lovely hostess should make a toast, but I have an announcement to make and if I know Sophie, she won't mind."

I smiled at him.

"The big news is that I have finally hired a new pastry chef for The Laughing Hound—Ms. Nellie Stokes!"

A cheer went up along with applause. At Bernie's prodding, Nellie stood up and took a bow.

But it was Aly's expression that brought tears to my eyes, and I knew I had done the right thing.

Recipes

Piled High Strawberry Pie

Graham Cracker Crust

1 8-inch pie pan

9 sheets honey graham crackers
4 tablespoons butter

Pie Filling

2 pounds strawberries
1 cup sugar
5 tablespoons cornstarch
1¼ cup water
2 tablespoons lemon juice

Preheat the oven to 350 degrees.

Melt the butter. Pulse the graham crackers in a food processor until they are fine crumbs. With the food processor running, pour in the butter. Press into the pie pan with your fingers. Bake 8–12 minutes. Remove from oven and set aside to cool.

Wash the strawberries, hull, and cut into quarters lengthwise. Place two cups of the strawberries in a heavy-bottomed pot, add the sugar, and mash with a potato masher, leaving some clumps of strawberry. Add the cornstarch and mix until dissolved. Stir in the water and lemon juice and bring to a boil over medium-high heat. Cook at a simmer (you may need to turn the heat down a bit) and cook until it thickens and turns red, approximately 2 minutes.

Pour enough of the uncooked strawberries into the prepared pie pan to cover the bottom in a single layer. They should not be perfectly arranged. Some should be turned up and others down. Ladle ⅓ of the hot strawberries over them. Add another layer of the uncooked strawberries, mounding them toward the center. Ladle another ⅓ of the cooked strawberries over them. Add the remaining un-cooked strawberries, heaping them toward the middle. Ladle the remaining hot strawberries over top, **slowly.** (If you pour it too fast it may overflow.) Try to cover all the bare strawberries. Refrigerate until set. Serve with sweet-ened whipped cream. If you're feeling festive, pipe the whipped cream around the edge for a knockout appear-ance.

Sweetened Whipped Cream

1 cup heavy cream
⅓ cup powdered sugar
¾ teaspoon vanilla

Beat the cream until it begins to hold a shape. Add the powdered sugar and vanilla and beat.

Quick and Easy Blueberry Cobbler

1.5 quart baking dish

3 pints of blueberries
⅓ cup sugar (taste the blueberries and add more accord-
   ingly)
2 tablespoons cornstarch
¼ teaspoon dried lemon peel
¾ cup water
1 cup flour
1 cup sugar
1½ teaspoons baking powder
½ teaspoon cinnamon
½ teaspoon salt
8 tablespoons melted butter (one stick)
1 cup milk

Preheat oven to 400 degrees.

In a medium bowl, mix the flour, 1 cup sugar, baking powder, cinnamon, and salt. Stir well to combine. Mix together the butter and milk. Add to the flour mixture and beat with a spoon until smooth.

Wash and pick over blueberries. Set aside. In a large pot, mix the ⅓ cup sugar with the cornstarch. Add the water and the lemon peel and mix until dissolved. Pour in the blueberries and bring to a boil. Turn the heat down and allow to simmer for about five minutes, stirring occasionally.

Pour the blueberries into the baking dish. Pour the dough over the top of the hot filling. Place on a baking sheet in case the blueberries spill over the sides while baking. Bake 45 minutes or until the blueberries bubble and the dough on top is light brown.

Serve with vanilla ice cream or lightly sweetened whipped cream.

S'mores Pie

1 9-inch pie pan
Note: Do not use Pyrex, glass, or ceramic pie pans under the broiler.

Graham Cracker Crust

9 sheets cinnamon graham crackers
6 tablespoons unsalted butter

Filling

1½ cups heavy cream
pinch of salt
12 ounces semisweet chocolate chips
2 tablespoons unsalted butter
2 teaspoons vanilla
1 bag miniature marshmallows, divided

Preheat oven to 350 degrees. Melt the butter. Pulse the graham crackers in a food processor until they are fine crumbs. With the food processor running, pour in the butter. Press into the pie pan with your fingers. Bake 8–12 minutes. Remove from oven and cool briefly.

Scatter the miniature marshmallows on the cooked and cooled graham cracker crust in a single layer.

Pour the cream and salt into a heavy pot and heat over medium. (It does not need to boil.) When it warms, pour the chocolate chips in and stir continuously until it's smooth and all bits of chocolate have dissolved. Add the butter and vanilla and stir until the butter is dissolved. It should be very hot. Pour over the marshmallows. With the back of a spoon, push down any marshmallows that are not covered with chocolate. They will float to the top, which is fine.

Cool the pie completely and refrigerate. When cold, add enough miniature marshmallows to cover the top. They're cutest if they all lie in the same position. Place under the broiler just long enough for them to brown lightly, 45 seconds to 1 minute.

An apple pie without some cheese is like a kiss
without a squeeze.
—Old English Rhyme, circa 1750

Salted Caramel Apple Pie

10-inch pie pan

Note: Use a metal pie pan for this recipe. Pyrex, glass, and most ceramic pie dishes cannot go from the freezer to the oven. They will break from temperature shock.

Pie Dough

2½ cups flour
1 teaspoon salt
2 sticks (16 tablespoons) **frozen** unsalted butter
ice water

Place the flour and salt in a food processor and mix with a fork. Using the shredding disk, insert the butter into the feeding tube and shred. Save any bits that stick to the top. With the machine unplugged for safety, remove the shredding disk and replace it with the pastry blade. Add the bits of butter that stuck to the top. Put the top back on and plug the machine in again. Pulse to combine. Add four tablespoons of ice water and run about 20 seconds. Pulse and add water (not much!) as necessary for it to begin to clump together. Remove the dough from the food processor and, mold into a ball. Cut off about ⅓, wrap it in wax paper, and refrigerate. Roll out the remainder immediately.

Note: This can also be made by hand with butter that is cold but not frozen.

Combine the flour with the salt. Cut the butter into small pieces and add to the flour. Work in with your hands, sprinkling with ice water as needed to make a ball. Cut off ⅓. Wrap the two pieces in wax paper and refrigerate for at least 30 minutes before rolling out.

Roll out the larger piece of dough and lay it on the bottom of a metal pie pan.

Filling

8 large apples (not crisp Fujis or MacIntosh)
juice of 1 lemon
2 teaspoons apple pie spice (or 1 teaspoon cinnamon and
    a pinch of nutmeg)
pinch of coarse salt
¼ cup heavy cream*
¼ cup sugar*
¼ cup dark brown sugar*
2 tablespoons unsalted butter*
1 whole egg
1 teaspoon water
1 tablespoon coarse sugar
½ teaspoon coarse salt like Maldons

Preheat oven to 450. Peel the apples and slice them as thin as possible. In a large bowl, toss them with the juice of one lemon and the apple pie spice.

Combine cream, sugar, dark brown sugar, and butter in

a tall microwave-safe container. (I use a 2-cup Pyrex measuring cup.) Microwave at 30 second bursts, stirring in between, until it bubbles up and the ingredients are combined. Pour ½ of it onto the apples and toss. Pour half the apples into the prepared pie pan, sprinkle lightly with a pinch of coarse salt. Pour in the rest of the apples and pour the remaining caramel sauce over them. Add lattice dough strips across the top, crisscrossing them.

Whisk the egg with 1 teaspoon water. Brush onto the lattice and the edge of the dough. Sprinkle with sugar. Sprinkle with coarse salt.

Bake 15 minutes, and check the top. Cover it with aluminum foil to prevent it from burning or getting too dark. Bake another 60 minutes (for a total of 1 hour and 15 minutes). Allow to rest at least 4 hours before cutting.

Make another batch of the caramel (marked on recipe with an *) just before serving. Top each slice with a scoop of vanilla ice cream, and pour a little bit of caramel over top to dress it up!

Ice Cream Pie

1 9-inch pie plate that can go from oven to freezer

Gingersnap Crust

40 gingersnap cookies
6 tablespoons butter

Filling

1 pint chocolate ice cream
1 pint dulce de leche ice cream
1 pint coffee ice cream

Melt the butter. Pulse the gingersnaps in a food processor until they are fine crumbs. With the food processor running, pour in the butter. Press into the pie pan with your fingers. Bake 8–12 minutes. Remove from oven and set aside to cool.

Soften the ice cream slightly at room temperature. Slide them out of their containers. Slice off the wide end of the dulce de leche in a 1-inch-thick round for the center. Slice the remaining dulce de leche and place around the piece in the center. Slice the coffee ice cream into 1-inch-thick pieces and place around the dulce de leche. Slice the chocolate ice cream into 1-inch pieces and place around the coffee. Smooth the top. Freeze immediately.

Toppings

Cheat and use store-bought caramel and fudge sauces or make your own!

Caramel Sauce

¼ cup heavy cream
¼ cup sugar
¼ cup dark brown sugar
2 tablespoons unsalted butter

Combine cream, sugar, dark brown sugar, and butter in a tall microwave-safe container. (I use a 2-cup Pyrex measuring cup.) Microwave at 30-second bursts, stirring in between, until it bubbles up and the ingredients are combined.

Fudge Sauce

1 can sweetened condensed milk
1 cup semisweet chocolate chips

2 tablespoons butter
1 teaspoon vanilla

Place all milk, chocolate chips, and butter into a pot and heat until the chocolate chips have melted and are smooth. Remove from heat and stir in the vanilla.

TiJuana Odum's Easy Chicken Pot Pie

9x9 casserole dish

2–3 cups shredded cooked chicken breast
1 can cream of chicken soup
1 can of chicken broth
½ cup frozen peas
½ cup frozen corn
salt & pepper
1 cup milk
1 cup flour
1½ teaspoons baking soda
½ teaspoon salt
1 stick (8 tablespoons) unsalted butter

Preheat oven to 450 degrees.

In a large bowl, mix cream of chicken with chicken broth. Add the chicken breast and vegetables. Add salt and pepper to taste. Pour into a greased 9x9 casserole dish.

Melt the butter and mix with the milk. Mix the flour with the baking soda and salt. Whisk into the butter mixture and pour over the chicken in the casserole.

Bake for 45 minutes until the crust is golden brown.

Grilled Cheese BLT

Sandwich bread
Butter
Mayonnaise
Dijon mustard
Salt
Cheddar cheese, shredded or sliced
Lettuce
Tomato
Cooked bacon

Tip: For easy cleanup, spread the countertop with a sheet of wax or parchment paper or aluminum foil and build the sandwiches there.

Butter four slices of sandwich bread on one side and lay that side down in sets of 2 (top and bottom for each sandwich).

On one piece of bread for each sandwich, spread a light layer of mayonnaise, followed by a small amount of Dijon mustard. Salt to taste. Top that with cheddar cheese. Add a lettuce leaf, a slice of tomato, and just enough bacon to have some in every bite.

Top with the remaining slices of bread and grill in a Panini machine or cook in a pan at medium heat. Turn the heat down so it doesn't burn. Cook on each side about 6–9 minutes.

Strawberry Bourbon Lemonade

2 cups strawberries plus extra for garnish
1 cup sugar
½ cup fresh lemon juice
2 cups water
½ cup bourbon

In a pot, mash the strawberries with the sugar and bring to a boil. Cook until sugar is dissolved. Allow to cool. Pour into a large pitcher with the lemon juice, water, and bourbon. Stir.

Cut a slice in the tip of the strawberry about halfway up and slide onto the rim of the glass as a garnish.

S'mores Cocktail

Chocolate syrup
Graham cracker crumbs
2 ounces marshmallow vodka
4 ounces chocolate liqueur

Dip the rim of the glass in the chocolate syrup and then into the graham cracker crumbs. Pour the vodka and liqueur into the glass and stir.

Turn the page for a preview
of Krista Davis's next
Domestic Diva Mystery . . .

The Diva Spices It Up

Coming May 2020
from Kensington Publishing

Chapter 1

Dear Sophie,
My mother-in-law takes great pride in her cooking.
But it's so hot that I can't eat it. Seriously, my
tongue goes numb. I watch the others eat with
gusto. Do you think she's adding something to my
plate so I won't come to dinner at her house?
        Numb Tongue in Hazardville, Connecticut

Dear Numb Tongue,
Next time, surreptitiously swap plates with your
husband. I think you'll have your answer soon
enough.

                            Sophie

Daisy, my hound mix, sniffed along the Potomac River
and followed her nose. She wore a halter and a long
leash so she could wander in the park. I let her investigate
scents that I couldn't smell and trailed along after her.

A gentle breeze blew off the Potomac River. The summer humidity was beginning to abate, and the air already

held the promise of brisk days ahead. Sun glinted on the water as it churned with the wind.

Daisy had stayed with my ex-husband for the last four weeks. I had promised her a long walk and a visit to the river as soon as I wrapped up a marathon of events. As a professional event planner, I realized that I had scheduled myself non-stop, without so much as a hint of a breather, but when you're self-employed, sometimes you just have to keep going while the opportunity is there.

I shared Daisy with my ex-husband, Mars, who had thoughtfully brought her home to my house on Sunday. When I arrived in the afternoon, sweet Daisy had been waiting for me. I had quickly swapped my suit for stretchy jeans and taken her for that long-promised stroll while I wound down.

A shout from the pier alarmed both of us. On this beautiful Sunday afternoon, quite a few people were out walking or fishing. Daisy tugged me in the direction of the pier, and I went willingly, thinking someone might need help.

"I've caught something huge!" The man was a stranger to me, into retirement age and well fed. "Must be a catfish. It's fighting like the dickens! Here, can you hold on to my fishing rod? Good and tight, now. That's my lucky one."

I took it from his hands and immediately felt the pressure of the fish. The rod bent precariously. I hoped it wouldn't snap in two. "This is really heavy. Can the fishing line take this much pressure?"

"I sure hope so. He's a big one. Keep reeling in. I'll try to snag it with my fishing net . . ."

He had stopped talking and I understood why. I didn't know of any bluefish that came with a handle on top.

He lay down on the pier and as the object came within reach, he nabbed it with a bony hand.

I kneeled on the rough wood and helped him pull a blue suitcase out of the water.

The man looked at me with rheumy eyes. "I have no idea how to cook this."

I giggled. "Do you think it's packed full or just water-logged?"

"We're about to find out." He clicked the latches and opened the top. "Mmm. This is a pretty skirt. But it's not my size."

He was very cute. I found myself smiling even though I was wondering why and how a woman's suitcase had come to be in the Potomac River. "I think we'd better report this to the police."

He stared at me with obvious confusion. "I don't think they'll be interested."

"Don't you find it odd that someone's suitcase is in the river?"

The fellow scratched his head. "Well, now that you mention it, I can't think of a good reason for it to be there among the fishes."

I called the Old Town Alexandria, Virginia, police department on my cell phone and told them about the suitcase.

"Ma'am," said the 911 operator, "is this an emergency?"

I winced. "No."

"No one is drowning?"

"No. But why would someone lose a suitcase in the river?"

The operator laughed aloud. "Why would there be garbage, motorcycles, or furniture? People are slobs. One lady dumped her husband's golf clubs in the river to get back at him for seeing another woman."

Clearly this was not a priority for them. "Thank you for your time." I hung up. "I guess it's yours if you want it."

The old fellow was peering into the water. "I can't see anything. Do you think the owner is down there, too?"

I hoped not.

He stood up and held out his hand. "Sam Bamberger."

"Sophie Winston. Can I help you carry it to your car?"

"Naw. I'm old but I can still carry a lady's suitcase. Even if it is drenched."

I said goodbye to the funny man and headed home, looking forward to a quiet evening.

The next morning, I fed Mochie, my Ocicat, who was supposed to have spots, but his fur pattern looked more like that of his American shorthair ancestors. But instead of my usual routine, I suited up Daisy in her halter and headed to my favorite coffee specialty shop for a treat.

The barista at the takeout window waved her hand at me, refusing my money.

I squinted at her in confusion. "I'm not sure this is my order. There's an extra drink and two chocolate croissants here."

"The gentleman paid for it."

Gentleman? I groaned inwardly. I hadn't showered and wore no makeup. I had pulled on elastic-waist stretchy jeans and an oversized top, feeling secure in the knowledge that the entire world was busy. It was ten o'clock on Monday morning. Why wasn't everyone at work?

Trying to hang on to Daisy's leash without spilling my mocha latte and her Puppy Paw-Tea, I twisted around to see who the barista was talking about.

My ex-husband, Mars, short for Marshall, came to the rescue. "It's my two favorite girls!"

Daisy made a fuss, wagging her tail and turning in circles at the sight of him. I was more subdued. Even though we had divorced, Mars and I got along well. Neither of us could bear to give up Daisy, so we had arranged a schedule and she went back and forth, living with both of us. But I didn't have to worry about my appearance. He had seen me without makeup and in far worse clothes before. I relaxed. "Thanks for picking up the tab."

Mars took Daisy's leash and led us to an outdoor table. Daisy didn't know whether to be more excited about Mars or her Puppy Paw-Tea, a dog-safe scoop of ice cream with a dog bone-shaped cookie on top.

"Are we celebrating something?" asked Mars.

A chilling fall breeze blew, making me glad I had worn the cozy fleece pullover. I sipped my hot drink. "Four back-to-back medical conventions are over. I worked nonstop for a month. I'm looking forward to a break."

Mars held out his coffee in a toast and touched it to the latte I held. "A break. How fortuitous."

Fortuitous? Ugh. What was he up to?

Mars smiled at me. "Soph, I need a big favor."

I never should have looked into his eyes. They crinkled at the outer edges and always softened any resolve I had to stay out of his business. A political consultant, Mars had been blessed with looks that could compete with his telegenic clients.

"I'm taking a break," I said very clearly, imagining that he probably needed me to arrange a party for five hundred people in two days.

He ignored my protest. "The wife of one of my clients is writing a cookbook."

That wasn't what I had expected. "Cool."

"Except she's not really writing it, she's using a ghostwriter."

"That's interesting. Why doesn't she do it herself?"

"She says all the celebrities use ghostwriters for their cookbooks."

"Celebrity?" I inquired.

"She's the wife of a congressman, and she's Tilly Stratford."

I'd heard the former TV star had moved to Old Town Alexandria. "No kidding!" Just to be sure we were talking about the same person, I asked, "The one who played the daughter in *American Daughter*?"

"The very same."

I chomped into one of the chocolate croissants. The chocolate was still warm and soft inside. The favor Mars needed was becoming clearer. He probably needed someone to arrange a huge party for the debut of the cookbook. I might be an event planner but, most of the time, I dealt with conventions and large events.

"But the ghostwriter quit on Friday." He sipped his drink and then said casually, "I was thinking maybe you'd be interested."

"In ghostwriting a cookbook? I don't know the first thing about that."

"Nothing to it," he said with way too much confidence for someone whose cooking expertise was limited to grilling meats and mixing cocktails. "And it pays very well."

"Is she difficult?" I asked out of curiosity.

"Who?"

"Tilly."

"Not at all. She's very sweet. You'll like her. She's . . . a little intimidated by the congressional scene. She's out of her element. But you'll love her."

"Then why did the ghostwriter quit?"

"We don't know. She told Tilly she was sorry, but she had to quit and that was it. She walked out, leaving poor Tilly high and dry. No one has been able to reach her since Saturday."

I tilted my head and gave him my best doubtful look. "Mars, that doesn't make sense. People don't take a job and quit in the middle of it."

"Are you kidding me? People do that all the time. One

of my clients advertised a job and hired six people. Guess how many showed up on the first day of training."

It was clearly a trick question. "Three?"

"Zero." He made a zero with his thumb and forefinger. "Not the best example, but my point is that people don't always come through with what they promise. I'm told that there has to be a personal connection between the ghostwriter and the chef. I feel a little guilty because I was the one who hooked her up with Abby Bergeron. She came highly recommended. Maybe they just didn't mesh."

Daisy finished her Puppy Paw-Tea and watched us, probably hoping we had another one hidden somewhere.

Mars persisted. "Tilly is a sweetheart, Sophie. She's so disappointed. It would mean a lot to her if you could help out."

I slurped the remains of my mocha latte in a most unladylike manner.

Mars wrote something on a napkin and slid it across the table to me.

I took a look and felt my eyes widen. "Is that a dollar sign?"

"I told you it paid well. They're in a hurry to get it done and willing to pay extra. The thing is"—he looked at me with his best imitation of Daisy's puppy eyes—"I know *you* wouldn't let them down."

He didn't need to shower me with empty flattery. I was torn. The money would be nice, but I had been looking forward to some downtime. "Mars, thanks for thinking of me, but I'd really like to have a little time off. Besides, a cookbook is a huge project. We'd be working on it for a year, and I would need to get back to my real job soon."

"Ah! But the bulk of it is done." He leaned toward me. "Tilly is very disappointed. This cookbook is a big deal for her and"—Mars locked his eyes on mine—"I know I can depend on you. I don't want some other highly recommended person coming in and making a mess of it or walking away."

"I'll think about it." I scowled at him. "In spite of your assurances that it's easy, I don't know what's involved in ghostwriting a cookbook."

"There's nothing to it. You write down recipes. How hard could that be?"

I stood up and collected Daisy's leash. "I'll let you know."

As I walked away, Mars called out to me, "You were my favorite wife!"

I was his only wife. He had lived with our friend Natasha, but she never did manage to get him to walk down the aisle with her.

Fall was my favorite time of year in Old Town. It was way too early for pumpkin, but they already decorated the front stoops of some historic homes. Others had wonderful wreaths on their doors, featuring dried flowers and giant sunflowers. The leaves on the trees that lined the streets were still green. It was that transitional time between summer and fall. School had started and weekend beach trips had ended.

Traffic had picked up and people had begun to leave their offices in search of lunch. At an intersection with King Street, Daisy and I paused and waited for the light to change and the line of cars to stop.

A man paused near us. About my age, his neat appearance reminded me of my old beau, Alex. His brown hair was neatly trimmed. He wore a blue oxford cloth button-down shirt with a striped yellow tie. Quintessential Old Town attire for gentlemen. He smiled at me, which made me totally self-conscious. He even reached down to pat Daisy.

But the second the light changed, he was off in a hurry, walking across the street in great, confident strides ahead of the crowd. When he reached the sidewalk on the other side, he lifted the end of his tie and placed it in his mouth. In one swift movement, he raised the lid on a public garbage bin, bent over, reached inside, and pulled out a red soft drink can.

I was so stunned that I stopped walking in the middle of the street.

He dropped the top of the garbage can back in place, let his tie fall back to his chest, and strode away.

I looked around; no one else seemed to be watching him. Hadn't anyone else noticed what he just did?

A car honked at us and we dashed across the street. I couldn't help myself, I turned right and followed him.

Chapter 2

Dear Natasha,
I love your TV show. You inspire me! I'm throwing
a party and I'm planning to serve your jalapeño
poppers. What do you recommend as a drink to go
with them?

Hot Mama in Volcano, Hawaii

Dear Hot Mama,
As much as I love those jalapeño poppers, I'm
afraid they're passé. Look for recipes involving
smoked salts or peppered fish and meats. Or go all
out with fermented garlic! That's what's on trend
right now.

Natasha

Unfortunately, Natasha intercepted me. "Sophie! Sophie! Where have you been? I went by your house half a dozen times last week but you weren't home. You really should let me know if you're going out of town."

I watched the man round the corner at Cameron Street and debated whether to run to catch up to him. It was ridiculous, of course. Even if I saw him go into a house or building, it would be meaningless. And then I did something completely out of character.

"Excuse me, Natasha." I took off after the man with Daisy romping alongside me. I was out of breath by the time I reached the intersection where he had turned. He was gone. I stood there for a moment, scanning the sidewalks. They were nearly empty. I'd have seen him if he hadn't turned somewhere or entered a building.

I sucked in some deep breaths of air. Maybe I had lost my perspective. I thought there was something sinister about the suitcase in the river, and now I was chasing a man who had caught my attention. I was being ridiculous.

When I turned back, Natasha stood where I had left her. She wore an angry expression and had crossed her arms in irritation.

I trudged back. "Sorry."

"What was that about?"

"I thought I saw someone I knew," I lied. If I told her about the soda can she would think I had lost my mind.

"I was saying that you should keep me informed if you leave."

"I have a phone," I said wryly.

"But this is important. It's the best thing that ever happened to me. I wanted to tell you in person."

I bit back the temptation to be snarky. "What is your wonderful news?"

Natasha looked me over. "What are you wearing? Oh, Sophie! I don't know what to say. Have you fallen on hard times?"

I laughed. "Natasha, are you going to tell me your good news?"

"I thought we might get a cup of coffee, but if you're dressed like that . . ."

I paid no attention to what she was saying. I had known

Natasha since we were in grade school. The two of us had competed at everything except the beauty pageants that Natasha had treasured. She still maintained the kind of figure that clothes were meant to hang on. No elastic waist-bands for her. She wore a black sweater with the sleeves pushed up, and a black-and-white plaid skirt. The kind with a gathered waist that I longed to wear. But unlike Natasha, I was short and not slender. I would look twice as wide as I already was. She wore black leather boots and, while part of me hated to admit it, she looked chic.

And now she gazed at me, raised her eyebrows, and nodded. "You will, won't you?"

Oy. Natasha was prone to outlandish ideas. I didn't dare say yes without knowing to what I was agreeing.

She tilted her head. "I would offer you something to wear but I don't think you would fit in my size."

"Thank you. It's really not necessary. I'm heading home." I started to walk in the direction of our houses and she went with me. "Now, what was it you wanted me to do?"

"Come to my party? I'm worried about you, Sophie. Didn't you hear a word that I said? I found my sister!"

Chapter 3

Dear Sophie,
My boyfriend's mother uses black pepper in one of
the cakes she likes to bake. I try to be open-minded,
but that strikes me as odd. Who would bake sweets
with black pepper in them?
                    Girlfriend in Pepper Pike, Ohio

Dear Girlfriend,
Pepper is used in cookies from South Africa to
Norway. It's not uncommon to find it in spice cakes,
either. You might like it!
                                        Sophie

Now I was the one who was worried. "But you don't have a sister."

"Okay, so she's a half-sister, but you know how I've always loved your little sister, Hannah. Now I'll have a Hannah of my own!"

I was quite certain that her mother was no longer of child-bearing age. And the biggest blow in Natasha's life was her father's disappearance when she was only seven years old. Where could a half-sister have come from? "Your mom adopted a child?"

"No! I told you. I sent off one of those DNA saliva tests, thinking I might be able to find my dad. And this woman popped up as my half-sister. That means my dad is alive! I always knew it. It was like a visceral thing that he was out there somewhere in the world. And get this. She lives right here in Old Town! What are the odds of that? We might have been shopping side-by-side or eating in the same restaurant at the same time and we never knew it!"

I was stunned. If I hadn't heard so many stories about killers being tracked down through DNA for acts committed decades before, I might not have believed her at all. "Have you met her yet?"

"No. That's why I'm having the dinner party. I want all my friends to meet her."

"You didn't run right out to meet her immediately?"

Natasha stared at me. Not a muscle in her face moved. Had she gotten Botoxed?

"It took me a while to work through the situation. Please don't mention this to your parents. I don't want my mother to know yet."

My parents and her mom still lived in the town where we had grown up. It wasn't as though they were close friends, but a new half-sister was the kind of thing a person might mention in a casual conversation at the supermarket. "No problem. But I think your mom would love to meet her."

"I'm not so sure. It might be very painful for her."

Natasha would know. The fact that she even considered her mother's reaction suggested to me that it had been painful for Natasha. And why wouldn't it be? It meant her father had left his family without so much as a fare thee well and went off to start another family.

"We talked on the phone. You won't believe what she asked me."

I could hardly believe Natasha had found a half-sister. I didn't think anything could top that! "What?"

"She wanted to know where Dad was."

"He left them, too?"

"I don't know all the details. I hope she'll tell us when she meets us. You're good at prying into other people's business. You'll get it out of her."

I ignored her slight. She was probably right. Among my many faults, I was definitely nosy. "What's her name? Maybe I know her."

"Charlene Smith."

"Doesn't ring any bells with me. I look forward to meeting her. When is the party?"

"Tomorrow evening."

"What can I bring?"

Natasha's expression turned to horror. "Oh Sophie! Please don't bring a dish. Everything has to be perfect. This is my night to shine."

Natasha had a local TV show about all things domestic, and a rabid fan base. I couldn't help wondering if she was being set up somehow. "Did she know who you are?"

"If she did, she didn't mention it."

We had reached my house. "I look forward to meeting her, Natasha. I truly do. And I'm super happy for you."

Natasha smiled at me. "Wear your best outfit, even it's last year's fashion."

I turned on my heel to stalk away and with total horror realized suddenly that the half-sister might be just like Natasha. After all, Natasha's mom was an interesting woman who worked in a diner, believed in spirits and potions, and was an incurable flirt. What if the annoyingly pompous side of Natasha came from her dad? Not two of them!

I unlocked the front door of my home and stepped inside with Daisy. Mochie, my Ocicat, came running and meowed complaints about being home alone. I unlatched Daisy and swept Mochie up into my arms. "You wouldn't have liked it. We didn't see a single mouse."

He purred as I carried him into the kitchen and spooned some salmon delight into his bowl.

I looked forward to a leisurely hot shower and headed upstairs.

Sometimes fate just toys with a person. On that particular day, while I was in the shower, a green tile fell off the wall and crashed into the bathtub in which I stood.

Daisy and Mochie came running to see what had happened.

Three more tiles fell in quick succession. I could see the row of tiles beneath them beginning to bulge. This was fate's way of telling me I had put off the bathroom renovation long enough. I felt fairly certain that the black and green tile and the green sink perched on weird aluminum legs that splayed like a colt standing up for the first time must have been the height of fashion once. For years I had longed for a modern bathroom, but I had taken out a whopping loan when I paid Mars for his half of the house in our divorce, and it didn't leave much for pricey renovations.

Green and black tile bathrooms excepted, I loved the old place with its creaking floorboards, tall windows, and huge double lot. Houses were pricy in Old Town Alexandria, Virginia, and I was lucky that Mars's aunt had left us this house. She had been a terrific cook and loved nothing more than to entertain. So much so that she had renovated the house by extending the dining room and living room to accommodate large gatherings.

I wrapped a towel around myself and gazed at the space where the tiles had been. I could probably pry off a few more tiles, then glue them back in place and caulk around them. It was the kind of fix that might work, but only for a while.

The figure Mars had written on the napkin hammered at me. Maybe it wouldn't be so bad helping Tilly with her cookbook. I tried to imagine the bathroom in white, with a vanity, and drawers for storage. There would be a place for the blow dryer and, be still my heart, maybe even a closet for towels!

If the tiles hadn't fallen off, I would have averted my eyes and continued to live with the ghastly old bathroom. But the truth was that the tiles had sounded an alarm. I knew the kind of damage that would occur if water leached behind the wall. Then I would be paying even more to repair the damage.

I had noticed that things in life often happened with an odd synchronicity. I wasn't particularly superstitious, but the timing was certainly interesting. Maybe it was a sign.

Connect with U(s)

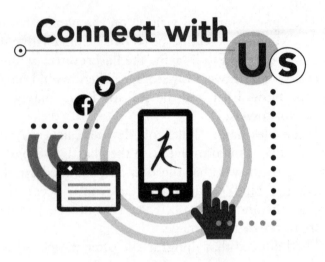

Visit us online at
KensingtonBooks.com
to read more from your favorite authors, see books
by series, view reading group guides, and more.

for sneak peeks, chances to win books and prize packs,
and to share your thoughts with other readers.

facebook.com/kensingtonpublishing
twitter.com/kensingtonbooks

Tell us what you think!
To share your thoughts, submit a review,
or sign up for our eNewsletters, please visit:
KensingtonBooks.com/TellUs.